BEAST

A TALE OF LOVE AND REVENGE

LISA JENSEN

CANDLEWICK PRESS

*For Marcia and Bruce Mcdougal. I would never have known
the fairy-tale magic of France without them.*

*And for the rest of The Gang—Donna Mekis, Morton Marcus,
and James Aschbacher—our companions in adventure.*

Copyright © 2018 by Lisa Jensen

First edition 2018

Library of Congress Catalog Card Number pending
ISBN 978-0-7636-8880-6

18 19 20 21 22 23 LSC 10 9 8 7 6 5 4 3 2 1

Printed in Crawfordsville, IN, U.S.A.

This book was typeset in Adobe Caslon.

Candlewick Press
99 Dover Street
Somerville, Massachusetts 02144

visit us at www.candlewick.com

Give me back my Beast!

—Greta Garbo, after viewing the Jean Cocteau film
La Belle et la Bête (Beauty and the Beast)

Lucie

It wasn't all the witch's fault.

She was just the one he saw as his spine hunched forward, as claws sprang out of the furry paws that had been his elegant hands only moments before, as long tendrils of mane erupted out over his eyes.

"What have you done to me, Witch?" he bellowed, although it was difficult to understand him with the lengthening of his snout.

"I have done nothing," she told him with a coolness I had to admire, as if he weren't crouching before her with animal horns and shaggy, pointed ears sprouting from his head and long rows of raptor feathers cascading down his back. "This is the truth of who you are inside."

"Change me back!" he thundered.

"I cannot," she told him. "That power lies with you, not me."

Well, that wasn't the whole truth. I had something to do with it, although even I didn't know it at the time. So I was surprised when the witch suddenly turned to me in her awful majesty. "And you, girl. What do you want?"

All I wanted then was my revenge, to see him groveling on all fours, his handsome face and manly form reduced to beastliness. Things might have been very different had I left it at that, run off with the other servants on that terrifying night, and taken up a new life in some other place. But as soon as I had what I most wished for, I found I craved more.

"I want to see him suffer," I breathed. I was drunk on my own hatred, more powerful than anything I had ever felt before.

"As you wish," she said, and that was the end of it. And the beginning.

I didn't know then the journey I was on. I could never have imagined any power that burned brighter than hate.

I had so much to learn from the beast.

My Beast.

Until *she* came.

BEFORE

· CHAPTER I ·

The Château

They say it's a turbulent household, where I'm going. They whisper behind their hands and cast baleful glances at me when they think I'm not looking. But I am always looking. I see them nudge one another and smirk at my expense. "Château Beaumont," they whisper knowingly.

Before darkness fell at the inn last night, I glimpsed this place, set like a gem in the distance above the wheat fields and vineyards, shining like gold on the green hill, like a royal palace. But the innkeeper's wife told me it's only a château, so I mustn't give myself airs. She said to beware of beauty, for it can deceive.

It's no disgrace to be a servant. That's what my father used to say.

Working for a wage is proof that you have value to someone, he told me. "Even though your station in life may be low, your character might yet soar. Poor folk have little enough say over their circumstances," he would say, "but your character is always yours to shape as you will."

My father looked at the world with joy and hope, and so he found joy and hope everywhere—especially when he looked at me.

"You are the light of the world, my Lucie," he would tell me. "Open your heart to life. You are the best of what will be."

While Papa was alive, the world was full of possibilities. Our village was just another cluster of drafty stone cottages and hungry faces, but it was my home. I never knew there was any other place on earth. I never needed any other place.

But that's all changed now.

Mama hoarded her wages for a whole season to send me here, what few coppers she could put by after the sowing and reaping and milling. She says it's well for me to go now, before my stepfather takes any more notice of how I've grown.

It's harvesttime, and the perfume of crushed grapes sweetens the air as I make my way up the steep, winding road to Château Beaumont. The town of Clairvallon, where I spent last night, seems very far below me now. At last, I climb to the top of the hill, and there it stands, Château Beaumont, floating like a golden island in the middle of a moat, surrounded by vast, green parkway. I cross a stone bridge over the moat, its water shimmering like jewels in the sunlight. Black-eyed swans glide over the water, ruffling up their white feathers for my admiration.

I pause at an enormous gate of gilded iron, whose keeper comes grumpily down, a rough-hewn man with a long, drooping mustache and an old scar along one cheek. He demands to know my business. I don't wish to be taken for a vagrant, so I lie and say I've been sent for by my aunt, the head laundress. That part is true; she is my stepfather's sister, although no blood kin to me. But we have never met, and she has no idea that I have come to beg a position.

The gatekeeper directs me to empty my pockets — simple enough, as there is nothing inside them — and inspects the underside of my cloak. Satisfied that I carry nothing but the clothes on my back, he opens the gates and nods me inside.

The courtyard I enter could hold my entire village. Two long wings of the château enclose it on either side, a west wing on the left and an east wing under a row of stone arches on the right. The main house stands beyond the courtyard, three stories of honey-colored stone with a black-domed turret at each corner. A broad gravel drive-way sweeps up to the main house, flanked by terraced gardens, so that the château seems to rise to heaven in a cloud of flowers. Ornate balconies, filigree spires, domes, and chimneys clamber over one another in a rush to the sky, under a single high tower with a colored glass window that glows in the sunlight.

Can this really be my new home?

My interview with Aunt Justine does not go well. Although we have never met, I recognize her by the same small eyes and sour expression I have seen in my stepfather's face. I find her in the laundry room, presiding over a roomful of steaming tubs and dishevelled girls. Strands of long, greying hair droop from under her wilted white cap. Her face is red, her hands chapped, and her bodice sweat-stained from the steam and heat. She casts a skeptical glance at me.

"I have more lazy girls now than I can manage," she barks.

She would like to send me away, but I can only hope the shame would be too great for her family if she could not find a place for her relation. "I'll work hard," I say.

All around us girls are thrusting long poles into the tubs to turn the linen. Others are on their knees, pounding articles of clothing in a wide, flat stone basin with a groove along one edge to divert water outside. It may be a challenge for my character to soar here, but I'm determined to prove myself worthy of my father's faith in me. Besides, I have nowhere else to go.

They thought me unnatural back in my village, a

girl my age with no suitors. Did I care nothing for my future? But I saw where it led, their gaming. They paired off because they have always done so, because the winter is cold and the nights are long. Next winter there would be a new baby to feed and their own small share of land to work, and then more babies and more work and their sporting days would be over. I knew my future all too well. I saw it every day in my mother's careworn face. That's why I am here.

I am only a girl, a servant, if God wills it. I possess nothing of value but my character, but that is mine to make of what I will. I cannot choose my circumstances, but I can choose to live nobly in this fine place. That will be my strength—if only I am allowed to stay.

Aunt Justine wipes her hands on her apron—large, rough hands like her brother's. "Go see Madame Montant, the housekeeper," she tells me at last. "She wants a girl." And she nods back toward a warren of rooms leading to the main house.

Mumbling my thanks, I turn to go, but not before I see her staring at me with a shrewd and critical eye.

"Do not disgrace me," she commands.

"Watch yourself, girl," cautions Madame Montant. She can never remember our names; there are so many of us.

"Yes, Madame."

It's my third day here, and I'm still learning my way around the lower rooms where I am employed as a maid-of-all-work. The château is so large and full of shadows, I often lose my way. This is not the first time Madame Montant has had to redirect me, nor does she bother to conceal her impatience. I am here only on trial at the moment; she might yet dismiss me on a whim if I do not please her. Madame is a solid figure in her black gown with modest lace at the points of her collar, and since there is no mistress of Château Beaumont, she keeps the keys to the wardrobes and coffers on an iron ring at her waist. They jangle with irritation as she leads me back to more familiar terrain.

The chambers I clean are mostly reception rooms, chilly and neglected, where coffers are kept and the Beaumont silver is stored and displayed, little seen by anyone but the servants. But the rooms are expected to be spotless, whether anyone will see them or not, so I sweep and polish and scrub. I'm told the master takes great pride in his beautiful things.

"The master cannot abide slovenliness," Madame reminds me as we trudge along. "And he has a particular aversion to spiders; woe be to any lazy girl who allows a spider to touch his person out of careless housekeeping."

We arrive again at my morning chamber, and I can't resist peeping through the doorway into the formal entry hall, its floor an enormous chessboard of black-and-white marble tiles. In its center stands the grand staircase panelled in rosewood that leads to the mysterious floors above, where I have never been. But Madame catches me looking.

"Attend me, girl," she says sharply. "What goes on outside your chambers is no affair of yours!"

"I understand, Madame."

"Be very sure that you do." Her gaze is unrelenting. "Do not let me ever hear of you straying into the entry hall."

"No, Madame."

"And never, ever go abovestairs," she warns me. "That is where Master lives. And, mind me, girl, you will do very well to escape the master's notice."

Master is away from home, attending to business in Paris. But he and his suite of gentlemen are expected back soon, and there is a great deal more bustle about the château now. I hear this from Charlotte, a kitchen girl. She's been here longer than me but has yet to rise above the hearth. We share a straw-stuffed pallet in the close, dark cubbyholes behind the kitchens, where the servants sleep, near enough to choke on the sooty air at night, yet too far off to feel any warmth from the kitchen fires.

I prefer to keep my own counsel; I'll not be one of those servants who gossips and pries. Charlotte, however, has no such scruples. She considers everything that happens at the château to be her affair and eagerly pours all she has gleaned into my ear at night when I hunger only for sleep. She tells me how fortunate I was to come along now, when a position had just opened up at the château. Madame Montant recently had to dismiss a chambermaid who'd let one of the noblemen of the region get her with child.

"It was no use her weeping and sobbing," Charlotte tells me eagerly. "Madame would not have her in the house, even though she was the daughter of Madame's own cousin."

I am reminded how tentative my own position is.

"The silly girl even went to the curé. Can you imagine the humiliation?" Charlotte goes on. "But she hoped he'd compel the one as done it into marriage. Claimed he'd promised to wed her, the little fool. Of course, gentlemen always say that," Charlotte adds with the absolute conviction of one who speaks from hearsay alone.

"And did the curé help her?" I ask, hoping to speed the tale along to some conclusion or other.

She stares at me, slack-jawed, appalled at my ignorance and delighted by her own superior knowledge. "Of course he did not," she exclaims. "There would be far more scandal in a gentleman of noble birth wedding a commoner—a servant!—than in the birth of another bastard. The curé could lose his living for even suggesting such a degraded union." She shakes her head at me pityingly. "Don't be a goose!"

I am not goose enough to encourage her further, and I say no more.

But Charlotte's tongue is accustomed to prattle on, whether or not anyone is listening. "The gentleman in question was one of Master's companions-in-arms in the war. He is under Master's protection, and so he may do as he likes." She wriggles closer to me on the bristly pallet. "No one opposes the master."

This morning, I patrol my chamber with a hand brush and dustpan for any dirt that might have collected in forgotten corners of display shelves or behind cabinets beyond the reach of my broom. Near the doorway to the entry hall, I'm surprised by a fragile tinkling sound from a nearby room and a gasp of alarm.

No official person is in the hall at the moment, neither housekeeper, footman, nor steward. There is no answering sound of rebuke. Perhaps no one else heard. But the sudden silence after the odd noise is all the more profound.

I take my brush and dustpan out into the back passage and peep around the next doorway. I see only a sideboard with fine things on display against one wall and two cabinets in the center of the room. But between the cabinets, a figure kneels before the sideboard like a penitent at an altar, dressed plainly in grey, like me—another chambermaid. She frets over a little pile of shiny debris on the marble part of the floor uncovered by the central carpet. Then I notice a smudge of red blood on her white apron as she clutches one finger in her hand.

I ought to turn away and pretend I didn't see. What happens in other chambers is no affair of mine. But even as I give myself this sensible advice, I hear another voice in my head, my father's voice, gentle and persuasive. *Come, Lucie, it takes only a moment to be kind.*

And because I cannot bear to disappoint my father, I hurry into the room. The girl turns huge, terrified eyes in my direction. She can't be above fourteen years old, younger than me. She reminds me so much of the sister I used to comfort through all her childish traumas, I feel a sudden wave of homesickness.

"I didn't mean it!" she whispers. "It slipped out of my hands!"

There's no way of knowing what the thing was she dropped, reduced now to a few brilliantly enamelled porcelain shards and gold dust. Some small ceremonial plate, perhaps, or the sort of delicate, shiny bauble I've heard wealthy folk present to each other when they have won a war together.

"They'll turn me out," the girl keens softly. "Where will I go? How will I live?"

Blood still coats the finger she cradles in her lap. I dig into my apron pocket for a scrap of linen I was going to use for mending, squat beside her, and take her bleeding hand.

"No one has to know," I tell her, and I bind the linen around her finger before her blood can stain anything else. "Go to the kitchen and wash your hands as you fill your mop pail. I'll clean this up." I tilt my head toward my brush and dustpan.

Her expression is disbelieving, but she slowly begins to nod.

"There are so many beautiful things here," I point out. "Surely no one will miss this one."

Wide-eyed, she nods again and dares a fleeting smile. "Thank you."

"Quickly now," I whisper, and she scrambles to her feet and dashes out.

I creep over and brush the glittering remains into my dustpan, the marble floor cold under my knees, even through my skirts. Rising again, I notice the empty space in the row of decorations on the sideboard. With trembling fingers, I nudge the other objects closer together.

I take up my dustpan again, brush held firmly over the elegant debris, and hurry out. At the back of the great kitchen stands a barrel for sweepings and leavings, but I must weave my way past cooks and potboys and scullery maids to get to it, expecting at every moment to be stopped, my guilty burden discovered. Yet I arrive without incident, dump the contents of my dustpan into the barrel, then poke my brush around inside to conceal the wreckage with ashes and other bits of trash already there.

I pause briefly to steady my breathing, then go back through the great kitchen. I spy the little chambermaid in a distant corner, rinsing her hand in her mop pail; she glances up at me for an instant, gratitude in her face, but we are too prudent to take any more notice of each other. A spiderweb of shadowy back passages connects the grand rooms of the château, and I am eager to return to the one that leads back to my chambers. But I hear the stern voice of Madame Montant in a nearby room, scolding some other servant for some far lesser infraction, and I hurry into an unfamiliar outer passage to avoid her.

I choose the darkest path, hoping the shadows will render me invisible until I can get back where I'm supposed to be. But a bend in the passage, beyond the last of the fine chambers, ends abruptly at a small door. It's rare enough to find any doors to interrupt the flow of splendor between these grand rooms, and this one seems so humble, with plain iron hinges and no ornamentation, I hope its purpose is to lead servants to a more direct route between wings. But when I try the handle, a graceful curve of iron, I find the door is locked.

"What do you think you're doing there, girl?" cries Madame Montant, emerging out of one of the larger rooms behind me. "This will not be tolerated!"

CHAPTER 2

The Beaumont Curse

"Sorry, Madame." I can scarcely speak. What can I possibly say in my defense?

"That room is forbidden to servants!" Madame glowers at me.

Room? This locked door? I do not even know where I am. She says nothing about broken porcelain, but her manner could not be more threatening.

"Disobedience is not tolerated. Get your things—"

But before she can order me off, as I'm sure she means to do, another chambermaid comes breathlessly down the passage to tell us that Monsieur Ferron, the steward who manages the household, is calling for the entire staff to assemble out on the front steps immediately. As the girl runs off, Madame spares me one last glare, then mutters, "Well, then. Don't dawdle, girl."

I am still part of this household! I hardly see where we go, I'm so relieved, but I follow Madame's black figure down another twisty passage. It opens onto the forbidden entry hall, and with a firm grip on my wrist to prevent me wandering off, Madame drags me across a corner of the black-and-white marble tiles and out onto the porch above the courtyard.

What a lot of us there are! The household servants crowd the porch and cascade down the front steps, and the outdoor staff gathers in the flat upper courtyard and the broad driveway between the terraced gardens.

Monsieur Ferron has called us together to tell us that the master is on his way back to Château Beaumont. We are told to be swift about our duties, obedient, invisible, and above all, silent. On no account is the master to be vexed with idle chatter from any of us upon his arrival.

"Pray God his lawsuit has prospered," mumbles one of the gardeners to another. But not so softly that Monsieur Ferron does not hear him.

"The master's business is no affair of yours," the steward says icily. He stares us all down over the long nose in his thin face. "However," he goes on after a lengthy pause, "as it is a matter of some concern to the operation of this household, I can tell you this much: the suit is not yet resolved."

There is a great deal of mumbling among the servants at this news. Cooks, maids, grooms and gardeners, stableboys and huntsmen, all cast one another fearful glances and mutter darkly. The rugged gatekeeper with the scarred face looks even more grim than usual and shakes his head. I have no idea what it all means, so I'm grateful when Charlotte appears at my elbow.

"The master is pursuing a claim to an estate in Clamecy held by the Villeneuve family," she whispers breathlessly. "He's taken it all the way to the Paris *parlement*. He says his claim through his grandmother is more valid than that of the Villeneuve cousins who hold it now."

"He's bringing a suit against his own cousins?"

She nods back eagerly. "He fostered out there as a page when he was a boy. That's how he comes to know how rich a place it is, in rents and dues and fees."

"Silence!" Monsieur Ferron commands us. "Do not," he warns, "give the master any cause to complain of you. Not if you value your positions."

The grumbling lowers in volume but not intensity. The mood of the folk is black as we are all dismissed back to our duties—myself included, for none of us can be spared now that the master is coming home.

Most of us are forbidden to return through the entry hall, so I trot down the steps to join a swarm of household servants crossing the courtyard for the kitchen wing. On the way, I pass the gardener who spoke up before.

"Small wonder his suit comes to nothing," he mutters to his companion. "It's the Beaumont Curse!"

"Oh, be off with you both," scoffs the head gardener, coming up quickly behind them to shoo them back to their duties.

The Beaumont Curse? I turn about, hoping for an explanation, but for once, Charlotte is nowhere to be seen.

Each nightfall casts longer, colder shadows inside the château as the days grow shorter. This is the time for slaughtering and feasting in my village, but there are no such celebrations here. Tempers shorten along with the days as our work increases. Stableboys row with gardeners out in the yard; kitchen girls fling accusations at laundresses. In the evening when we servants take our meal around the worktable in the great kitchen, I recognize the little chambermaid who broke the fancy ornament. But we dare not look at each other, much less speak, for fear our shared guilt will crackle between us like lightning. Madame Montant watches me like a falcon, ready to swoop down on my every misstep, so I take extra care not to make any.

Tonight a frazzled Aunt Justine sent me off to deliver clean linens to a distant storeroom where I have never been. I found the place, but with only a single candle to light my way through the gloom, I'm not sure how to get back to the kitchen. These passages all look alike in the dark. I listen for the distant talk of the servants to guide me, but their chatter has faded.

Instead, I hear a soft, sweet sound, a kind of humming, from somewhere nearby in the dark. I follow it around a corner and find myself facing the humble little door to the locked room I encountered the other day. Forbidden to servants, I was told. But even as I begin to back away, a feeling of warmth and comfort steals over to me, as if the door itself were beckoning me. The singing seems to be coming from the other side, soothing, like a lullaby, and I move closer; perhaps whoever is inside can direct me back to the kitchen. I scarcely touch the curved handle, and the door opens, drawing me in.

No one is inside. The hearth I glimpse across the little room is cold, yet it seems warmer in here than in any other place I've yet been inside the château. By candlelight, I see that it's not nearly so grand as the other chambers, nor so ferocious in its finery. Its few furnishings are simple. I bend down slightly to inspect a rocking chair standing before me, woven from twigs and saplings, its worn cushion plain linen, not velvet. It seems homey and comfortable, as few other objects do in this place, and so well-used, someone might have been sitting in it only a moment ago.

I straighten up, and something moves in the shadows.

I thrust out my candle and jump when the thing in the

dark responds. But despite my pounding heart, I realize it's only my own reflection in a large looking glass obscured in shadows above the hearth. I draw nearer. I never saw a looking glass in my village; such things were too dear and far too fragile. But I see myself reflected in this one: plain and pale, brown hair plaited back beneath my linen cap, my eyes as grey as the stones of my village.

And over my shoulder, in the room behind me, the twig chair is rocking.

I spin about, heart in my throat, but the chair is utterly still as I stare at it. I turn again to the glass — and nearly drop my candlestick in alarm. Seated in the chair, calmly rocking, is the figure of a young woman.

I freeze before the looking glass, not daring to turn around again. The woman is beautiful, dressed in the most elegant gown I have ever seen. Her dark hair is swept up in a golden net, but for a few renegade curls brushing her pale cheeks as she rocks a small bundle in her lap. She is humming the melody I heard before, a lullaby for the little bundle moving and cooing softly in her arms, although the babe is too swaddled in blankets for me to see it. By candlelight, I see that she is weeping.

Her tune breaks off, and she sighs and lifts her face. Her dark eyes are lovely even as they overflow with tears. She raises a hand to sweep a damp curl off her cheek, and something flashes in my light, a gold ring she wears with a tiny red jewel shaped like a heart. Then she turns her face up to me, meeting my eyes in the glass.

"Won't you help us, Lucie?"

I am so shocked, I nearly drop my candle again as I turn about once more, but the chair is as empty and as still as it ever was. When I look back into the glass, I see only my own terrified face reflected there.

A curse! Château Beaumont is cursed!

I hurry out of the room, shaking, and pull the door shut behind me. Out in the passage, I hear the low, distant rumble of conversation once again and follow it back to the kitchen. A part of me wants to bolt outside right now and run back to my village, my home, and take comfort in my mother's familiar scolding. But there's no longer any place for me under my stepfather's roof. I can never go back.

Returned at last to the familiar bustle of the kitchen and the gossip of servants, all anxious over the master's homecoming, I begin to view my encounter in the forbidden room as no more than a fanciful trick of the mind, brought on by too much idle prattle about curses and suchlike. I'd best learn to control my fancies. Madame Montant will not tolerate foolishness, and I have nowhere else to go.

He is coming! The master! This taskmaster, cause of so much distress among the staff, is coming home.

I am at work in one of my chambers when I see them through the window, Master and his suite of gentlemen, thundering up the drive in a cloud of dust and gravel. The talk of the men is loud, and their horses are steaming and snorting. The courtyard seems smaller with all of them in it. The gentlemen are all richly dressed, although their fine boots and cloaks are coated with dust from the road. The master is their leader, gold trim bright on his wine-colored cloak as he rides in at their head, pulls up his mount, and leaps off.

The master sweeps off his plumed hat to reveal russet-colored hair, dark eyes, and a full, curving mouth, his smile like the sun.

He is beautiful!

· CHAPTER 3 ·

Le Chevalier

The master hands his hat to one of his gentlemen, then strips off his riding gloves and tosses them to another. He is tall and straight; I can see the shape of powerful shoulders beneath his fine doublet as he throws his cloak behind his shoulder and hurries up the steps. He is slim-waisted, with long legs below his richly embroidered breeches. Madame Montant would punish me for even noticing such things, but I cannot help what I see.

His stride is long, his movements agile and forthright, like a noble knight, like the thoroughbred animal he is. There is nothing indecisive about him, nothing hesitant. His youthful features suggest he cannot be above five-and-twenty, yet he is in complete command of himself, of this place, of this vast green and fertile region. To think, I almost let my foolish fancies and the prattle of servants poison my mind against him. Jean-Loup Christian Henri

LeNoir, Chevalier de Beaumont. Handsome, noble, and good, master of us all.

They will not leave off warning me, but now I know better than to listen to them. "Come away, girl. Master will be down soon," cautions Madame Montant when I contrive to catch sight of Master at his daily rendezvous with Monsieur Ferron. "Master has no time for chambermaids," Charlotte tells me loftily.

It is true. Master will never notice me. I know I am no beauty; my virtue, my character, are all I possess of any value, and they are not visible. And yet I watch him nonetheless. It gives me pleasure to hold him in my sight, as few other things do in this forbidding place. So I tarry too long at my morning tasks, earn slaps and scoldings and extra work, all for a glimpse of him.

Since the master has come home, Château Beaumont has become a magnet for all the young noblemen of the countryside. Charlotte says most of them rode with him during the war against the Spanish invaders. The king himself, good Henri Quatre, conferred upon Master the title of chevalier, presenting him with a *lettre de chevalerie* for his service. Now his companions-in-arms make free with his hospitality at the château; they come to dine at his table and ride to hounds in his fine park.

I've trained myself to rise in the cold dark before dawn on the days a hunting party is arranged. That's the best time to steal a glimpse of Master. This morning a party is assembled at breakfast upstairs in the dining salon. From the kitchen, I see legions of liveried servants parading up the back stairs, cold plates heaped with cheeses and fruit, mountains of bread, flagons of wine, and made dishes steaming under silver covers. Enough to feed all the people and livestock in my village for a week. I take up a broom and sweep my way into the nearest of my chambers. I creep through the drowsy morning shadows until I gain the chamber adjoining the entry hall. I nudge the broom idly about near the open doorway until I hear them clattering down the grand staircase, the master, members of his household suite, and his noble guests.

"Who is that gargoyle who keeps your gate, Beaumont?" one of the guests is demanding, a blustery fellow in a violet habit.

"You mean Andre?" responds the master. He's dressed in fawn and gold to set off his coloring.

"You must dismiss him," says the man in violet. "He's an eyesore."

"But a very effective gatekeeper," says the master, pausing at the foot of the stairs while his valet drapes his cloak about his shoulders. "He frightens off the rabble. Keeps a family in town as well. Obscenely large, I'm told," he adds, shrugging into his cloak and waving off his valet.

"And what about you, Beaumont?" another gentleman cries. "When are you going to marry?"

I had not thought of Master wed. Not yet, I hope. My eyes have not possessed him long enough.

"You sound like my late father," Master says lightly, "and I shall answer you as I answered him: I'll marry when it suits me and not before." In the shadows, I breathe again, as his gentlemen chuckle. "I've only lately come into my own inheritance," Master continues, "and I mean to enjoy it before I saddle myself with the responsibility of a wife."

"But it's time you had heirs," chimes in the man in violet.

The master's face darkens. "I suppose you had heirs in mind when you assaulted my chambermaid, Laprise," Master remarks coolly. The man in violet chokes on his last chuckle, his expression suddenly wary, and I realize this must be the gentleman Charlotte told me about.

"If you haven't any better taste, you might at least cast your pole into some other fellow's property," Master concludes, and they all laugh again, Master and Laprise most heartily.

"For my part, I shall worry about heirs when I have something to settle upon them," Master continues, "when

I have won my claim to the Villeneuve property, which by all rights should be mine."

"And what of your other suits?" asks another of the men. "With those members of the fair sex whom discretion compels me to identify only as the Lady A and the Lady B. How do they prosper?"

The master shrugs and smiles. "I continue to pay court to each, as time permits."

"Rather say the fathers of Ladies A and B are paying court to you," observes one of the men.

"Or to your fortune," chimes in another.

The master turns again to his valet, extending his hands, but the valet only dips his head in a bow of mute apology. The awkward moment is interrupted by a sudden pounding on the stairs. A young page of about thirteen comes hurtling around the last bend in the stairway and races down the stairs clutching a pair of fawn-colored riding gloves.

"Speak of the very devil," says the master as the lad hurries over to him. "Gentlemen, may I present the newest member of my household. Or should I say the latest? My young cousin Nicolas. From the branch of the house of Villeneuve that still values the patronage of the LeNoirs."

"F-forgive me, monsieur le chevalier," stammers the boy, hunching over into an ungainly crouch as he proffers up the gloves.

Master glowers down at him without taking the gloves. "I served in his mother's household when I was a lad," he says to the others. "Out of the great affection I bear for her, I have taken him in."

"Was there an estate in all of Burgundy to which you were not fostered out?" pipes up one of his men.

"My father believed my education would benefit from experience in several noble houses," Master responds with an elegant lift of his chin.

"I heard you were hounded from place to place for your youthful indiscretions," says his companion.

"Was it my fault my female cousins found me so attractive?" Master laughs. He smiles charmingly at Nicolas. "And their mothers?"

Nicolas's face flames pink to the very tips of his ears as the gentlemen all laugh. I feel the boy's discomfort, but this may be a test of loyalty; a man in Master's position can't afford to have renegades in his suite. The page is still frozen in his submissive posture holding out the gloves, his reddened face lowered, but he says nothing.

"How sweet were her entreaties on her son's behalf," the master murmurs, gazing down at the lad. "How persuasively I was coaxed to yield at last to her desire. How shamed she will be if he does not prosper."

Master gazes at Nicolas a moment longer, an edge to his smile, as the other gentlemen stifle their chuckles. "You see how well he learns the habits of a gentleman," says Master at last, plucking the gloves from the boy's hands. The young page staggers backward into something like a normal posture, although his head is still bowed. Master spares not a glance for the gloves but drops them to the floor. "These are soiled." He sniffs. "Bring me another pair."

Without daring to look up, the page sinks to the floor and gropes for the fallen gloves. He is still on his hands and knees as Master and his men march across the hall in a great flurry of boots and weapons and laughter. Something uneasy stirs inside me, an anxious sympathy for the shame-faced page. Yet I cannot pity him, for he exists in the master's sight in a way that I do not.

At the door, Master gazes back around the entry hall. I realize I am still lurking in the doorway when his restless gaze lights on me—it must be me because no one else is nearby—and his mouth slowly forms into a radiant smile. Then Master turns again to his valet.

"Have the girl bring them," he says, nodding sideways at me.

I can scarcely breathe. It's as if I am watching someone else cross the forbidden marble tiles and wait for the boy to come lurching back down the stairs with the gloves—Master's gloves!—which he gives to the valet, who grudgingly hands them to me. I proceed out the formal front doors to the grand porch like someone in a dream.

I never make it past the third tier of gentlemen, however; one of them takes the gloves from me and trots down the steps with them to the broad gravel drive, where Master and his companions are readying their mounts. But it doesn't matter. Master has seen me, if only for an instant. My new life has begun.

I am up late. The air is close and heavy, but the fat, wet clouds have not yet delivered their burden of rain. The other girls are snoring in their beds, but I am up and about.

I didn't see Master all day, and tonight he is out. I think of him so often, I've grown careless in my work. I've just remembered a plate I left out of its cabinet today while I was cleaning. I must go place it back on its rack behind the glass before Madame Montant finds it in the morning. I cannot risk a reprimand now; one more misstep, and she will turn me out. I'm sure of it. And how could I bear to leave Master's service now that he has noticed me?

I creep out of the maids' quarters and into the housekeeper's private cubbyhole. Madame Montant keeps her ring of keys on a little end table beside her bed at night, but she takes drops to help her sleep. The little bottle of inky purple liquid stands on the table as well, and I find her bundled up in her dressing gown, her breathing wet and heavy. I crouch beside the little table, careful not to let the keys clank together, and fiddle off the one I need.

I slink out into the great kitchen to light a candle from the hearth fire, then make my way into the chamber to unlock the glass door of the cabinet. That the silver commemorative dish, a gift to the master for some noble service, still sits forgotten on the table before the cabinet is testament to how few people ever come into these rooms. As I replace the fine piece on its rack, I gaze for a moment at the Beaumont coat of arms etched into its surface, a Beast Rampant, disparate parts of eagle, lion, and stag, on a shield above a row of spearheads. The arms of a noble warrior. The beast's mouth is thrown open in a savage roar.

The shadows around me suddenly seem more menacing; I hastily close the cabinet door, turn the key in its lock, and pluck it out. The flame of my candle blazes in the glass panels — and something thumps in the dark at the far end of the room. My heart flies into my mouth, and I drop the key as an indistinct shape lumbers up in the opposite doorway.

· CHAPTER 4 ·

Little Candle

"A light! A light, by God's good grace!" It is Master's voice, and I almost sob with relief. He shambles toward me, toward the light, without his body servants or any of his gentlemen. All alone. He enters into the circle of flickering light and peers at me.

"You, girl. You're one of mine, aren't you?"

I bob into a breathless curtsy. Perhaps he doesn't recognize me out of my uniform. And a new kind of anxiety grips me, as I realize just how out of uniform I am in my chemise, barefoot, with my hair down. I can't think what to do. Madame Montant would have the flesh off my hide for not fleeing at once, yet I dare not behave rudely to the master.

"New about the place, eh?" The effort of craning forward for a closer look nearly topples him off his feet.

Servants are cautioned to be silent above all things, yet surely I must answer a direct question. "Yes, sir."

"It speaks!" He raises an eyebrow. "Have you a name?"

"Lucie, sir."

"Lucie," he exclaims. "A light, in this most black of nights! Oh, I have great need of your light tonight, little candle." Up close, I see the state of his clothes, his collar carelessly open, doublet mishooked, the hem of his shirt hanging out in back like a forgotten tail. His hair is unbound, swinging free about his shoulders. He sways a little toward me again, but he's sure enough on his feet to keep himself in balance.

"Light me upstairs, girl. I've had a beastly night, and there's no point in rousing the others at such an hour."

"I cannot, sir." How do I dare refuse him anything? But I must not be caught flaunting the rules of his household, if I wish to keep my position. "I'm not allowed upstairs," I manage to explain.

"Not allowed?" He reels up to his full height, his expression as dark as the thunderous clouds outside. "Who is master here?" he barks.

I cower before him, alarmed by this outburst. But his anger clears in an instant, and he composes his features. Perhaps he was only testing me. Perhaps my virtuous character has pleased him.

"Come along, Lucie." His voice has softened as he

nods toward my candle in its dish. "I shan't breathe a word to a soul, I promise you," he whispers confidingly.

What can I do? I'm not allowed to disobey him. He gestures out the door to the entry hall and the grand central staircase so long forbidden me. All is swathed in shadows, but I can light his way in the darkness. Praying that Madame Montant will not waken and catch me, I take up the candle, and with Master at my heels, I cross to the stairs and ascend.

The dark rectangles of paintings on the staircase walls flicker in and out of the light, portraits of Beaumont ancestors following me with their disapproving eyes. But the master has given me an order, and I must obey.

Past the first bend in the stairway, we climb to the second-floor landing. He directs me through a grand passage to the tall, handsome doors of what must be his private apartments. My hand trembles on the ivory handle, but he is beside me, nodding me on, so I take heart, plunge the handle down, and enter.

He takes the lead now, with me scurrying alongside to light his way. We pass through a long, formal salon; in the moving light, I half glimpse the dark shapes of chaises and bedsteads where his household gentlemen must sleep, but none of them are about. We proceed into a more comfortable sitting room, where he signals me to stop. In the shadows, I see an enormous white marble fireplace. The head of a god protrudes from the mantelpiece, and leaping stags are carved over the looking glass above. Opposite is a tall wardrobe, its panels of inlaid wood glistening in the candlelight. Master's hunting boots are tossed aside at the foot of the wardrobe, one propped upright against the cabinet, the other slumped across the carpet; there is something so intimate about their wanton disarray. But he has gone to a corner occupied by a stuffed velvet chair and footstool. He grasps a heavy glass decanter off the end table but, finding it empty, sends it clattering back to its tray with an oath. He strides to another pair of doors and throws them open into the dark.

"Come along now, Little Candle," he commands me, and I bring the light. But I pull up short when I see an ebony bedpost curving out of an alcove in the shadows. Surely, he cannot expect me to enter his private bedchamber?

"Ahh!" he cries. From where I stand in the doorway, my candle illuminates a hunting wineskin on a strap over the bedpost, and he races to it. He pulls out the cork with his teeth and spits it out. He tips the skin up to his lips and smiles, even as he savors its contents. I stand there, watching him in the light, his head tilted back, eyes half-closed in rapture, his mouth working industriously. It embarrasses me to witness such a private moment, and my gaze skitters aside, in search of somewhere else to land.

When he notices me again, he nods toward another marble fireplace that overlooks the foot of the bed. Fat beeswax candles in iron holders stand on either end of the mantelpiece, and I am directed to light them. But I dare step only one bare foot across the threshold, when I think how gladly Madame Montant would turn me out if she ever found out I was even upstairs, let alone here in this room. But Master could dismiss me tonight, this minute, as late and dark and cold as it is, if I were to balk at his command.

"Don't dawdle there, girl!" Master barks, sounding so much like Madame Montant that I am startled into obedience. I am a servant, I remind myself, invisible. A candle to light his way. My only duty is to be silent and obedient, to light his rooms and take myself off, not to annoy him with foolishness.

So I enter the room and light the candles. I glance furtively into the glass above the mantelpiece, half dreading, yet almost hoping to see the lady in the rocking chair again, to feel less alone in this awkward moment. But I see only a dim reflection of the far corner of the room, the indistinct shape of a dressing table in the shadows, and the folds of a heavy curtain drawn across a window, perhaps, or another alcove. I feel a servant's anxiety that the hearth is cold below me, and Master's next words speak to my thoughts.

"Gave my men leave to see to their own affairs," he grumbles. "Never thought I'd need 'em again tonight. Never thought to be sent packing. Damned impudent bitch."

I turn back in some alarm, only to find him sprawled in a stuffed chair just outside the wide, deep alcove where his bed is enthroned, grinning up at me. His angry words must have been meant for someone else.

"You see the state I'm in on my own. Helpless as a babe. You'll have to do my boots for me." He cocks his head like a quizzical bird, and his grin broadens. "If I may presume."

"Of course, sir." My hand shakes at the impropriety of this moment, even as I blow out my candle and set its dish on the mantelpiece. How many household rules have I already broken tonight? I can only pray that no gossiping servant caught sight of me on the forbidden stairway and that I can leave just as invisibly.

I go to his chair and kneel before him, and he stretches out one long leg. I hope he can't feel how my hands tremble as I brace his square boot heel on my knee and wrestle down the deep cuff of fawn-colored leather. I tug at the heel, but my grip shakes so, I lose my purchase. As I grope in too much haste, I jam a finger into one of the razor points on his gilded spur. The prick startles me, and I pull my hand away, but I do not drop his foot. For an instant, we are both transfixed by a tiny bead of red blood on my white fingertip.

Then his eyes narrow. "Be more careful, girl."

I am too much of a goose to respond with anything more than a nod of apology as I bend again to my task. The boot's muddy sole stains my chemise, but I finally get the thing off. He lowers his stockinged foot, and I seize the other raised boot and prop it in my lap, handling the spur with better care. This second boot comes off without incident, and there is a moment when I cradle Master's muscled calf and elegant heel in my hands. He reclines in his chair, watching me. But he does not pull his foot away, and I dare not insult him by dropping it to the floor.

"You'd never turn a fellow out of your bed, would you, Little Candle?"

What a thing to ask! My heart races. My eyes drop. What answer can I give that will not make me seem wanton or ignorant?

When he speaks again, his voice has ripened. "Never had the opportunity, is that it?"

"N-no, sir."

"A creature of virtue—what a rarity!"

I can't tell if he is mocking me, but my cheeks flame, and he laughs, a cold, mirthless sound. I wish I were far away from here.

"I'm sorry, sir," I mumble. Servants are accustomed to apologize, even when we have done no wrong.

"Why, there's nothing shameful about *virtue*," he says with a sly emphasis on the last word. Then he yawns and prods at me with his foot. "Do the bed, girl."

I stumble up, glad to be farther away from him, yet even more eager now to finish up and be gone. I go into the alcove that cradles Master's bed like a shrine. The polished bedposts gleam in the soft light, framing the dark jewel colors of the satin counterpane and a mountain of gold-braided pillows. I curl my pricked finger to my palm and reach forward, digging under the pillows with my other hand and fingers, feeling for the hems of sheets to turn down, when I hear him rise to his feet behind me.

"But there's no point to virtue, either."

His voice is right in my ear, and I am shoved facedown into the pillows, my flailing hands sliding over satin. My fingertips are so roughened from scrubbing that they snag at the fabric, but I'm still unable to get a purchase, as my chemise is thrown up around my waist and my legs are pried apart.

"Chevalier!" I gasp. "Please! No . . ."

But I am crushed with the impact of Master's weight and his heat and all his fury as he falls on me from behind, tearing me up inside.

How it hurts, the sudden shock of it, the furious impact

again and again. But humiliation ravages me more completely than any pain. I am weak, foolish. I can't defend myself. His arms are stronger than mine, pinning me down as my clutching fingers rasp uselessly over the satin counterpane.

Searing pain and shock and shame overwhelm me. If only I could die, right here on this spot, yet I continue to feel everything, every lurch of his body against mine, every gust of his sour breath on my shoulder, my neck. Each instant is an eternity. The longer he bores into me, the less able I am to fight him, the less of me there is to defend, until I am an empty nothing. An object to be used at his whim. A thing.

He goes on grunting and sweating until he expels a last rush of wet, foul air, and he is finally done with slamming into me. He sprawls forward over my back to hiss in my ear.

"Your virtue is cured, Little Candle."

Then he rolls off me into the embrace of his pillows, chest heaving. The tone of his words tells me how pleased he is with himself. He makes a dismissive gesture with his hand, and the empty thing I have become peels itself away from the fine counterpane.

I stagger for the door on shivery limbs, aching everywhere, mopping feebly at my legs with my chemise. I leave the candle behind, and I stumble through the dark rooms for the passage, bruising my toe on an end table, my knee on a door frame. But I cannot bear the light; I am too filthy to be seen, not by him, nor the ancestors hanging in the stairwell, nor what is left of myself.

I can hear the rain outside racketing at the glass windowpanes like savage laughter. Deep-bellied thunder booms, and I shrink from a flash of lightning, feeling my way to the stairs to crawl down them slowly, painfully, almost on all fours, hand over hand on the balustrades. I imagine I'm leaving a trail of slime behind me, like a garden snail, oozing over each carpeted stair. I can't hide my shame. Everyone will see it, follow it, and know what I've become.

I am too filthy to live.

· CHAPTER 5 ·

Beast Rampant

It grieves me to waken. Last night I felt snuffed out, a candle flame disintegrating into the black nothing, yet this morning my eyes open again. Death has not released me. But I am no longer alive, for a thing cannot live; it only is.

I go about my toilette as well as I might, reeking of shame. I'm certain they can all smell it on me. It is almost midday when he calls for his bath. Half a dozen stout body servants carry up buckets of hot water drawn from the well and warmed over the kitchen fire, baskets full of thick towels and fragrant oils that foam and soothe. But I will never be clean, never again.

What can I do? There is no one here I can confide in, no one to whom I dare confess my shame. The stranger who is my Aunt Justine will not comfort me for disgracing her. Madame Montant will turn me out, as she did the last foolish girl in my place. And where should I be then?

Mama will not have me back. Without my situation, I am ruined, beyond all redemption, without friends or money or skills to sustain me. All I possess now is my shame, the burden I can never escape. It meant nothing to him, robbing me of my virtue, but a poor woman who loses her virtue has lost everything.

There was some disturbance this morning when Madame Montant, making her rounds, found the key to the cabinet I opened last night on the floor where I dropped it. But the cabinet was locked, nothing inside had been stolen, and since there was no obvious place to lay blame, the housekeeper could only conclude that it must have worked its way off her ring yesterday.

Days stretch into weeks, and I am quicker about my duties to avoid any contact with him, not even a glimpse. Madame Montant stops scolding me, pleased with my improvement. I speak to no one, and no further notice is taken of me. I try to believe that if I'm quiet enough, insignificant enough, someday I might disappear altogether, like the dew off a rose. I will escape my memory, my shame, even my flesh, and the torment of my life will end. I pray for that moment.

And yet I continue to live.

I can't always get away quickly enough. This morning, he's ridden early to hounds, and before I am done with my scrubbing, he and his men come roaring out of the park into the vast yard that lies out beyond the back of the moat, the dogs yelping at their heels. My chamber window affords a better view of their clamor than I wish to see, as the men form a hasty circle and restrain their dogs, then shout for the servants. It is even more distressing when I see what they're playing at. A young doe has been wounded in the chase, and the servants drive her into the open for the hunters' sport, into the circle of laughing men and slavering hounds. Blood gushes from a wound in her haunch, and the tormented creature limps about drunkenly as she struggles to leap on her lamed leg. Pawing desperately at the ground with her forehooves, she careens this way and that within the circle, veering away in panic from the noise and the scent and the thickening bloodlust of her captors. No one laughs more heartily than the chevalier. At last he gives a signal, and they loose the dogs. The doe freezes at the sight of the mad eyes and foaming mouths of hell that bear down upon her from all sides, the last thing she will ever see before they tear the life from her body.

He calls off the hounds while there is still enough carcass left to salvage, which he carries across the back bridge over the moat and into the house in triumph for Cook to clean and dress. Through the chambers he goes, trailing mud and blood from the kill that the maids will be expected to clean—again—as his hounds snarl and howl outside. I am ordered to the kitchen with my pail, and he appears to take no notice of me as he marches past; what is the ruination of a housemaid to him, after all? But at the last moment, he turns his fine head and looks directly at me with a look of smug satisfaction, of possession, the way he looks at any of the other things that he owns. And I wither where I stand, reduced to an object once more, in his sight. It makes him smile; my humiliation amuses him. He will never let me forget it.

As the frazzled kitchen staff scurries about, he calls for wine, and I see Charlotte nearby, all agog, wrestle out a goblet from some shadowy corner. A senior member of the kitchen staff grabs the hammered pewter goblet out of her hand, hastily pours in a tot of wine, and presents it to the chevalier. As he grasps the stem and turns about, I am near enough to see a long-legged spider appear around the curve of the bowl and crawl down onto the chevalier's fingers. He bellows an oath, sends the goblet flying under an angry red arc, shakes his hand as if he had palsy, and stamps furiously on the floor where the creature landed.

"The wine is foul!" the chevalier shouts to his companions. Then he rounds on Charlotte. "You, girl! Out! Off my property. Now!" He turns to the trembling Cook. "See to it!" Then he strides out again, his face like a sudden cloudburst.

Poor Charlotte can only stand there, ashen-faced,

speechless for once, as the older women move in to carry out the chevalier's order. I grieve at this injustice done to Charlotte, although she might be luckier than she knows to escape this place. But I know nothing was wrong with the wine. And I nurse one tiny pinprick of pleasure, amid my misery, to know there is something the chevalier fears.

Still his every glance, every smirk, hammers me raw anew and multiplies my shame. I can scarcely bear it, it smothers me so. I shall die of it. And please, God, soon.

I've kept out of his way since the incident with the deer, but today I dread hearing his voice and another's above the tread of their boots as they come into one of my chambers. I grab up my scrub pail and brush and flee into the next room. I am well out of sight as the chevalier and one of his household gentlemen, his secretary, come into the room I've just left. It's the secretary's task to account for the chevalier's fortune down to the last denier, and the burden of this task makes him perpetually earnest and wary.

The room they've just entered is furnished with a writing table and a chair, besides its grand display of chests and cabinetry. This is where the chevalier conducts his business, and he seats himself in the chair while the secretary lays down his burden of papers on the outer corner of the tabletop and stands respectfully to one side. I am trapped in the next room; the door between them is only partway closed, and I dare not retreat any farther, for fear of being seen by him. So I hold still, peering furtively at them through the crack between the door and the jamb.

"I'm in no mood to be bored with petty matters today, Treville," the chevalier declares, lounging back in his chair and stretching out one long leg under the table.

"Of course not, monsieur le chevalier," Monsieur Treville agrees. "It's only a small item. I've received a petition from one of your tenants—"

"A written petition?" the chevalier interrupts. "That must have cost dearly."

"The curé wrote it on his behalf," the secretary explains. "The man is called, eh . . ." And he begins to consult his papers.

"Never mind what he's called," mutters the chevalier. "What does he want?"

"He's a laborer from the wheat fields beyond Clairvallon," the secretary goes on. "The rent he owes you is nearly due. He begs for an extension of one more year to pay it off."

"A year?" echoes the chevalier. "I loaned him cash to pay his royal taxes against a higher yield. If that yield has not been forthcoming, he must bear the consequences."

"With all respect, monsieur, consider that crops have failed everywhere," the secretary points out. "The weather—"

"I am not responsible for the weather, Treville. The terms of our arrangement were very clear. If he can't pay, he must forfeit his plot."

"But where will he go? His family has worked that parcel of land for generations."

"At the pleasure of my family. If he can't raise a yield on it, I'll rent it out to someone who can. These parasites can't expect to take advantage of my good nature forever. My resources must produce if I'm to see to my own affairs."

Treville clears his throat and shuffles his papers. "Yes. Your suit is proving to be a costly affair, indeed. There are lawyers' bills, recorder's fees, testimonies to be bought—"

The chevalier's eyes narrow. "If you are suggesting my funds are in arrears, there is something very wrong with your accounting."

"Your fortune is intact, monsieur," says Treville. "I only wonder if there might be other . . . detrimental costs if you pursue it."

"It's the richest estate in Clamecy, well worth pursuing. The expense will be recovered once I have won it."

"Until then, is it not wise to practice some . . . economies?"

The chevalier stares at Treville as if he has never before heard the word. Perhaps he has not—I'll wager few enough have ever dared to utter it in his presence.

"Economies? I am the Chevalier de Beaumont. All

that is mine must inspire respect. The Villeneuve estate will ornament the entire seigneurie. Its splendor shall be a source of pride through all of Burgundy. If my suit is too costly, I'll raise my tenants' rents, charge more at my mill."

"But the weather has been foul and harvests poor throughout your lands. Your people may not be able to pay anymore."

"Of course they will pay! They must share the expense, just as they'll presume to share in my prosperity when the suit is won."

"I'm afraid the expense may be twofold," murmurs Treville. "Some of your people may resent your extravagant habits in this and other matters when they have so little."

"Who dares to say so?" cries the chevalier, leaping to his feet. He rounds fiercely on his secretary. "I'll have it known that I will not tolerate rebellion."

"Of course not. There is no such talk abroad," Treville assures him hastily. "But if you would maintain the good-will of your people, might it not be advisable to limit your rents and dues to what they can pay? And your spending to what is most necessary?"

"And do you set a limit on what my honor is worth?" the chevalier demands. He paces angrily about the room. "The Villeneuve estate is mine by right, and I'll not betray the memory of my father nor my grandfathers by letting it slip through my grasp, whatever the cost. What is the goodwill of a few peasants when the honor of my family name is at stake? I am the lord of Beaumont, and I shall conduct my business with all the resources Beaumont affords—including your salary, Treville, should occasion arise."

He stalks back to his writing table and flings himself into the chair. He draws a fresh page of parchment out of the box, reaches for his pen, and dips its point in the inkwell. "Now," he commands Treville, his pen hovering above the page, "who speaks against me in the town?"

"Monsieur, there is no such talk."

"There must be, Treville, or you should not have heard it. Give me their names."

Treville does not know how to respond. At last, the chevalier snorts in disgust, flicks away his pen, and shoves himself out of his seat. He marches to the outer doorway and calls for the captain of his guard. The call is raised among the spiderweb of servants and messengers always hovering within the range of the chevalier's voice, and a moment later, the captain of the guard appears in the doorway opposite mine. He's a big man trying not to pant with the exertions of his arrival, but his medals jangle on his chest, and his sword shivers against his boots.

"Your orders, monsieur le chevalier?"

"Monsieur le capitaine, I have heard a report that tongues are clacking against me in the town," says the chevalier. "Monsieur Treville here will supply you with the names of persons whose seditious talk is to be silenced by a day in the public stocks. I choose the Feast Day of Saint Martin next week; it will give the people something to ponder while my bailiff is collecting their quarter rents. If no names are forthcoming," he adds, glancing briefly at Treville, "you will put Monsieur Treville in the stocks on that day."

"But . . . my lord—" The secretary gasps, then lowers his eyes and wisely says no more. The captain of the guard accepts his commission with a nod. His expectant gaze fastens onto Treville as the secretary collects his papers and goes meekly out of the room with his escort.

It's unheard of, a gentleman in the stocks. Apart from the humiliation, he would be the target for offal and refuse, even stones, hurled by every malcontent with a grudge against the nobility—and there are many. Even poor folk are often stoned to death in the stocks by vagabonds and outcasts who have no better target for their rage. What poor man's liberty and pride will Treville sacrifice to save his own? What a terrible choice to have to make.

I thought myself proof against any further shock at the chevalier's cruelty, but I feel a sudden revulsion in my stomach. I turn and flee through this chamber and the next until I gain the kitchen and spill my breakfast into the slops pail.

· CHAPTER 6 ·

The Wisewoman

How foolish I was to think I could bear no more. As if wishing alone could put a limit on my suffering. But there is always more to be borne; that's what living is.

I can scarcely eat. The sight of food turns my stomach. Everything turns my stomach: the gurgle of onions boiling in a pot, the bitter stench of damp ashes swept from the hearth. When it finally comes to me, I don't want to believe it. I struggle desperately not to believe it. But I've seen it often enough, in my own mother with every one of the little ones. First the sickness, then the belly. Then the child.

I can't have his child inside me! I'll go mad. I'll claw it out with my bare hands! Now I am truly ruined. How long before my belly shows, before I am mocked and denounced and turned out? Without a coin to my name, with no hope of maintenance or support, growing bigger with his burden, my shame made visible for all to see. Sleeping under bushes, starving in the road. A part of me might almost welcome it, but I've seen starvation in the lean times in my village, and I know how slow and painful it can be.

If I were clever, I would find a way to end it more quickly. God's punishments are severe for taking a life, even one's own, but hell can be no worse than the endless torment I now suffer every day. Yet how is it to be done? I can't throw myself from the château tower; I'd be chased off before I ever got upstairs. I should not be able to keep a poison in my stomach long enough for it to act, even if I knew which kind to take, and as to raising a weapon against myself—no, I can't bear it. I'm too cowardly.

At last, I remember the river. I am river born, of river blood. As grey and muddy as it is, the river sustains the village I grew up in. It must flow green and clear near Château Beaumont; everything looks so beautiful here. I will give myself to the river, and the river must decide my fate. That way, it can't be murder, can it?

They say God can see into your true heart and knows your deepest secrets despite the lies you tell, even to yourself. But if God can read what's in my heart, He must see that I have no other choice. If God is truly just, He'll forgive me for what I must do.

Château Beaumont is chiselled out of the crest of a hill overlooking acres of vineyards and wheat fields. A great forested park carpets the rear of the plateau, where the Beaumonts do their hunting, but the park gradually gives way to dense, dark wood as it slopes down into the river valley.

I finish my chores early but make my appearance at table for midday dinner so my absence will not be noticed. When the meal is done and all the others are bustling over the dining things, I return to my chamber. When I am certain no one is about, I dart across the grand entry hall and into the rear vestibule behind the staircase. Its door gives onto the little back bridge over the moat, which leads out to the stable yard and the park. I hurry over the bridge, sucking in the fresh air. It seems like centuries since I've tasted the freedom of outdoors. It makes me bold.

I once climbed this hill in a single morning, so long ago now it seems like a different lifetime. I was a different person then. It should not take me longer than an afternoon to find my way down the other way, into the wood. It doesn't matter if they miss me at supper tonight. By then, I'll be past caring.

It's one of those chill, crisp, sunny days, the prime of autumn before cold winter rises from his frozen bed. Some of the park is planted in greenwood, some not, and the trees shimmer with leaves of gold and scarlet, chattering in the breeze. But it's all greenwood deeper into the wood; the trunks grow closer together, and their foliage makes a canopy that shuts out the sun. It might be day or night in the wood, winter or spring. It's all one in the heart of the wood.

How green the river runs here! When I finally glimpse the curving ribbon of it, down in the valley, I make my way toward it with more eagerness. Even in this dark wood where the sun can scarcely penetrate, it doesn't look cold, as I had feared, but soft and inviting, like pale velvet the color of sage leaves. It flows so gently, hardly a ripple, even up close, as I scramble down at last to the bank.

I find a purchase on a flat corner of rock protruding from the bank and gaze into the green water, transfixed. It's so soothing, so inviting. I'll give myself to the river, and I'll be clean and whole again. Such a small price to pay, a life.

"I hope you're not thinking of fouling my river, girl."

It's as if the wood itself has spoken! I jump inside my skin at the words, and as I half turn, I see a figure standing on the bank beside me, only an arm span away, an old woman, bent under a grey hooded cloak. I jump again at the shock, and my foot slips on the mossy rock; the wood somersaults all around me, and then I plunge backside-first into the water, the surface closing over my head, sealing me up. It's cold after all, and dark, and rushing so fast

I can't get my bearings. Water floods into my nose and ears, sharp edges of rock scrape my body and tear at the skin of my hands as they claw for any support, and I'm tumbled through rushing blackness in utter terror. The blackness covers my eyes and weighs on my chest, bearing me down. One of my grasping hands breaks the surface to feel the tingle of cold, dry air for the last time before the river sweeps me away.

But my hand closes suddenly on warm flesh. The river sucks mightily to keep me, but a greater force tugs at my hand. My arm, my shoulder, and my head emerge, and I gulp air into my lungs, choking on the water already there, hacking and rasping. My body is limp in my sodden clothing as I'm dragged up the bank, and I roll over at last onto solid earth, spitting and coughing.

When I have emptied my lungs of water and the world has stopped spinning, I look up. But no one is there, besides the old woman in the grey cloak peering at me, leaning on a stick that looks like an immense tree root upside down, her two hands clasped over the gnarled root ball at its top. From what I can see of them, her arms look as frail and withered as the limbs of a long-dead tree, and her sleeves are dry. Surely she cannot have pulled me from the river.

"Life is a stubborn thing," she croaks at me. "Not so easy to throw away."

And it comes flooding back to me, with the force of

the river itself, the reason I am here. I have failed again. I had only to lie still and breathe deep under the water, and my ordeal would be over. Now I'm worse off than I was, and even more humiliated.

"Well, come inside and get warm," clucks the old gnome. She turns on her stick and shuffles off into the gloom. Beyond her, just a few trees away, I see a small hut with a thatched roof. I'm certain it wasn't there before, or I would have chosen a more solitary place.

But how did it get here?

A voice inside me urges me to roll back down the bank into the river and try again. Surely this time I'll be too weak to resist. But I am cold now, and wet, chilled and shivering in the unfriendly dark. Discomfort and exhaustion cure me of my recklessness, and I rise from the carpet of twigs and needles and leaves and stumble after her, my wet woolen skirts tripping up my legs.

At the hut, she throws open a small wooden door carved with a sun and the phases of the moon and other characters I can't begin to understand. My legs are still shaky, and it's awkward for me to bend low enough to squeeze through the doorway that fits her so perfectly. But I find I can stand upright inside. Indeed, the interior is much more spacious than you'd think from looking at the outside. The floor beneath my feet is laid in dark green and ivory tiles. A cozy bed under a gauze canopy sits in one corner with a calico cat asleep among the pillows. A welcoming fire blazes in a fireplace of bricks, although I swear I never saw any plume of smoke rising out of the roof when I was outside.

Kitchen things are in the corner near the fire, and rustic carved cupboards are on the wall above a table laid with bowls and cups. Another larger table is half concealed in shadows, under a string hung with bunches of drying herbs. Two small armchairs are drawn up to the hearth. I smell chocolate steaming on the hob.

"Sit, girl," instructs the old woman as she crosses the room, pointing to one of the armchairs with her stick. As I move toward it, I realize my frock and shoes are already dry, as if they had never been wet.

"What is this place?" My voice quavers. I've heard stories of the uncanny folk, but I've never seen one before.

The old woman leans her gnarled stick against the fireplace and turns toward me as she tosses back her hood. Her bearing is straighter, somehow, and her face, when it is revealed, looks less gnomish and wrinkled. It's still a face older than time, full of experience, but she wears her age with serenity. She no longer seems frightful. She gazes at me, a thoughtful smile playing at her lips.

"This is my home. And you are my guest." She nods again at the little chair, and I sit, surprised at its comfort. She lifts the beautiful china pot off the hob—the heat hasn't cracked it, nor does it burn her fingers—and pours a cup of chocolate for me. The aroma is rich and beckoning; my first sip leads to a deeper draught as she sits in the other chair, facing me. "And now I must know why you've come to see me."

I swallow another mouthful. "See you? I don't even know who you are."

"Folk call me Mère Sophie."

"But I wasn't looking for you," I tell her.

"Ah, no." She nods. "You came to throw yourself in the river."

I shift uncomfortably in my chair, hiding my face in the steam from my cup. "I didn't think anyone would be in the wood."

"But the wood is full of life. Nothing happens here in secret."

My humiliation is complete. All of nature has witnessed my shame. I hold my cup with both hands and stare into what's left of its contents, rich and sweet and comforting, even with my heart in such turmoil. A tear slides off my nose and into the cup, disappearing into the dark foam.

"I know God will punish my wickedness—"

"Ptah! That's a matter for the priests to debate," she interrupts me with a careless wave of her hand. "It has nothing to do with the lives of women. Why should you suffer when you've done no wrong?"

I glance up, shocked, to see so much wisdom and understanding in her eyes—black eyes, like small, ripe olives. It's as if she knows all the secrets of my heart. Fairy, witch, or wisewoman, she knows everything about me.

"The young Chevalier de Beaumont," she goes on calmly, nodding at the badge on my bodice. "I know his livery. He is often spoken of in this wood, by mothers needing remedies for their hungry children. By tenants turned off their land and seeking refuge." She leans confidingly toward me. "Do you think you're the first woman who's ever fled into the wood because of him?"

My gaze falls again to my chocolate.

"I carry his seed," I whisper. And all of the desperation and despair that drove me to the river seizes me again, icy fingers clenching my heart. "It festers inside me. I can feel it! It will consume me."

Mère Sophie reaches out one ancient hand to touch my arm with the gentlest of fingertips. "A seed need not bear fruit."

I look up again. It is terrible to consider. It's no fault of the thing itself that it was conceived. But even if I wanted it, what mother could willingly bring a child into such a life, knowing that only poverty, shame, and starvation would be its fate? I struggle to muster my resolve.

"Will it hurt?" My voice quakes.

She squeezes my arm very gently. "It is done."

A part of me is fearfully alarmed, wants to leap up and dash the cup to bits in the hearth. But the wisewoman's comforting presence gives me courage, and her reassurance is so beguiling, I cling to it, as I clung to the powerful hand that pulled me from the river. By strength of her will alone, by the serenity in those black eyes, the festering inside me eases a little. And yet, something gnaws at me still, troubles me, goads me.

"It will take time to heal your heart," says the wise-woman. It's as if she knows all about me, by her touch alone. "Be strong. You are not to blame for what happened, and you are not the one who deserves punishment. Arrogance, cruelty, beastliness . . . those are dark sins, more difficult to absolve." Her fingers slide down my arm, and she takes my hand in hers. I recognize her grip from the riverside. "He has taken a great deal from you, my dear. Don't let him have the rest. Prove you have the stronger heart and survive."

I have no other choice. But her words give me comfort somehow, or perhaps I am simply relieved to have my story known to someone. Yet I dread the prospect of returning to Château Beaumont.

"But . . . I will have to see him," I say. Until this moment, I never expected to go back, and now the prospect chills me. "I will have to face him. Every day."

The memory of his smirks, his slanting glances, the

callous way he used me, all come flooding back to me. I am outraged, and my rage burns off the last of my despair. In that instant, as if they were sparks leaping out of the fire, I see the face of Treville, the secretary threatened with the stocks; Nicolas, the young page so cruelly humiliated; the maimed doe torn apart for the sport of his dogs. A kind of power surges through me as my fury rises against him. Perhaps my hatred will give me the strength I need.

The wisewoman gazes at me, head cocking very slightly to one side, as if my thoughts were written in the air for her to study. She nods slowly.

"I see. Then watch and wait, Lucie." I don't even question how she knows my name. She sits so alert before me, her black eyes bright in the firelight. "There will be a reckoning at Château Beaumont soon enough, I promise you."

But when I beg to know more, that is all she will say on the subject.

It must be fearfully late by now, and I know I must go back. As I get to my feet, it occurs to me that I have accepted her hospitality and her potion and have nothing for her in return.

"I can't pay you," I apologize. "But I will have my wage at year's end, in silver coin, and I will bring it to you."

"And what would you normally do with your wage?" she asks.

"Send it home to my mother."

"No doubt she will make better use of it than I." Mère Sophie smiles. "I have little need of coins, child. Your company is payment enough."

She must get few visitors if she counts me as company, a mewling chit she's had to drag from the river like a drowning cat. And yet she thinks mine is a life worth preserving. Few enough ever have before, not since I lost my father, and my mother sent me here. But now that she's given me back the gift of my life, I suppose I must treat it with more respect.

At the door, I hesitate. Mère Sophie has restored my life, but more trouble is brewing. "It's nearly nightfall. How shall I find my way back in the dark?" I ask her. "How can I explain where I've been?"

She pushes open the door with her stick and gestures outside. I see early-afternoon sunlight slanting in through the tree trunks, no later than when I first set out after dinner.

"But it's been only a moment, a blink." She smiles at me again. "You shall be home before you can blink again."

I set out into the wood, then pause to turn back and thank her. But the thatched cottage is nowhere to be seen. There are only silent tree trunks and the giddy laughter of the river.

And a soft breeze that rustles in the leaves. It whispers, "Watch and wait."

· CHAPTER 7 ·

Acts of Charity

When I casually mention Mère Sophie at the château, they all claim to know something about her.

"She's a witch!" a housemaid tells me gleefully. "I've seen her! Riding her switch across the moon, dressed all in cobwebs! They say the toads dance in the marsh when she flies overhead."

Madame Montant scoffs. "She's an old hermit who lost her reason and took to the wood." The housekeeper narrows her eyes at me. "Don't let me ever hear of you going down there, girl. Her foolish talk can beguile a person's wits."

I pretend I have only heard the name from the other servants. But I know what I've seen, so I watch and wait.

The floors in my chambers want scrubbing. There is no urgency today as there was the day I ran into the wood, so I decide to follow the long route to the well: out a side door in the kitchen wing and across the front courtyard to the gap between the carriage house and the main house. I'm told the main house occupies the site of the original Fortress Beaumont, and the side wings were added later as the fortune and the grandeur of the LeNoir family increased. The kitchen wing to the west connects directly to the main house for convenience, but the carriage house opposite the courtyard is a separate building. A horse track under a covered archway divides it from the main house, and this track continues over an ancient drawbridge that crosses the east side of the moat. This route circles around the east wing of the château and back to the stable yard that lies beyond the rear of the moat. The original intent was to provide a way for horses from the stables to be brought into the protection of the courtyard if the fortress were under siege. Now it's used mostly to bring in horses for the chevalier's carriage when he wants to make a splendid progress through his gilded gate. Or else by servants going to and from the well.

The swans are paddling lazily in the water as I round the outer edge of the moat and turn the corner for the back bridge. A great deal of water is still in the moat from the last storm, but the water is grey, like the lowering skies we've had of late. Behind the château, I make my way to the line of sculpted hedges that screen the back of the moat from the yard and the stone well beyond. But I have to skitter off behind a hedge when I see him coming, striding out of the park with his favorite hound, heading for the well. I hear the boisterous talk and laughter of his hunting companions still some distance behind him. But he and his dog approach the well alone. He draws the water himself, laughing as his dog leaps and capers and bares its teeth in impatience. He splashes the water out of the bucket into a gilded dish and sets it on the ground, and the dog greedily slurps it up.

He's dressed for the hunt—collar thrust open, shirt-sleeves rolled up to the elbows, tan leather jerkin, over-the-knee boots. A magnificent animal, I suppose, as he goes down gracefully on one knee to stroke the hound's withers, but I can't think how I ever found him beautiful. Master and beast. Two of a kind.

We all three look up, suddenly, at an odd noise: soft, shuffling footfalls in the gravel pathway and a heavy wheezing on the far side of the well. I peer out between the leaves of the hedge as he rises. The dog sniffs the air and growls. I see him lace two fingers through the dog's jewelled collar as a small figure swathed in a grey cloak approaches the well.

"Good day to you, good sir." It's a quavery female

voice, frail with age. She leans upon her gnarled stick, and he responds with a curt nod. "Can you spare a cup of water for an old woman?"

"Use the river. It's free to all," replies the chevalier.

"Yes, I am going that way. But it's a long walk for these old limbs, and I am thirsty now."

I catch my breath, eager, for I recognize Mère Sophie's voice.

"Please, kind sir, as an act of charity," she goes on. "A swallow only, and I'll be on my way."

"Be off with you!" he retorts. "I want no beggars about the place."

The growling dog now sets up an agitated barking, catching the scent of its master's anger. The old woman withdraws a step, looking at the creature, then turns her gaze once more to the chevalier.

"One drop would fortify me, sir. It would be a great kindness."

"Why should I be kind?" he cries. The dog is lunging in his grip now, up on its hind legs in a frenzy of baying. "This is my well and my land, and you are trespassing. Be off before I set the dogs on you!"

There are answering howls from the park, as other dogs and other hunters appear at the tree line. More men are emerging from the stable to see what's amiss and do their master's bidding. But I know the wisewoman's strange powers. Surely she will serve him some reprimand for his cruelty!

But she shrugs deeper into her cloak. "As you wish." She sighs and turns away. We all watch her creaky progress as she heads for the trees and the wood far beyond, keeping clear of the place where the snarling hounds are held in check.

"Crone," mutters the grand Chevalier de Beaumont. "Witch!" Something more than impatience is in his voice. Could it be fear?

He bends over his agitated dog, petting and stroking. "Quiet there, Zeus. Good boy. Easy now," he soothes, softening his voice, drawing deep breaths. He might as well be speaking to himself. Then he looks around to see his gatekeeper trotting toward him, alerted perhaps by one of the other servants.

"Andre!" the chevalier shouts. "How did that damned insolent hag get on my property?"

"Hag?" echoes the gatekeeper, mystified. "But . . . I saw no such person, monsieur le chevalier—"

"If you can't do your job, I'll find someone who can!" roars the chevalier. "Get your things and go!" And before poor Andre can utter another word in his own defense, the chevalier is marching back for the park with his hound at his heels.

But my heart is sinking. I let Mère Sophie beguile my

wits, but she has no more power against him than I have. She's just an addled old woman after all. I have no champion, no ally against the chevalier but my own hatred. I will nurse and suckle it. It is my only comfort.

Storm clouds are gathering as we clear away the dining things a few days later. The metallic scent of rain makes the dogs too uneasy to hunt, and their master is upstairs, brooding, for want of amusement. The chevalier's nights have been restless; the upstairs servants whisper that he cries out in his sleep, waking in a fever, disturbing his gentlemen. He is more ill-tempered than ever with all of us since the day the crone came to the well. I dare to hope that Mère Sophie has visited some spell upon him after all.

I'm cleaning the windows in one of my chambers when I see a coach of astonishing finery enter the courtyard, pulled by four snow-white horses. Its gilded surface blazes like a sun, even on this grey day, as it climbs the drive between the flower beds and pulls up at the foot of the broad front steps.

From my window in the west wing, I see Monsieur Ferron, the steward, appear at the top of the steps as the coach pulls to a halt. A footman in emerald livery leaps off the back, plants himself on the bottom step, and cries up to the steward, "My lady seeks sanctuary!"

Monsieur Ferron frowns down at him. "Do you take us for a church, my good man?"

"Indeed not! The last church was miles away! But this storm will break soon, and my lady requires shelter."

"Neither are we a house of charity," sniffs the steward.

"Ferron!" cries the master of the house, emerging from the grand doorway behind him. "Do I dream, or are you debasing yourself on my steps arguing with a footman?"

"My apologies, monsieur le chevalier," the steward grovels.

"You may prattle like a peasant in the streets if you must, but I caution you to have a care for the honor of my house."

Monsieur Ferron bows nearly to his knees at this unjust rebuke, for he is second only to the chevalier himself in guarding the reputation of Château Beaumont and its master. Meanwhile, the footman has been called to the side of his coach, where an elegant gloved hand rests on the sill of a small window, and a soft female voice declares, "I shall speak to this gentleman."

The footman bows and pulls open the coach door, then tugs down the hinged step and hands the lady out. She is beautiful beyond measure—hair upswept from her face and done up in jewels, with long golden coils trailing down her back and a pale, perfect complexion. Her throat is long and elegant, her bosom alluring above a gold-worked bodice that fits her like a second skin. Her gown and cloak are of the richest velvet in a soft shade of heather green. All eyes seek her out, and for that moment, all conversation ceases. She raises her gaze to the face of the chevalier, and something blazes between them. I can see the transformation in him. The bored, petulant knight disappears; in his place stands Jean-Loup, the predator, regal and charming.

"My lady," he murmurs, bowing rakishly low, his fingertips all but sweeping the top step in a grand gesture of welcome. "Your presence ornaments my humble home. Pray tell me whom I have the privilege to address?"

"I am Lady Honoree D'Auria Reveaux, Comtesse Du Bois." She inclines her perfect head, and Jean-Loup himself glides down the steps to take her hand. He rattles off his own titles to her and dares to place a chaste, obedient kiss upon her gloved hand.

"Shall I have the pleasure of entertaining Monsieur le Comte this evening?" he asks.

"Alas, the count, my late father, is beyond the pleasures of this world. I journey to meet my bridegroom-to-be but find myself at odds with nature this afternoon."

"Then praise nature for delivering you into my care, my lady." His eyes are earnest, his smile hopeful, not yet dazzling. He plays the components of his handsome face like a puppet master, teasing this string, nudging that, until all the pieces work in concert for maximum effect. How can the poor creature not melt at the sight of him? Indeed, she lowers her beautiful eyes. Her first gesture of surrender. "Please come inside, my lady," he urges her. "Whatever is in my poor power to provide is yours."

He dismisses her men to the carriage house and orders refreshment laid for them in the kitchen. He sends his steward to the kitchen as well, to order wine and brandy and a meal, then escorts the Comtesse Du Bois up the steps and into the hall. My stomach is churning as I watch. The Lady Honoree is a noblewoman who has declared herself en route to wed a husband; she believes the Chevalier de Beaumont's behavior will be as gallant as his words.

How wrong she is!

· CHAPTER 8 ·

Transformation

I can't bear it. Wealthy and noble she may be, but with her father dead and herself not yet under the protection of a husband, she is as vulnerable as I was. And she may be deceived and ruined, as I was, unless I try to interfere on her behalf. No one else will dare to cross the chevalier, but I can't sit idly by; I can't. Not if it's at all in my power to stop him.

I tell Madame Montant I am off at the bidding of the under-housekeeper Marie, and I tell Marie I'm running an errand for Madame Montant. They are in too much of a frenzy belowstairs over the master's houseguest to take any notice of me. In a far corner of one of my chambers is a door that leads to one of the four turrets that mark the corners of the house. Each turret encloses a hidden stairway for the use of the upstairs servants. I have never used them before, but now I open the door and slip inside.

The stone steps, worn smooth by generations of slippered feet, spiral ever upward in the narrow cylinder of stone, giving way at last to a long utility passage. I follow this until it opens onto the spacious upper hall that surrounds the central staircase.

Now I recognize my surroundings. Beyond the staircase lies the dining salon, where the chevalier entertains, and beyond, the ballroom. Servants are already bustling the plates and knives and serving platters out of the dining salon. I retreat back into the utility passage so as not to be seen by them, but they are using one of the other turret staircases. I hear no music coming from the ballroom, so I know the chevalier and the comtesse must be elsewhere.

Fighting down my anger and shame, recalling the last time I was in this place, I turn toward his private rooms. The door to his outer salon is open, and I shrink back into a shadowy niche when a figure appears in the doorway. It is Monsieur Ferron.

"That will be all, Ferron." His voice comes from inside. "See to my lady's apartments."

"Very good, monsieur le chevalier."

"And you may leave the door ajar." His voice has turned charming, humorous. "We have no desire to scandalize the servants."

How kind of the chevalier to consider my lady's delicate

reputation! But of course, his gentlemen-in-waiting have taken themselves off, now that he has company.

"As you wish, sir." Monsieur Ferron bows and retreats, then turns on his heel and marches off toward the wing of private apartments beyond the dining salon and the ballroom. The other servants have all melted away, leaving the chevalier utterly alone with the Lady Honoree.

Or so he believes.

Assuring myself no one else is about, I creep through the salon to the open doorway that leads to his private sitting room and peer inside.

A small, rosy fire burns in the grate of the white marble fireplace. A crystal chandelier with cream-colored candles hangs before a mirror above the mantelpiece, reflecting more warm, soft light into the room. It shimmers in Lady Honoree's golden hair and on the folds of her lush gown. The young comtesse stands at a tall, arched window that gives onto a small balcony, watching the rain. The chevalier perches on a chaise longue in a corner of the room, watching her. It appears they have been speaking lightly of nothing in particular, their dinner, perhaps, or the weather, or the state of this year's wine. But now, they have grown quiet as my lady leans her golden head against the glass.

"See how it rains," she murmurs. "I may be a burden on your hospitality for days to come, monsieur le chevalier."

"Please, call me Jean-Loup. And it is no burden, Lady Honoree."

"You must allow me to repay your great kindness to me."

"But your beauty and virtue are recompense enough, my lady," he assures her, this great champion of virtue. "I shall carry them always in my heart to sustain me."

She turns her face from the window to look at him. "Sustain? How so?"

"After you are gone and I return to my solitary pursuits. When the memory of your beauty and virtue shall be all I have left of you."

Her hand rises to her bodice as she regards him. "But—you speak like a suitor, Jean-Loup."

"Would that I had the opportunity to press my suit, my lady." He rises in agitation. "But you are but a step away from the altar, and I am far too late."

"We are ever pawns in the hands of fate, people of our station," she agrees sadly.

"And yet, fate has brought you here," he reasons, daring a step closer. She turns again to the window, lowers her head, and sighs, so she does not see him come one step closer still.

"Only to wound you, it seems," the comtesse murmurs. "It grieves me to think you will suffer because of me."

She cannot see what I see, the smile slowly spreading across his handsome face as he looms behind her. When he speaks again, his voice is low and urgent.

"But there is something you can do for me . . . Honoree. Something that would ease my suffering."

"You have but to name it, Jean-Loup." Her voice is small, fluttering like a fan. "You have been so kind to me. What may I do for you?"

"A small thing only, a token," he murmurs, lowering his face close to her bent head. "The smallest of kindnesses, to carry in my heart for all the rest of my lonely days." He raises one hand to rest on her shoulder; the other inches around her waist.

Lady Honoree's posture stiffens immediately. "But, monsieur le chevalier—"

She tries to twist out of his grasp, but he does not let go.

"Come now, Honoree," he says, more urgently still. "We may never meet again. Why should we not be kind?"

How dare he speak to her like a mistress, like one of his maids!

"You must let me go, Jean-Loup!" exclaims the comtesse.

"Grant me a kiss, and we shall see," purrs the chevalier, tightening his grip.

Rage boils up inside of me; I mean to throw open the

door, upset the wine decanter, overturn chairs — anything to disrupt the scene. But my hand is frozen to the door handle, my feet will not leave the floor, and my words stick in my throat.

"A kiss? A kiss only?" echoes the lady, and there is something strange about her voice. It's less melodious now, more harsh. She seems to shrink into her gown, eluding the chevalier's groping hands, and he pauses, bewildered. She whirls around to face him again, and he cries out and staggers back several steps. Lady Honoree's golden hair uncurls into long, straggly grey-and-white strands, and her dazzling raiment dissolves into shapeless grey rags. Her skin withers, her features wizen, and her black eyes blaze. She is Mère Sophie at her most frightful.

"So that is the price of your kindness, Chevalier de Beaumont!" she crows at him. "A kiss! Had you only told me so at the well, we might have made a bargain. But it's too late now, as you say. You have sealed your fate."

"Hag!" he cries as he stumbles backward. "Witch! What do you want with me?"

"My wants?" she taunts. "When have the wants of others ever mattered to you? I'm here to see to *your* wants."

"Ferron!" he roars. "Andre! Guards!"

But his gatekeeper was dismissed, and the rest of his men fail to appear.

"You want to dishonor women for the sport of it,"

Mère Sophie goes on. "You want to pursue your pleasures without restraint, whatever the cost to others. You want to live like a beast, and so you shall."

The storm outside has suddenly risen to a horrendous pitch; lightning cracks across the sky, and hailstones rattle the window. And yet, I can hear the panicked shrieking of horses in the stables and dogs howling in fear from the kennels. His yelping for his servants goes unheeded. The nervous buzz of the servants downstairs escalates into frantic shouting; an atmosphere of calamity, sorcery, and doom now grips all within these walls, a fear of unnatural forces greater even than their fear of the chevalier's wrath. What has become of Lady Honoree's golden coach? I wonder. Is it crumbling to dust before the servants' eyes down in the carriage house? Are her footmen turning into frogs skittering away under their feet? Have her snow-white steeds flown off as bats?

In the next heartbeat, the household servants are all in flight, terrified of witchcraft. I see them emptying out of the upstairs rooms and fleeing down the staircase. Their footfalls are pounding down the turret steps, amid wails of mounting alarm. Down the stairs flee Monsieur Ferron, Nicolas the page, and Treville, the abused secretary. None of them come to aid the chevalier. The babble of a hundred terrified voices fills the entry hall below and then bursts outside like a fist shoved through the door. I hear shod feet crunching on the wet gravel in the courtyard as they stream out of the house. And I realize I am suddenly in command of my own limbs again. I might join the others and flee. But I don't. I am mesmerized by the spectacle of Jean-Loup, Chevalier de Beaumont, crouched low on his haunches now, cowering from the fearsome Mère Sophie, arms thrust up to cover his face, bellowing like a wounded animal.

"You will know what it is to be wretched and alone," the wisewoman tells him calmly. "What beauty will want you now?"

The chevalier cannot seem to rise. Something is wrong with his body. His trunk is thickening, swaying lower to the ground; his hind end is rising. His howls are deepening, becoming more savage.

But my heart is leaping. Can this be the reckoning Mère Sophie promised me? I am astonished, fascinated, but not afraid.

The chevalier lowers his hands to support himself, and they are covered with hair; they have become large and furry paws. His jacket, tunic, and breeches, his shoes and stockings all split apart and fall away, revealing a thickening hind haunch covered in short, curly brown fur, over goat legs tapering to heavy, sharp-edged cloven hooves. And his head! Devil horns sprout between shaggy, pointed ears above a broad neck. His profile lengthens into a snout, eyes forward, like a predator. A ragged, goatish beard decorates his chin, and great tufts of straw-colored mane erupt from his sloping forehead and down the back of his massive neck, to cascade over his chest. Long rows of raptor feathers sprout out of his fur-covered shoulders and ripple down his back.

He is hideous!

He shakes back his mane in a fury, his expression full of rage.

"Wha . . . what have you done to me?" It's hard to understand his words because of his new animal snout and the lower, rumbling pitch of his voice.

"I have done nothing," Mère Sophie declares. "This is the truth of who you are inside."

"Change me back!" he thunders.

"I cannot. That power lies with you, not me."

Then Mère Sophie turns to me; her voice seems to be right in my ear, but she is still standing above the chevalier, across the room. "And you, girl." She lifts her face and fixes me with her black eyes. "What do you want?"

"I want to see him suffer," I breathe.

The wisewoman nods. "As you wish."

"Witch!" the chevalier rages. "Undo this spell you've put on me!"

Mère Sophie rounds back on him, her words precise

and full of rage. "You are such a champion of virtue, Jean-Loup. Find a maid of good virtue to marry you as you are now, and you shall be restored."

I hear him suck in a breath, shocked at the impossibility of such a task. But I am delighted; what use will Jean-Loup's wealth and honeyed words be to the beast that stands before us now? With a nod of satisfaction, the wisewoman turns away.

"You cannot leave me like this!" he bellows after her. "Release me, you foul, vile—"

Mère Sophie waves a hand in irritation, and his hateful words freeze on his lips. He rears all the way up on his hind hooves, pawing at the air, his awful mouth open in mute rage. The wisewoman neither shrinks away nor quails, and he hurls himself away from her as if to march out the door. But his heavy chest sways lower and lower toward the ground; he is nearly on all fours when his head swivels around to stare at me for an instant, where I stand in the doorway. Then he lunges past me out the door, through the outer salon, and into the dark, deserted hallway.

Mère Sophie walks toward me. I am surprised at how large she's become; she towers above me. She bends low, stretches out a hand, and takes me up in her grasp. How still I've become, how small. I feel that my arms are upraised, but they don't ache in that awkward position. My legs seem bound together. She lifts me up and shuffles over to the fireplace. When she sets me on the mantelpiece, before the glass, I see how I, too, have been transformed.

I am woman no more. I am flesh no more. I am made of silver, sleek and smooth and slim. My arms curve upward to hold two long, tapered candles; a third rests in the crown of my head, or what was once my head. I have no human anatomy, no vulnerable parts to be hurt or betrayed, no face, no eyes, and yet I see.

I am beautiful!

· CHAPTER 9 ·

Shattered

Time passes, but it matters little to me. My tapers burn at all times, day or night, dark or light.

I am not a waxen candle, subject to every whim of heat or weather, draining away my life in service to others. I am proud, strong silver, holding up the candles. Their wicks burn, but they are enchanted; hot wax never drips down my silver arms, my tapers never shorten, and their flames never die.

But the candles in the crystal chandelier are ordinary wax and subject to the laws that govern ordinary things. They have all burned out, and the chandelier hangs dark and forlorn from its gilded chains. The fire in the hearth below me has gone out as well. It's so quiet now. No servants to bustle about. No hounds to bay.

His dogs set up a fearful racket when he went down to the kennels the next day; they could be heard all over the property. They might have torn him to pieces, but in the end, they seemed as frightened by the witchcraft as the servants and ran away. From my perch, I can see out the window and over the balcony to a great deal of the grounds and the park behind the château. I saw the dogs' dark shapes racing away into the park and the wood. He tried to follow, perhaps to join their company, for want of any other. But he was not yet in command of his strange new limbs and was left panting at the edge of the park, snarling and cursing.

Even his brutish hounds abandon him.

He is the only thing that moves in this place. I often hear the distant clop of his hooves on the marble floor or his heavy tread upon the stairs. Or sometimes a crash of pans in the kitchen as he searches for food. There are no servants to cook for him now. No one dares to come here anymore. His companions have forsaken him for other sports, other tables. He has only himself for company. And poor enough comfort he must find it, for I often hear him howling at night in his misery. A pitiful, beastly howl. Yet it warms me to hear it. Let him know what it is to feel despair!

I despair no more. I am elegant and strong, with no clumsy human body to be abused, no heart to be shamed. I feel no pain, no weariness, no anxiety of any kind. I do not thirst or hunger. I am sustained by his misery, and I feast upon it.

He never comes back here. I suppose he can't bear to return to the place where his life was destroyed, can't bear to go into his old apartments where everything is still laid out so luxuriously for the man he was. I am the only sentinel here, watching the nights lengthen outside the window as the winter comes on, that brooding time of year when all the country appears cold and dead.

But tonight I hear a sullen footfall out on the stairs, and he appears in the doorway, hunched forward but not quite on all fours. He hesitates there, then enters the room gingerly, still in a crouch, peering into the shadowy corners as if he expects Mère Sophie to come cackling out of the dark, flinging more curses at him. Finally his paws touch the floor, and he follows his snout around the room, sniffing at everything. Perhaps he hopes to pick up the scent of Jean-Loup in the last place he ever existed, to find some trace of his old self that will make him whole again. He creeps up to the chaise longue, sets his heavy paws upon the seat, and snuffles at the cushions. From up here, I gaze down at the mottled rusty brown-and-white stripes on the black-tipped feathers that cover most of his back; they tremble slightly as he roves about. He circles around to sniff at the cold fireplace below me, then turns his face up toward the mantelpiece to peer at the light reflected in the glass. My light.

He rises slowly, steadying his paws on the marble ornaments until he is up on his hind feet, balancing carefully on his heavy hooves. He cocks his giant head to one side. His eyes are still strangely human-shaped; stony dark under his new, thick, beastly brows and shot with a cold light, reflecting my flames.

"What, still alight?" His words are thick but intelligible; the wisewoman has not permanently denied him the power of speech, although he hasn't had much cause to use it of late. He snuffles at me with his long snout, his animal breath hot, fogging my smooth surface. I am mute, of course, and serene.

"Little Candle," he breathes. I see recognition dawning in his eyes and a fleeting shadow of that crafty look, that possessive smugness I remember from the night he called me by this name. Once it would have made me shudder inside, but he has no power to hurt me now. I wonder if he has sniffed out some trace of my former humanity, as he came looking for some trace of his.

"Of course," he rumbles. "Who else could you be? Come to light my way again, have you?" His expression darkens with anger. "To mock me? To show me what . . ."

His words fade away as his eyes shift from me to the

mirror behind me, where his reflection hovers in the glass. Horns, snout, ratty, strawlike mane—he sees it all. By my light.

His roar of rage would split my ears, if I still had ears; the tapers rattle in my silver grasp. His huge paw closes around me, and I'm lifted off the mantel; then my heavy base is dashed into the looking glass. A hailstorm of glass bursts over us both, but I am undamaged. I feel no pain. My candles and I are unbreakable.

This is what he thought of me once, an object to be used and discarded. But look at me now! I am strong, as I never was before. I am here to show him what he has become. I will illuminate his crimes.

Still howling in rage, he stumbles across the sitting room, wielding me like a club, throws open the wardrobe, and smashes me into the looking glass bolted inside the door. Then he carries me into his bedchamber and smashes me into the mirror overlooking his bed.

Glass crunches beneath his hooves as he lurches, half-upright, back out through his apartments. He smashes me into a mirror on the wall outside his chamber door in the entryway across from the staircase. Holding me in one paw, he crosses to the dining salon. We dispatch a huge mirror in a gilt frame above the sideboard, then proceed into the ballroom. It is an enormous cavern of a place in the dark. I have never been here before. Every wall is hung with panel after panel of full-length mirrors, veined with gold. Each one reflects my light, which of course has not gone out, will never go out. Each one shows him what he is.

Still gripped in his paw, I am hammered into one glass panel and the next and the next. With each crash, glass splinters, flies into the air, and rains to the floor, each explosion amplified in the vast, echoing room. It sounds like a battlefield, like the end of the world. It's exhilarating, his rage. I am glad to be the instrument of his self-loathing.

At last nothing is left but four blank walls marked with gilded brackets and a carpet of shattered glass. Spent and panting, he props himself by one heavy paw against the wall and lets me slide from his grasp down into the broken glass. My candles still burn; the glass bits glitter with their light. They illuminate his face as he stares down at the destruction we've wrought.

He no longer has breath to bellow, but as he sinks down on his haunches, he makes a different noise, a wounded-animal sound, mournful and hopeless. His paws rise to cover his horrible face, and he crouches there, shuddering. I recognize his hopelessness. I revel in it.

At last, he lowers his paws. His eyes search the floor, then he springs at something. His paw rises out of the rubble, clutching a long shard of glass with a wicked point; its edges are so sharp, I can see blood on the thick pads of his paw where he grasps it.

He rises on his haunches and claws aside the thick tendrils of his mane that fall over his chest, revealing a heaving expanse of matted fur. He grasps the glass shard in both paws and aims its point at his exposed breast.

Oh, if only I had a mouth to cry "No!" He must not take his life! He cannot rob me of my revenge!

He draws a breath — and pauses. He angles the point a little higher, toward his throat, lifts his tufted chin, and closes his eyes.

But his resolution fails him again. Try as he might, with all the best intentions he can muster, he can't plunge the weapon home, cannot deprive himself of his life, however wretched it's become. At last, with a howl, he casts the bloody shard back into the rubble in disgust. Relief wells up inside me, and no little glee, to witness his cowardice.

Then his gaze falls back on me, my light still sparkling in the broken glass. His dark eyes narrow. "You shall mock me no more, Little Candle!"

He scoops me up again and picks his way across the room, hooves crunching the splintered glass until he reaches a dark passageway and a small door in a far corner. It opens into another of the turret staircases. We climb the spiraling stone steps to the topmost floor of the château, its rooms long unused. We come out into a narrow passage and turn off into another longer one, the gloom too deep and our pace too quick for my light to illuminate much.

He has no need to see by my light, I am sure; his beast's eyes sharpen in the dark. He must have some other purpose in bringing me here.

We arrive at last in a large room under steep, slanting roof beams, dark and dusty with neglect. I see chests and pieces of furniture stacked here and there, some of them nursery things, all items for which Jean-Loup, the bachelor chevalier, had no use. An old cupboard stands in one corner, turned sideways toward an arched window through which nothing can now be seen but black night. The beast who was Jean-Loup yanks open the cupboard door and thrusts me inside, setting me on a shelf tall enough to accommodate my tapers. There is no other object on this shelf; my flame illuminates nothing. For the first time since my transformation, I feel anxiety as he begins to shut the door on me. How will I enjoy my revenge if I can't witness his misery? And perhaps he hears something of my thoughts somehow, or simply guesses them, because I see a wicked smile kindle in his cold eyes.

"You are so eager to watch me suffer? I will give you better than that, Little Candle," he growls. "You shall suffer with me. Shine as bright as you like, but see me no more."

And I am shut up in empty darkness.

CHAPTER 10

Beast

I should have known he would find a new way to be cruel to me, even in my present form. Time has no meaning for me. I can't feel its passage as I once did; I no longer feel hunger or weariness. But I notice subtle changes in the nothingness within this cupboard. A strip of morning daylight alerts me that the cupboard doors are ajar; the impact when he slammed the one shut must have loosened the other. There is a space through which I can peer, and beyond it a mullioned glass windowpane.

Daylight comes and goes many more times, and the unlatched cupboard door sags open a little wider, so I can resolve what it is I see. The window looks out over the courtyard, its flower beds beginning to run ragged, the blooms all gone, the stalks unpruned. This room I am in is near a corner of the château, and another wing juts out nearby, framing the courtyard below. From where I perch,

I can look into a broad bay window, one floor down in the adjoining wing. It is always dark inside, and I can never see what lies within. But tonight, as the full moon rises, it casts its curious beam through the glass to illuminate what's inside.

Visible now within the bay window is a beautiful sunken bathing tub inlaid with Moorish tiles — deep blues, rich greens, purple, and turquoise, like a small private ocean. A half-drawn curtain separates it from the larger room within, and as I peer beyond the curtain, I glimpse an ebony bedpost. His bedchamber. His private bath.

The curtain is pulled all the way back, and he is standing in his room. He surveys the bathtub for a long time, and finally turns and lumbers away to the fireplace at the opposite end of the room. I can just glimpse his feathered back as he crouches before his hearth, working intently at something. At last I see the flickering of firelight in the hearth; by some miracle, he has managed flint and tinderbox with his clumsy paws. When he's satisfied that the fire has caught, he turns and gallops away; I hear his heavy footfalls echoing in one of the stairwells below.

He hauls the buckets of water up himself, with no servants left to help him. My hands are fit only for holding candles in this dark place where light is banished. He wants the fire not for light, but to heat his bathwater, and

I marvel at his determination to savor what must be the only pleasure left him—even as I gloat over all the pleasures he has lost. First he brings up the cauldron from the kitchen and sets it on his fireplace grate. Then he hauls up the water, two buckets at a time, slowly filling the cauldron. Whenever it gets too full, he bails hot water out of the cauldron and carries it over to the bathtub by the bucketful, then races downstairs for more water to feed the cauldron.

At long last, the tub is full and steaming, and he stands above it. It's a terrible sight, all of his animal parts joined together—huge horned head above massive shoulders and a broad chest matted with motley fur. His trunk is pelted with long, tangled hair. From this angle, only a few ruffled edges of the useless feathers that cover his back are visible, silhouetted in the firelight, but I can see the curly fur that covers his broad haunches, from which his thick hind legs emerge above heavy cleft hooves. His muscled shoulders and heavy paws provide power, his hindquarters speed, but surely his patchwork parts were never meant to be joined to the same creature. He is breathtaking in his hideousness.

He clambers over the side of the tub and slides into the water on his back, like a man, deeper and deeper, until nothing is left above but his hairy paws covering his face, lest he glimpse his awful reflection rippling on the surface of the water. A straw-colored forelock looks soft, almost boyish, as it spills over his paws. But something odd happens when at last he dares to lift his head.

From my high perch, I swear I can see his former body, his human body, shimmering beneath the surface of the water. Illuminated in the silver moonlight, it's as well-formed as when he was human—broad chest and shoulders unobscured by fur, tapering waist, narrow hips, long human legs. Naked and poignant, the image floats like a dream, a memory, under the water. His great head jerks when he glances into the water and sees it. But when he hastily raises a dripping leg out of the water into the air, it's still coated in animal fur with a hoof on the end. The vision is only an illusion of water and moonlight or a trick of Mère Sophie's or some last, lingering memory of Jean-Loup, haunting his rooms. And I hear his voice begin to rise, not roaring like an animal this time, but sobbing like a man who has lost everything. His elegant tiled bath provides no refuge; moonlight, water, and all of nature mocks him, even here.

I would smile, if I could, that my revenge has borne such fruit.

There must no longer be any comfort for him in civilized pursuits. He goes no more into his private apartments; his fine clothing, his wineskin, and his crossbow and arrows all lie untouched. I sometimes hear him prowling about the rooms at night, his movements quiet and stealthy, no more banging and crashing about. By day, he seems to disappear, for I never hear nor see him. Curled up in some dark corner, I suppose, hiding from the light.

Some movement catches my attention, far below my window, and I peek out into early winter twilight. A hare creeps about in the courtyard foraging among the gnarled, overgrown flower beds. The small creature pauses for a moment; his ears prick up as he scents the air, then he goes back to his nibbling. But I see another movement, a dark shape poised in the long shadows thrown by the buildings. He watches the hare with feral intensity, his powerful haunches tensed.

He shifts his huge body into a better position and freezes, waiting. The hare, unconcerned, swivels about, presenting his backside as he takes the next shoot of withering grass in his paws. The larger animal rises imperceptibly, then springs over the flower bed dividing him from his prey. Startled by some natural instinct, the hare bolts off to the left the instant before the heavy paws would land on him. He's fast, skittering this way and that, but the predator has size and strength and cunning. The hare wheels about three times, but the fourth is anticipated by a lunge from the larger animal, who falls on the hare with his deadly claws. The hare is slammed to earth, and a mighty paw crushes his backbone. Quick. Clean.

He crouches on his haunches and lifts the hare's lifeless body in both paws. Holding it belly-up, he sniffs at it, touches his tongue to the still-warm flesh. He angles his head sideways, rips open the small body with one savage tooth, and begins to feed. Ravenously. Tiny bones break under his powerful jaws. Gore drips from his snout whiskers. Blood drenches the matted fur of his chest.

He is man no more. He is Beast.

CHAPTER II

Blooming

My cupboard door is drawn open. Beast stands outside. Days or perhaps weeks have passed, and daylight streams in again through the window.

"I felt that someone was in here," he rumbles as his gaze searches these empty shelves. His eyes look different in the daylight, still strangely human, but a warmer shade of brown, flecked with gold. Then he frowns at me. "What fool left lighted candles in a cupboard? It's a miracle they didn't burn the place down."

What game is he playing at? Has Mère Sophie's spell erased his memory along with his handsome face?

My candles stand as tall as they did when he first shut me up in here, however long ago that was; my wicks burn constantly, but they never diminish. Tilted briefly upward, as he lifts me down from the shelf, I see my flames have not blackened the shelf above. He notices it, too.

"Are these flames not real?" He draws me farther out, snuffles tentatively at my candles, but pauses when he glimpses his reflection in my silver surface. We have shattered all the mirrors, but I am still here to show him what he is.

"I know there's been enchantment here," he murmurs at last. "I can sense it." And his whiskers quiver slightly. That's all he says; no raging at his image, no flinging me across the room. He looks around one last time, but all is silence and dust. He glances again at me.

"Perhaps you are enchanted," he suggests after further consideration. As if he didn't know. Why does he pretend not to recognize me? "But whatever you are, your light is wasted here." And he carries me out the door and downstairs. I could not agree more. I have nothing to illuminate up here, but now I can enjoy my revenge once more.

The solitary clopping of his hooves echoes in the stillness. "I thought this house would be full of people," he murmurs as we go. "But it's so empty."

How can he not remember how all the servants fled in terror from witchcraft? From him? How can he have forgotten so soon? But I have vowed to never let him forget!

Gloom and neglect hang like cobwebs on all the once-fine things in the château. Beast has not kept up his housekeeping, and now no one will come in to do it for him. I can imagine the tales put abroad in the town by his fleeing servants. Witchcraft. Ruin. The Château Beaumont is haunted. A terrible monster lives there.

I wonder if this is the Beaumont Curse fulfilled at last, this monstrosity conferred upon the chevalier? But I know this monster has always lived here, for all that he once had a pretty face and comely form. Still, the rumormongers have done their work well. The château remains utterly deserted; no one is left on whom to spend his silver coins and his scorn. Only me.

On the second floor, he hesitates for a moment, then carries me toward his private apartments and through the outer salon. But he goes no farther than the sitting room, frowning down as his hooves crunch over the shattered glass that still covers the hearth. From here, I can see through the tall, arched window overlooking the grounds. It's late afternoon, and I'm astonished to see how ferociously the wood has overgrown the park. Wild-growing thicket and bramble smother the stately, manicured trees and riot across the green. At this rate, they must soon devour the entire château.

Beast is also gazing out the window. "That is where I make my bed," he says. "In the thicket, under a canopy of thorns." Is he thinking aloud to pierce the silence or speaking to me? And why should he imagine I care? I am not here to listen to his prattling, at any rate, but to witness his suffering.

His uneasy gaze sweeps all around the sitting room, where his own nightmare began. He frowns again. "I feel that something terrible happened here," he whispers.

I would stare at him if I could. *He* is the terrible thing that happened here—his beastliness! If he forgets his own hideous transformation, and all he has lost, how can he suffer? He *must* suffer, or I shall have no revenge! And without revenge, what use is my life?

Rage at this injustice so boils up in me that I feel bubbles explode out of one of my upheld silver cups. Tiny globs of hot wax, eternally burning, splatter over his paw, scorching him. He yelps and sets me firmly on the mantelpiece. Rumbling to himself, he marches out, clawing the hardening wax out of his fur. Let him suffer his own company a while longer. Let him know what it is to be truly alone.

The winter sun is cold and pale, shrouded in white gauze. It appears only briefly each day in the arch of the window near the fireplace before drifting off again, consumed by dark night as the park below is consumed by the wood. What little light the sun provides glistens off the ice and snow that covers everything outside now and glitters feebly in the bits of broken glass on the floor. It's a silent, sleeping world, abandoned by time—abandoned by life.

Only Beast disturbs the deathlike serenity. Sometimes

I hear him stomping about belowstairs or out in the yard, barking in the cold moonlight. I don't know what he finds to feed on in this season. I am more fortunate in my transformation; I feed on his misery.

It's cold afternoon again when Beast comes back to the sitting room. He crunches over the glass to the mantel where I stand. I see my steady flame reflected in the gold in his eyes as he peers at me.

"I feel certain that something I said or did offended you last time," he rumbles at length. He rubs absently at the spot on his paw where the wax landed. There can be no doubt that he is speaking to me, not merely airing out his lungs for his own benefit. "I regret it, whatever it was."

The words astonish me. It should never have occurred to Jean-Loup that he ever gave offense or to mind the consequences.

"It may be that you prefer your own company. For which I would not blame you," Beast goes on with a wry glance at his image in my polished surface. "But if you feel yourself trapped in this solitary room, there is a great deal more to see in this place, and I am eager to see it." He raises a shaggy brow hopefully at me. "I will try not to offend you again if you would like to come with me."

I consider his offer with the suspicion it deserves. I am not here to make him feel his loneliness any less, and yet I am eager enough to be out of these rooms. My purpose here is to witness his further humiliation, and I can't do so if I'm left on my own up here. So I make up my mind before he can abandon me again—which he certainly will if I do not find some way to agree to his plan.

Rage alone has fueled me thus far; my flames feed on it. But I wonder if I have other thoughts, other feelings, that might be as powerful; thoughts and feelings are the only parts of myself that still live inside this silver form. So I take a moment to center my thoughts on serenity for a change. Nothing can hurt me anymore. I am invulnerable. And for that moment, I feel my flames flickering lower on their wicks, although I cannot see them.

But Beast can. He visibly starts, sending a shiver through his unruly mane, to see all three of my flames dimming together. "By God's life, you heard me," he whispers, staring at me; were he not a beast, I could almost swear his mouth is forming into a kind of smile. He hesitates another moment, then makes a mock courtly bow, ridiculous in such an ungainly creature, and slowly extends a paw toward me. And, as I spew no more hot wax at him, he dares to lift me again, very gingerly, and we leave this cursed place at last.

What am I to make of this puzzling creature? Jean-Loup would never ask permission before doing whatever he pleased. Perhaps Beast's mind can no longer grasp the horror of that transformation. I am here to remind him, of course, but I resolve to bide my time and keep him under observation while I try to understand this mysterious new turn of events.

He carries me back to the staircase and down to the entry hall. My flame makes the shadows dance in the gloom, the only sign of life. Beast is less clumsy in his beastly shape than he was before, walking upright on his sturdy haunches. At the bottom of the stairs, he steadies himself on his hind hooves and glances about the hall.

"This place has become my mausoleum," he says, and begins to carry me slowly around the hall, tipping me toward doorways and into corners, as if to see for myself that gloom and loneliness fester in every shadow. "There is nothing to do, nothing to see," he tells me. "No one ever comes here. There is nothing at all to interrupt the days."

He can't expect me to respond, so he merely sighs and carries me into the front of the hall, across the black-and-white checkered tiles, to the grand glass panels overlooking the courtyard. The once-glorious flower beds are choked with desolation. Blooms have dropped, stalks withered, and unpruned limbs have become mazes of knotted grey bramble, all frosted with snow. It's a dreary sight, without warmth or color, without hope.

Beast frowns out the window at this ruin. "This was a

garden once," he murmurs. "It must have been so beautiful." He shakes his great head. "Oh, if only I had the power to make it so again."

Out in the courtyard, the flower beds begin to tremble, as if in the grip of an ague. Snow seems to dance in the beds, and frost and ice are shaken off the bramble. Tiny pinpoints of spring green erupt along the grey limbs, forming into tiny leaves that grow as we gaze. The leaves unfurl, and we see clusters of red growing instantly into buds. In less than a blink, they mature into roses of voluptuous velvety red, and suddenly all the flower beds on either side of the central drive are a riot of red and green. We stand transfixed as new branches burst out of old bushes, and layer after layer of blooming branches rise up and up until the thicket of roses is as dense as the wood and higher than the stone wall that contains the courtyard.

We stare in astonishment at this witchery. I feel myself trembling in Beast's paw, and when I glimpse his face reflected in the glass pane, I see his tufted jaw hanging open and his eyes full of awe. Slowly, his lips—if such they can be called—begin to curl upward at the corners in his beastly smile, but I am too amazed myself at this moment to mind.

"Roses," he breathes, his voice so humbled in wonder, even I can scarcely hear it.

They must be magical, these scarlet roses in the heart of winter. Yet their beauty is real enough, their lavish color a shock of vitality in the dead white landscape. Beast grips me more firmly as he throws open the door and trots down the grand front steps and into the enchanted garden. He cautiously extends a paw toward a rose on the nearest bush and lightly touches a petal with one padded toe. I brace for the instant when it will all vanish into the air, leaving us in cold white gloom once more. But witchcraft-born though they may be, these roses are all real and alive. Some hidden thorn pricks Beast's paw, but instead of howling in rage, he merely raises the wounded toe to his mouth, sucking thoughtfully as he turns around and around among his magical roses.

"Have I done this?" he whispers. "Did my wish make it so?"

Can it be that some forces of this enchantment are at his command?

But there are limits to his power. He wishes for companions and receives only contemptuous silence for his answer. But when he wishes away all the broken glass his fury has caused, it's gone in a twinkling, all of it. Not a speck, not a single tiny crystal remains.

Beast sleeps in the garden now, breathing in the

perfume of a thousand blushing roses that he tends like a proud mother hen. I wonder, do they sweeten his dreams? Do beasts dream?

The outside world is still frozen, but it's always warm in the garden. I see it all from my perch, a sill in the middle of one of the glass panels in the entry hall, overlooking the courtyard. He leaves me here when he goes into the garden at dawn, where I can enjoy the beauty of the magical roses all day. He lingers there as long as he can in the afternoon after he wakes, until the hour between sundown and night-fall, when his senses are most keen and his urges become irresistible — the hunting time, when he must feed.

After dark, I am a small beacon of light in the glass. Then he comes back for me. When the beast in him has been satisfied with the hunt, he carries me with him to dispel the gloom as he prowls the silent rooms of his châ-teau: my downstairs chambers with their fine displays of Beaumont possessions; the laundry room, its stone tubs dry and empty; the kitchens. He investigates the servants' quarters behind the kitchens, including the tiny, airless room where I once shared a lumpy pallet with Charlotte. In the small, private cell that belonged to Madame Montant, we find the little bottle of her sleeping drops still on the bedside table. Beast picks up the bottle, uncorks it, and sniffs at it. "Poppy juice," he rumbles, and puts it back where it was.

Across the vast entry hall and into the opposite side of the ground floor, we discover sitting rooms and morning rooms filled with more beautiful items — mahogany chests inlaid with gold, wonderful carpets, Chinese vases — that he himself seems never to have seen before. Has he forgotten them, the way he forgot the garden? Or was Jean-Loup simply too busy to notice them? But now Beast sees everything. By my light.

I have no notion how many nights we spend in these pursuits. One night is devoted entirely to the portraits of his ancestors that hang above the grand staircase; they rise up the panelled wall opposite the carved railing. It takes hours for him to inspect them, one paw on each gilt frame, his snout pressed up against each dusty surface as he contemplates their faces and stately clothing. These are the only vestiges of humanity left to him, these cold, dead portraits, and he studies them as if trying to remember who they are. Or what he was.

My view is more detached. I note the long noses and amber eyes of generations of LeNoir men, each more wolfish than the last. Handsome in their way, but cold and cunning. I believe I can trace the introduction of pride and cruelty into the family line — in the flinty gaze of an eye, the uncompromising curl of a lip — and see these traits flourish in succeeding generations.

One LeNoir has had himself painted before a landscape

with a keep of honey-colored stone in the background; this must be the original fortress upon which Château Beaumont has risen. Another portrait shows a stately, long-nosed gentleman with a severe expression identified by the small plaque on the frame as Auguste Henri LeNoir de Beaumont. Beside him hangs the portrait of a wraith-pale lady swaddled to the chin in minutely rendered lace, identified as Anne-Marie Villeneuve LeNoir de Beaumont. She must be the grandmother whose family estate Jean-Loup found so alluring.

Beast has moved on to the next two portraits. They hang above the first bend in the staircase, portraits of another man and another woman. The man is long-nosed and sandy-haired, but with dark eyes as hard and brittle as the shards of glass we once left glittering on the ballroom floor. Yet I recognize the cruel set of his handsome mouth, the challenging angle of his chin. He is dressed in fancy silver-colored armor painted to look so clean and shiny, I expect to see my flickering light reflected in its surface. He holds his helmet with its pointed visor tucked into one arm. The Beaumont device is displayed on his breastplate, a Beast Rampant above a row of spearheads. As I peer into that expression of self-satisfaction, it is Jean-Loup's face that comes to mind. This must be his father. I read the small plaque: Rene Auguste LeNoir de Beaumont.

Beast regards the portrait for a long time through

narrowed eyes, whuffling at the surface with his snout as if trying to pick up its human scent. But there is something more to his attention than there was when he inspected the other portraits. Perhaps he is moved by the image of the father to whose memory Jean-Loup was so devoted, whose honor he was so determined to uphold at any cost. Perhaps he is ashamed to appear before his illustrious sire in his present grotesque form. He shifts his head from side to side, studying the flat surface from every angle, pawing wistfully at the portrait as if trying to coax some response from the cold paint.

At last, he moves on to the woman's portrait. She is not at all like the others. Her features are soft and expressive, full of life. Sprightly ringlets of dark reddish hair frame her pale face, and her mouth seems poised to suppress a giggle. Her expression is so happy, I don't recognize her at first, and when I do, I very nearly shudder myself right out of Beast's paw.

She is the sobbing woman I saw in that secret room! The one who knew my name. The one who asked for my help. She's had herself painted on the porch with a view of the luscious gardens behind her, not surrounded by fine, expensive trinkets, like so many of the other portraits. I would gasp, if I could, as I see the silhouette of a humble rocking chair made of bent twigs on the porch behind her.

Beast's paw is warm, but I am suddenly cold. I'd

convinced myself it was all nonsense, cobbled together from careless prattle and foolishness. But now I see the sorrowing woman is real, or once was. How could I have had such a vision? I had never seen this portrait inside the stairwell back then. The wonder of it haunts me far more than all the other enchantments that have occurred in this place.

Calming myself, I study her face in oils, a warm, friendly face, without the LeNoir arrogance, although the little plaque identifies her as Christine DuVal LeNoir. She must be Jean-Loup's mother. Her eyes are as brown and sparkling as ale, shot with gold, even in this painted copy.

I remember how frightening it felt to have the full tragedy of those eyes, swimming in tears, turned upon me.

Won't you help us, Lucie?

What did she mean? What does she want?

But Beast knows nothing of this. He ponders the portrait in the glow that I cast. There is no snuffling or pawing of the painting this time. He only gazes at it in thoughtful silence.

At length, he moves on to the last painting, on the wall directly above the landing. It's a portrait of the most recent chevalier, Jean-Loup, elegantly clothed in all his wine-red and gold finery, standing with one hand resting on the hilt of his sword, with his favorite hound sitting up in sleek attention at his feet. The present Château Beaumont is painted in the distance, much grander than the plain stone keep we saw in an earlier portrait. The chevalier's handsome mouth is set in proud disdain. The painter has captured nature perfectly, down to the frank and predatory eyes that dominate the picture.

It hadn't occurred to me until this moment how different Beast's eyes are from Jean-Loup's. Jean-Loup had his father's eyes, dark and flinty, glinting like a sword. But Beast's eyes are warm, like his mother's.

I expect Beast to claw the canvas apart as furiously as we smashed the mirrors. But instead, he simply regards the image, without any kind of expression at all. His eyes lower to the little plaque on the bottom of the frame. "Jean-Loup," he murmurs.

Then he turns away and carries me to the bottom of the staircase, out across the entry hall, and into the warren of shadowy passages behind the grand rooms. We follow a passage that ends abruptly at a little door with a curved iron handle. I shudder again to recognize it. The door opens for Beast, and he stands in the doorway, holding me high, but this time there is no ghostly vision in the glass above the hearth. A neat little bed, plainly dressed, occupies one corner, a modest cupboard in another. The rocking chair I remember still sits in the center of the room, unmoving, the same one I saw rendered in paint a moment ago.

Why have we come here? I know this room has

something to do with Jean-Loup's mother—we were just looking at her portrait. This is where I first saw her. But Beast only gazes in silence for another long moment. Then he turns and carries me out of the room, closing the door on whatever memories may lurk there.

The next night, we inspect the rooms on the second floor with renewed fervor, relics of a life he seems to have forgotten he had. No object escapes his scrutiny. Once again, it's as if he is seeing everything for the first time.

What is he thinking when he sees these things, touches them, sniffs at them, caresses them with his padded paws? He no longer confides in me. Perhaps speech is becoming distant and strange to him. Or perhaps whatever he feels can't be contained in words.

I am standing in my window one afternoon when I hear a soft keening that works itself up into an angry rumbling and at last explodes into a full howl, tinged with enough pain to set me on edge. I would jump if I had the means, to hear such a cry. It rattles the windowpane beside my sill, and I am rattled, too.

It came from the rose garden. Two rows down from the front steps, where the end of a bed meets the driveway, Beast hovers beside the last bush in the row, pawing at the ground. He straightens again with another beastly wail, part outrage, part despair, holding aloft what he has found as if to plead his case before the judgment of God. With one paw, he grasps the dry stick of a spent rose blossom, the round hip open, its leaves spiky, bereft of petals. In the palm of his other paw I see a little mound of forlorn red petals, already turning crisp in the chilly air.

"Bring it back!" roars Beast. "Make it live!"

But there is no answer from the forces of magic that govern us, nor indeed from God. Beast's roses may be magic-born, but their life span is not eternal, so it seems. Once born, like all natural things, they are destined to die.

Beast falls to his haunches again and turns back to the bush from which he has plucked the withered stalk. He sets the dry stalk and the petals carefully down in the gravel track outside the rose bed, then begins to dig with his claws in the dirt beneath the bush. When he has made a ragged hole, he places the remains of the rose inside and covers it with a sprinkling of its petals, then shoves the little mound of dirt he's dug out back in over it all, patting the surface of the dirt into place with his paws. I expect him to mumble a few words over the grave like a priest, but Beast says nothing, only hunches there, staring at the dirt. Then he turns an accusing glance on the rosebush itself, as if it has betrayed him. He thrusts his head forward and sniffs and snuffles all around it, trying to learn its secrets the way he tried to draw some sort of understanding from his family portraits and the grand furnishings in his rooms. Indeed, he seems to take some comfort from the scent of the roses still in full bloom, breathing in their fragrance, reassuring himself. At last he cradles two voluptuous blooms in his upturned paws.

"Do not leave me," he begs of them as if they were companions. Indeed, they are the only companions he has left. Besides me.

Yet, while I expect to feel joy to see him so utterly alone, to hear his pathetic pleading, I am suddenly reminded how solitary my own existence has become.

He pries himself away at dusk to hunt and feed, but he does not drag himself up the steps to me afterward. Instead he comes back to the rose garden, to the errant bush that lost its bloom. On all fours he lumbers around and around its trunk, his deep chest low above his busy paws. When he has worn down a kind of track in the dirt surrounding the bush—the dirt must be dry as dust or it would not take him so long; soft, moist soil would give way more easily—he heaves himself into it, curling his massive body around the bush. And he sleeps, among the rest of his living companions.

CHAPTER 12

Water

I keep my vigil in the window throughout the night. My flame glows in the glass pane before me while the garden beyond sleeps in darkness. Sunrise is scarcely more than a white smudge above the stark winter landscape out beyond the château walls. But there is light enough to see the state of the garden. Beast still lies mounded up around the base of the rosebush, but his tawny fur is dappled with the red petals of dying roses. Indeed, every bush in every raised bed in the garden has dropped a litter of spent petals. Thousands and thousands of them cover the ground like splattered blood.

I brace myself for Beast's reaction when he wakes and sees it. He leaps up, shaking off his dusting of petals, and stares all around the garden, but the cry that erupts out of him is not the angry bellowing I expect, but a slow, steady keen of mourning. It's as if he grieves for the roses themselves.

Of course, there are means for keeping flowers alive that have nothing to do with magic. But Jean-Loup knew nothing of husbandry and cared less; he had servants and gardeners and groundskeepers for that. He took his pleasure freely from his garden, as he took it elsewhere, with no thought of how it came to exist or what it cost to maintain. It belonged to him; it was his due.

Beast can only stare helplessly all about him at the litter of petals, his massive head hung with grief. It angers me that he will let his beautiful garden die off again out of ignorance. He can't know how simple the solution is. Any peasant child who has ever had charge of a vegetable patch knows it. Even I know it, cold and inhuman as I am. Nothing alive can survive without water.

Water. The word echoes inside my silver being. *Water.*

I focus all my thoughts upon it. *Water, you great shaggy-brained fool. Water!*

Out in the garden, Beast stops turning around. He frowns at the dirt beneath the nearest bush and probes it delicately with one hoof. He squats on his haunches and pats the earth with his paws. Frowning again, he pats under the next bush. Even from here I can see how hard and caked the dirt in the rose beds has become, its surface split by parched gullies. At last Beast scrambles up to his hind feet and sprints away out of my sight to the track between the château and the east wing that leads to the stables and the well.

Soon enough, I hear the far-off commotion of his rooting around in the stables—tools swept aside; hay bales knocked about. Later, I hear the clank of iron handles against wood, the distant smack of wood against stone, and the sloshing of water. At length, he hustles back into my vision from the gap in the east wing, his paws clasping the handles of the two buckets he's found, the buckets so full of water they drip a wet trail behind him with every step.

Can he have heard me somehow? And why should I wish to help him, in any case? My happiness depends on his complete despair. But I enjoy the roses, too. It is not only Beast who will suffer without them, and he has the means of doing something about it, as I do not. Let him labor for my benefit for a change.

He carries them to the first row of rose beds, sets one down, and splashes half the contents of the other over the first bush. The ground beneath is so dry, the water puddles up on top of it.

He pauses, one bucket still grasped in his paw. He puts out one hoof and stamps lightly at the ground, then kicks at it. He sets down the bucket, crouches low, and begins to rake at the dirt with his claws. His first effort all but uncovers the root of the bush; he has to shove dirt back into the deep cavity he's made. But he's begun to understand the principle of the thing, clawing at the dirt more gingerly to break up the clods, then pouring out the water slowly, letting it seep through the broken dirt to the roots below.

I watch in fascination, trying to imagine any circumstance in which Jean-Loup would allow his fine, smooth hands to touch the raw wood of a bucket, let alone common dirt. But Beast doesn't seem to mind his dirty paws, nor does he mind it when the mud he's creating cakes his claws and sticks in wet clumps between his toes. He's too absorbed in his task to even notice.

But after tending only three bushes, his buckets are dry again. He trots off with the empty buckets, brings them back full, and sets to raking more dirt and watering the next two bushes in the row. Then he catches up the empty buckets and carries them off to bring them back full of water once again.

I am reminded of the night Beast drew himself a bath. But this time he can have no thought for his own luxury; on the contrary, the goal he's set himself is immense and exhausting. The sun is stretching for its midpoint by the time he's completed a single row of rose beds on either side of the drive. He rises up on his haunches and shakes back his shaggy mane, surveying the situation. Then he picks up the two buckets and carries them around the side of the château again.

He does not come back for a long time. I begin to think he must have given up on his project, consigned his beautiful roses to the devil, and stalked off. But I recognize more clattering of buckets in the well, followed by a measured creaking from the yard, and the rattling of some heavy vehicle over the wooden drawbridge that crosses the moat on the eastern side, until Beast emerges into the garden again. He is pulling behind him the yoke of a haying cart. The yoke was built for a team of oxen or mules, and Beast has to pause every few steps to get behind the T-shaped bar and press the contraption forward with the strength of his massive shoulders, an effort that sets him trembling to the very tips of the useless feathers on his back. And I can see why, for the open cart is heavily laden, not with hay, but with vessels. There are buckets from the stables and barrels that once held feed for livestock. There are basins and bowls and iron pots of every size purloined from the kitchens, even some crockery pitchers. Every one has been filled with water.

Beast is as lathered as any draft animal by the time he brings the cart to rest at the second row of flower beds. But his step is lively enough as he goes to inspect his load and withdraws a pitcher. He waters the first bush from this pitcher after he has turned the soil with his claws. When the pitcher is empty, he takes it back to the cart and dips it into a barrel to fill it again, then returns to the next bush.

He labors on in this manner all the rest of the day, breaking up the earth and watering each rosebush. When all his containers are empty, he hauls the cartful of them back to the well, draws the water to fill them all again, and hauls the loaded cart back into the garden to begin where he left off. The work is slow, but he keeps his pace steady. I wait for the moment he will throw up his paws in dismay or unleash a bitter tirade of impatience. But it never happens. Neither does he make any more demands of the magical forces, nor whine for their help. His resignation to his task is complete.

But no, Beast is not resigned. He is eager. Throughout the wearying day, his vigor never flags. He pauses only now and then to refresh himself with water from one of his vessels, and then he is back at his labors again. More labor I think in this one day than Jean-Loup ever accomplished in his entire lifetime.

The weak sun is drooping toward the west wing when the work is done. Beast stands at the bottom of the garden and gazes up at the rows of neat flower beds on which he has lavished so much attention. There is not much to show for his labors but that the soil beneath each bush is fresh and moist. Dead petals still litter the gravel walkways between the rose beds.

Beast turns to the cart and extracts an empty kitchen bowl of earth-colored clay. He makes his way along the pathways, picking up forlorn petals and collecting enough to fill the bowl, then climbs the front steps and carries the bowl heaped with red petals into the entry hall. He pauses in the doorway to look around, then carries the bowl to a sideboard against a wall in the shadows and places it just so. There are finer objects on the sideboard, but he removes them all and hides them away inside the cabinet, leaving only the rustic bowl of petals on the surface.

He considers the effect for a moment, and then he half turns to look at me, although he says nothing. It might have been mere chance that he thought of water at the same moment I did. But what if he heard me in some magical way? And I store away this tiny grain of possibility.

Beast keeps at his gardening for days. It absorbs his waking hours, except for those times when he must hunt and feed. He has lost interest in exploring the château and discovering its treasures. He does not come for me, but I watch him in his garden from my window perch.

One afternoon, as Beast is pruning dead heads from his empty stalks, I see a flash of scarlet amid the landscape of brown shrubs and grey sky. It's not a new bloom, but a little bird with a dapper, crested head. Beast lifts his muzzle, watching, as the creature flits about. It lands on an upper branch, warbling down at him. Beast is very still, getting ready to pounce, I suppose. But then Beast smiles a little, and a moment later the red bird cocks its head and flies off.

Beast waters his roses every day and feeds them from the pile of rotting vegetation and muck kept in a shed out beyond the stables. He brings a barrow of the foul-smelling stuff into the garden and dallies among his roses all through the night. Snow falls no more in his enchanted garden, but the night air can be bitingly cold. He spends another day hauling in hay bales, building a wall around the beds to keep off the night chill. And as the pale winter sun climbs a little higher and lingers a little longer in the sky each day, I see how his efforts are rewarded. New green shoots begin to thrust up from the old rose wood under tiny clusters of rust-colored leaves.

Soon enough, the frozen white landscape out beyond the garden wall starts turning to grey slush, and the nights no longer freeze. Beast now seems content to spend his time in the company of his roses.

It takes a sudden drenching rainstorm to drive Beast back inside the château one night. He drags the doors shut behind him, then stands in the entryway and shakes the water out of his fur and feathers so violently, he staggers on his hooves to keep his balance as tiny beads of water skitter across the marble floor. Yet he stays rooted where he is, fur knotted in wet clumps, dark eyes gazing all around the room. He sniffs at the air, and I suddenly know what has caught his attention. It's the bowl of rose petals on the sideboard. The petals are long dead; they have lost their bright color and velvety texture and curled into crisp, dry cinders. But their scent is alive and stronger than ever before, rich and heavy and seductive.

Beast follows his nose over to the sideboard, peers into the bowl, and stirs the brown papery petals gently about. The scent in the room intensifies. He lifts his paw and sniffs at the soft pads, heady with the perfume of dried roses. He shakes his great head in wonder.

"They are even sweeter in their transformation," he murmurs.

· CHAPTER 13 ·

The Library

The rains continue off and on, and Beast is obliged to spend more time indoors. A beast in nature cannot mind a little wet and must seek whatever poor shelter he may, but some memory, some instinct still roots Beast here, to his château. I am watching a light grey drizzle pattering down on the rose garden when I am aware of Beast beside me, gazing out the window. I notice his paw on the sill next to me, free of dirt and grime.

"I've done all I can for them," Beast muses, nodding out at his roses. His voice rasps, dry and dusty from disuse. "Now they must thrive on their own." He takes one step back from the window and sighs. "And so must I."

He turns his head to gaze at me with his brown, thoughtful eyes. "There is more to see," he suggests. "If you like."

I make no objection, so he takes me in his paw again. We climb the grand central staircase, past the portraits of Beaumont ancestors, past the formal hallway of the second-floor landing, and on up to the third-floor attic rooms—the rooms that contain the past, all the relics of previous Beaumonts that have been forgotten or banished over the generations.

Beast hesitates at the landing to gaze down the corridor. It's daylight outside, but all is shrouded in gloom up here. Is it my light he needs, or my company?

He heads for the center room facing front, where he once shut me up in the cupboard. But now he seems more intent on inspecting the other objects in the room: small headboards and footboards from children's beds that are stacked against one wall; forlorn pieces of cabinetry that have gone out of fashion; one or two battered, broken chairs that litter the room like corpses; an old carved rustic cradle that stands in one corner under a thick lacework of cobwebs. Beast thrusts me toward each thing in its turn, careful not to snuffle too deeply for fear of choking on the dry dust of centuries.

At the cupboard, he draws open both doors and gazes for a moment into the empty shelves. He sets me on the lowest shelf, then squats on his haunches to pull open the wide drawers beneath the shelves under my light. The first two are all but empty, yielding up only an ancient ribbon the color of dust and a few scraps of moldy cloth. But when he opens the last drawer, the thick, sweet musk of old roses wafts out. Beast draws back in surprise and sniffs the air. After reaching into the drawer, he extracts a flat bundle wrapped in old paper. He peels open the paper, much of which crumbles to fragments at his touch, and finds inside an article of creamy muslin and delicate lace. He handles it very carefully in his big paws, taking pains not to snag it with his claws. He lays it open at the folds and shakes it out, scattering a few dried rose petals to the floor, then holds it aloft. It looks like a christening gown, foaming with lace at the collar, broad and voluminous below, but oddly cut. It has no sleeves, and it shakes out to a remarkable length; it must have covered its infant wearer like a tent.

Beast gazes at it curiously, frowns, but does not speak. He sniffs at it gently, then lowers it again into what remains of its paper and lays it back in the drawer. Rooting around with one paw, he finally pulls out what must be the cap that was made for the gown. It's a simple mob cap with a white satin ribbon to gather it closed. But the cap itself is large and deep; it would easily fit the head of a grown man. Beast toys with one end of the ribbon before he lays the cap back with the gown. I hear the soft crackle of dried rose petals and brittle paper as his paw moves about in the drawer, but he withdraws nothing else: no tiny hose lovingly preserved, no miniature doublet embroidered in gold, no first pair of satin shoes. Perhaps the other infant clothing was passed down to Beaumont cousins in other noble houses or given to the servants. Only these christening things remain, salted away under their cover of dried roses.

Beast closes the drawer and rises slowly on his hind legs. I don't know what he's thinking. Jean-Loup was the last Beaumont infant to be born here. Did these things belong to him? Was it Jean-Loup's mother, the woman from the portrait, the woman from my vision, who folded these things up and put them away with such tender care?

Beast takes me up again in his paw, closes the cupboard doors, and makes his way out of the room. His tread is heavy. I can't tell if he is weary or troubled or simply brooding. Out in the corridor, he pauses and gazes again at the staircase. Perhaps he has had enough of the past. All the familiar things from Jean-Loup's world are in the floors below. But he turns down the corridor and proceeds to the next room and the next, although we find little more of interest.

At last, we circle around to a back corner turret, the only place we have yet to enter, but the door is locked. It's a small single door with an arched top, three beautiful wrought iron hinges stretched across its wooden planks, and a graceful ivory handle. A modest door, by château standards, but one that's been crafted with care. And one that remains stubbornly secured. The handle will not budge, and there is no longer any key in the keyhole to unlock it.

Beast wonders what to do about this obstacle; his quick dark eyes survey the door's height and breadth, and he angles his body to measure his massive shoulder to the old wood. But he doesn't assault it. Instead, with claws retracted, he gently touches one paw to the wood.

"Might this open for us?" he asks softly. "Please?"

The ivory handle, untouched by either of us, tilts downward with a soft click. Beast nudges it, and the obliging door opens inward. He has to stoop to fit his large, burly frame under the arch, but in we go.

We find ourselves in a small passage under heavy roof beams just high enough for Beast to stand upright. Opposite the door is a short flight of stairs, beautifully carved out of wood, tilting steeply upward through an opening between the beams. Beast holds me aloft as he climbs. As I rise up through the opening, my flame illuminates a plush red-and-gold carpet overlaying the wooden floor. Higher yet, my light falls upon some few pieces of comfortable furniture: an old stuffed armchair worn with use and draped with an ancient paisley shawl, a matching footstool, a small writing table and chair. Beast's head and shoulders rise up under me, and I am held high enough to cast my light on what is beyond these furnishings.

I see books—hundreds of books in shelves that line

every wall of the room. The shelves are not orderly; books are shoved in every which way, upright, or stacked sideways, or all atilt against various objects that appear to have been undisturbed for ages: an ancient teacup whose contents have long since evaporated; a fat candle half-melted into its saucer. Some are even piled up in corners on the floor, but they are everywhere. On three walls, the book-filled shelves rise nearly all the way up to the high vaulted ceiling, where painted nymphs and satyrs and mermaids frolic among star-dusted clouds. On the fourth, the shelves give way to a round window framing a picture in colored glass. The last of the daylight spills through the glass to illuminate a golden castle, a pink sun, a green dragon, and a princess dressed in blue. I recall a tower room I spied from far down in the courtyard on the day I first arrived at Château Beaumont.

Beast pauses on the stairs below me, one paw braced on the carpeted floor, and drinks it all in with his eyes, warm and shining in my light. Something stirs in his eyes that I've never seen there before. In any other creature, I might call it tenderness.

After climbing all the way into the room, frowning slightly in concentration, he begins to rove about, gently pawing and sniffing at every remnant of former habitation—a dust-covered plate that may have once held crumbs, long since carried off by mice; a sticky goblet tumbled to the carpet. He prowls along the shelves, snuffling at the spines of books, poking me into dark, dusty corners undisturbed for years, but there is a kind of warmth in the room not even dust and neglect can chase away. We get to the armchair with the paisley shawl tossed carelessly across it, as if its owner were coming right back. Beast caresses the shawl with great care, so as not to snag it.

At last, he carries me to the writing table. With one brisk puff, he blows the dust off the surface of the little cubbyhole shelf attached to the table and places me upon it. He unlatches the leaf—with no little dexterity for such large paws, maneuvering the catch with a single outstretched claw—and folds it out flat. In the cavity beneath the cubbyhole shelf, a small, slim volume is tucked away.

Beast gently lifts it out and sniffs at its cover. It's less dusty than the other volumes, having been shut up in the writing table for so long. From where I perch, I can glimpse the word *Sonnets* etched in gold on its spine. My father had me taught to read, although I've had little enough use for it since then. Poetry is not something with which I have much experience, nor can I imagine Jean-Loup as a boy whiling away his hours in rhymes. But Beast cradles the book as if it's something precious. When he opens the cover, we see something inscribed in a neat, beautiful hand on the first page.

Christine DuVal LeNoir.

Jean-Loup's mother. Was this her library? Perhaps she was reading this book on the last day she ever spent here.

He turns the book over in his paws, and something else glints and shimmers in my light. Beast inserts a claw gently between the pages and opens the little book flat. A long red ribbon marks the place, with the shimmering thing dangling from one end. Beast lifts out the ribbon and holds its ornament up to my light.

I would gasp if I could. It's a plain gold ring, decorated with a tiny red heart. She was wearing it the day I saw her in the mirror downstairs.

Beast closes his paw gently around the ring. He eases the book back onto the table, catches up the long, thin red loop of the ribbon, and somehow manages to pull it entirely over his head, stretching it over his horns and muzzle; it must be enchanted, to stretch so far. He paws up long tendrils of his shaggy mane until the ring dangles in the thick fur of his chest.

He reaches behind him for the wooden chair, lowers his bulk into it with no little care, shifts his tufted tail about to find a comfortable position, then draws himself up to the table and turns again to the open book. Nothing disturbs the silence for a while as he bows his huge head over the little book in the halo of light cast from my flames.

Suddenly, with a deep, rumbling groan, he rises again.

"Love verses!" he cries, sweeping the book to the

carpet. "What use are they to me?" And he charges across the room to the stairway and gallops down the stairs paws-first. Below, I hear the enchanted door slam shut behind him.

I am too high up now to hear Beast in the rooms below. I wonder if he's abandoned the château altogether.

Sunlight makes the stained glass brilliant in the high round window. Its colored figures dance on the carpet and the spines of the books as the sun moves across the sky. Sometimes their images fall on me, and my surface reflects dragon green or princess blue. I have an eternity to contemplate the colored glass, to wonder at its composition. A castle, a princess, and a dragon — all the elements of a fairy story. But where is the prince? Should there not be a prince to slay the dragon? That is how the old tales always go.

This is a room unlike any other in the château, a place for dreaming, apart from the world. Did Jean-Loup's mother come here to dream? Is this where her soul was nurtured, where her spirit soared?

And no sooner do I think these thoughts than I see her shimmering before me again. She kneels on the carpet in the pool of colored light thrown by the window. She wears the golden ring with the tiny heart, twisting it on her finger in quiet distress. Tears gleam on her cheeks, but they are shed silently as her gaze rises to the colored glass.

"Oh, my sweet child, what have I done?" Her tremulous voice seems to address the images in the colored glass. "How I have wronged you!"

This is no dream; I do not sleep. Is she here in fact, in some unholy reality between heaven and the grave? And what wrongs can she have done? Is Jean-Loup's transformation into Beast partly in payment for her sins, whatever they may have been? But it was Mère Sophie who created Beast. I was there. I saw it all.

She lowers her head onto her clasped hands for a moment, then lifts her face again, turning toward the writing table. Her brown eyes come up to rest on me, warm and full of feeling.

"Don't hate him, Lucie," she whispers to me. I am chilled to my silver marrow. How can she still recognize me as I am now? Why does she pursue me?

"He was so good and loving once, never a cross word for anyone. Before . . ." She shakes her head sadly, but her gaze does not leave me, her expression earnest. "You were so kind once, to another girl, a stranger," she murmurs. "Please, show him your kindness. Help him."

CHAPTER 14

The Moonstruck Poet

Help him? Me, help Jean-Loup? Never, not in this world or the next, no matter how pitifully his mother pleads for him! He stole my kindness from me, her son, as he stole so much else. She is some phantom, some fairy sent to drive me from my purpose, but I am unrelenting. Jean-Loup will get no help from me.

And even as these thoughts cross my mind, the vision evaporates before me, leaving me in peace once more.

After a few more circuits of the sun through the colored window, I hear the tread of agitated hooves as Beast races up the stairs. Newly resolved, I look forward to his next storm of helpless fury or complaint.

But when Beast's head emerges above the stairwell, his brown eyes are bright and eager. His mouth is open and curving upward in his animal smile, a smile of wonder. What has he found to be so happy about?

But I find out as soon as he clambers up into the room and hurries over to where I still stand on the shelf above the writing table. He shows me a rose cradled in his paw, red and ripe and dewy, its petals just beginning to unfurl. He holds it up before me.

"Look!" He pants, his breath so warm, so near, that it mists my polished surface.

Beast turns the rose slowly, eagerly before me, as if he needs my reflection to reassure him that his own senses have not lied. The rose exists.

"It's the first to bloom since the magic roses dropped their petals," he whispers in awe. "See how it grows! It lives!"

I can't imagine Jean-Loup ever sparing a single thought for a mere flower. But Beast's eyes are soft and adoring, gazing at the thing he has coaxed into life. No mother could be any more besotted with her newborn. He gently turns the new rose over and over in his palm by its short green stem. With every turn, it releases more of its sweet perfume into the air until the room itself seems to brighten, as if the sun has come out from behind the clouds.

Abruptly Beast stops his swoony reverie and frowns down at the rose. His gaze hurries all around the room, but he doesn't see whatever it is he seeks. Cupping his rose in both paws, he turns and disappears into the passage.

No sound from below tells me where Beast goes or

what he does. I am left alone again to ponder the pale sun's progress through the colored glass. But the scent of the new rose lingers in the room like a faint memory. It's not the heady, musky scent of the magic roses. It's lighter somehow but no less pleasing. It's the fragrance of rain and sun and air and earth, of living things. And something else, I think. The impudent sweetness of something beloved.

Jean-Loup could never love anything. But what of Beast? He must love his roses to have brought them so patiently back to life.

Before I can ponder this any further, I hear the tread of hooves on the stairs again. Beast rises into the room, his brown eyes beaming. He carries his rose in a plain, slender glass vase he must have found in the kitchen and filled with water from the well. He brings it over and places the vase on the surface of the writing table, in my pool of warm light, then stoops to pick up the fallen book of sonnets that he dashed to the ground the last time he was here. He gently shakes the pages out straight, closes the small book, and lays it next to the rose vase, nudging it a little with his paw to the most pleasing angle. When that is done, he resettles the chair to the writing table, slightly drawn back, as if someone reading the book and enjoying the rose has wandered off for only a moment, but will soon return.

I reckon time by the rose, watch its heavy petals uncurl and begin to spread open. Rainbows dance in the glass vase as the tinted sunlight touches it through the round window — dragon green, princess blue. Night shrouds the room in darkness, but for my persistent flame. I see no more visions of Jean-Loup's mother.

I've forgotten the number of days, but it is evening outside, and the rose is a sunburst of red above its vase when Beast returns. He gazes fondly at the rose and sniffs the air for its scent as if to assure himself of its continued life. And then he turns away, his paws locked behind his back, creasing the rows of feathers, as he assumes a studious pose and gazes around at the shelves of books. Finally, he returns to the writing table, seats himself on the chair on his haunches, his furred and feathered upper body held erect, and takes up the little book again. He reads until dawn warms the colors in the window, and then he disappears again.

The next night, when that book is finished, Beast prowls the shelves with brow furrowed, paws behind his back like the most doleful of philosophers, until he finds another, and the next night, another. This goes on for several more nights. When his prize rose finally exhausts its span of life and crumples, he replaces it with a fresh one and goes back to his reading. He can't get much pleasure from it; his expression is always melancholy. But still he comes, night after night. It's another kind of feeding.

This night, halfway through his latest volume, he suddenly shoves it aside and sighs again, a great, rumbling outrush of breath. He rests his face in his paws for a few moments, then raises his head with an air of resolution and reaches into a cubbyhole below me. He withdraws a quill pen and inkstand, and from another niche extracts a sheet of parchment.

I observe in fascination as he withdraws the stopper from the inkwell with his bared front teeth, drops it to the tabletop, and noses it aside. He wrestles the pen out of its slot in the stand, traps it between his paws, and nudges it upright with his snout. After steadying the quill with his mouth, he settles the shaft snugly between the first and second toes of his paw, lifts the pen, and dips its nib in the inkwell. For a long while, he does nothing more, poised with the pen dripping in his clumsy paw, but never applying pen to paper. He gazes abstractly out into the empty air. Then his gaze falls more tenderly on the rose. At last, he scratches out a few words. Then, tentatively, a few more. I can't make out the words from this angle, and his awkward scrawl is barely readable in any case, but the words are shaped like verses on the page.

Poetry? Can Beast be writing poetry? Oh, it is too delicious—love sonnets from the beast! Has he been so long out of the society of women, he must channel his yearning into verse? But verses must be poor substitute indeed for the caresses of a live woman. How Jean-Loup would laugh!

And my own mirth suddenly curdles within me, to think that I might share any impulse at all with Jean-Loup.

Beast pauses over his work, draws an inky slash across a word here, and scribbles a few corrections there. I see his mouth working silently as he holds up the paper to read what he's written. He frowns, sighs, and shakes his shaggy head.

"Moonstruck puppy," he mutters to himself. Something like an ironic smile plays across his expression. "'Puppy,' there's a fine jest. Would that I were anything so adorable as a *puppy*." He glances up at me, at his reflection in my polished surface. "Moonstruck gargoyle, more like."

He shifts his gaze away from the image of himself to me. "What is it about this place that makes me want to tell my feelings?" he murmurs, tilting his head to one side. "Like a human. Like a man." He glances at the quill still stuck between his toes and sighs. "All I lack is the skill. And the wit." With another wry glance at me, he plucks the quill from the grip of his paw with his mouth and drops it on the desk.

"But I find I am not suited to poetry," Beast rumbles on, rising from his chair with a sigh. "Out of doors, beyond these walls, I never think of such things. Outside, in the park, working in my rose garden, I grow stronger and faster every day. Everything is sharper, clearer, more . . . pure."

He turns about, his gold-flecked eyes full of wonder.

"Every day, I see things that fill me with wonder: a spiderweb drooping with pearls in the rain; the majestic circling of a hawk in the winter sky. I can hear the sigh of a snowdrift or the bustle of creatures tunneling underground, their tiny claws sifting through the soft dirt. When I water my roses, I can hear the water singing its way down into the earth. And the way the world reeks — the brassy stench of a coming storm, the sweet decay of rotting leaves, sharp, spicy pine. I can track an animal in the wood from leagues away. And when I feed, the smell of blood is maddening and irresistible . . ."

He pauses in the middle of this sudden cloudburst of words, the most I have ever yet heard from him, but then plunges ahead.

"And my roses! There is nothing on earth sweeter than my roses. They are the best of nature, blessedly free from the taint of . . . human folly." He gives his head one more little shake that ripples through his long, tawny mane. "In my garden, buoyed up by the fragrance of my roses, I feel I have the courage to do anything. Bear anything. Outside these walls, it's almost possible to feel that I . . . belong in this body. As horrible as it is. That there might yet be a place for me somewhere in the world."

Beast has a surer grasp of poetry than he knows, in speech at least, if not on paper. I know I ought to feel outrage that Jean-Loup is learning to content himself in any way with his new monstrosity. But, in truth, I am more amazed than angry to find Beast so awed by common things that Jean-Loup held in such disdain, or never even noticed.

"And yet, I am compelled to keep coming back here, to this library, to the world of ideas, the world of men." Beast sighs again. "Beneath this face, this fur, I think human thoughts. I have human feelings. I am gifted with speech, like a man, and cursed to desire the fellowship of other men."

If only Beast knew how useless those old companions were. Which of them has come back out of concern for the chevalier? They were ready enough to jest and laugh and sing at his table, so long as he provided food and wine and sport enough, but where are they now?

Beast picks up his discarded page of verses and casts his haunted gaze over it one more time. "But that was Jean-Loup's world. His life. Not mine."

And without rancor, without rage, he lifts his paper and burns it to ashes in my flame.

CHAPTER 15

A Voice

Beast carries me out of the library at dawn, but my thoughts are in such turmoil, I scarcely notice. What does he mean, Jean-Loup's life is not his? Are they not one and the same?

Yet, even I must admit, I can find no trace of Jean-Loup in Beast's behavior, as doggedly as I search, not since the night he shut me up in the attic cupboard. I can't believe Mère Sophie's spell would have erased Jean-Loup's memory on purpose, for what use is my revenge if he no longer knows what he's lost? It seems far more likely that he only pretends not to be Jean-Loup now, but why indulge in such an elaborate charade? What on earth would be the point? Not for *my* benefit. I'm scarcely a maiden. I'm not even human; my touch scorches and burns. I can't be tricked into releasing Jean-Loup from his curse. He has nothing at all to gain by pretending to me.

I am still chewing on these thoughts when Beast sets me in my old place on the windowsill overlooking the courtyard. This is the first time I've seen his new crop of roses in full bloom. He's planted emerald-green moss to carpet the rose beds, between the bushes, and it looks beautiful. The melancholy lingering in his eyes from last night evaporates when he gazes out at them. His glance shifts hesitantly to me. "Perhaps you might like to see them, too?" he suggests.

Beast senses more life in me than Jean-Loup ever noticed when I was human. Surprised by this unexpected kindness, I feel my flames fluttering all together for a moment—a brief little glimmer of gratitude. Beast smiles cautiously back at me.

Certainly, nothing is more beautiful to see than his roses. How they tower above the stone wall enclosing them! The buds are the size of lemons, the open blooms like red sunflowers.

In the time I have been upstairs, Beast has carted away the sheltering hay bales and trained the center bushes up on stakes to form an elegant arch over the drive from the gilded gate all the way up to the front steps. His roses must be visible all the way to the town. I recall my first glimpse of the château from the tavern at the inn, shining like gold on the crest of the green hill. What must it look like now, bursting with red roses in the late-winter landscape?

In another moment, the sun has drawn Beast outside. Indeed, he's in such a hurry to get to his garden, launching himself downstairs at a gallop, paws-first, that he misses his footing on the dew-slicked steps. I see his body stretch out in midair for an instant, paws flailing for balance, as he plunges helplessly forward. And then, impossibly, the feathers down his back spread apart into two giant sail-like spans that catch the air for a heartbeat until Beast can get his hooves under him again.

For that one moment, he is flying.

Beast is no less astonished than I am. After landing on the gravel track, he rises up on his hooves, his great shaggy head twisting backward as far as it will go, muzzle snuffling at the feathers that carpet his shoulders, under his mane. He reaches one paw back, grooming at the feathers with his claws, then straightens his posture a little more, poised on his hooves, and gives his shoulders a mighty shake. But the wings do not rise again; the feathers have all resettled themselves back into their dormant position. He is quiet for some time, pondering. Then he slowly turns his head back to look up at me, my light burning still in the window. His witness.

Beast retrieves me every evening after he has hunted and fed, and we make our nightly progress to the library. His touch is tender in a way it never was when his hands were human. He composes no more verses but still browses among the books. Sometimes he sprawls across the carpet as he reads or stretches his huge bulk in the armchair, his hooves propped up on the padded footstool. It's a curiously human posture, almost grotesquely so, yet it seems to suit him. His wings do not stir again; the rows of feathers down his back are just another mismatched body part, like his fur and mane and hooves, to be managed as best they can.

Tonight, when Beast takes me up to the library, he is also carrying a large leather pouch bound with a dark ribbon that he found in Jean-Loup's study downstairs, the room in which the chevalier once condemned his secretary to the stocks. When he folds the pouch open on the writing table, under my light, I see that it contains scores of papers, some loose, others bound in small ledger books; they are mostly marked with columns of figures, but there are other lengthier notations as well, in a neat, crimped hand that must be Monsieur Treville's. Beast is entirely absorbed in reading through the papers for a long while, his expression growing ever darker until he is scowling down at them. What can it matter now if the chevalier's accounts are out of order? But Beast finds them so disturbing that, at last, with an angry groan, he shoves aside pouch, papers, and all.

"What poor use Jean-Loup made of his life," Beast grumbles. "What did he need with more wealth, titles, and possessions?" He glances again at the pile of papers. "Fruitless lawsuits, crippling taxes, selfish extravagances," he mutters, shaking his head. "And what is there now to show for it? This empty house, these lonely grounds."

He rises to his hooves, catches me up, and sets me on a higher bookshelf nearby, as if to deny my illumination to the papers and the grim evidence they contain. He sinks down to the chair again, but he is still agitated.

"The Villeneuve estate," he goes on glumly. "What good was it? Was there not honor enough in this property, this house, this lineage? And never a thought spared for the welfare of the seigneurie or the dependents who labored for him. He did not value these things, or his affairs would not be such—such a testament to arrogance and cruelty."

It amazes me to hear these words in Beast's mouth, but it angers me, too, to think he would try to deny any part in Jean-Loup's crimes. I feel my flames burning hotter.

Beast glances again at the papers, shaking his head in disgust. "What a mess he made of everything," he mutters.

I suppose you *could have done better.*

Beast freezes to the spot for an instant, staring at me, ears pricked up, his tufted jaw dropping open an inch or two. Then he clambers up to peer at me more intently, his expression wonderstruck, his dark eyes aglow in my flame. "I heard that," he says, his voice hushed. "I am not dreaming. That was you! You can . . ."

Yes, I can, I agree, shaping my thoughts with care, the ones I wish to share with him. Never have I felt so moved to communicate with him, not since the day I urged him to water his roses. *When it's important enough.*

Beast peels his gaze off me for an instant to glance at the tabletop crowded with Jean-Loup's papers, and then his eyes rise again to me.

"I could scarcely have done any worse," he huffs, shaking his head, "if I had been here. But . . ."

Then a new thought takes hold of him; I can see it in his widening eyes.

"Were *you* here?" Then he frowns at me. "You weren't *him*, were you?"

My flames shoot up so suddenly in outrage that Beast actually backs away a step, but his expression looks relieved.

"Then who were . . ." He pauses, reconsiders. "Who *are* you?"

I was called Lucie.

If my name is familiar to him for any reason, he gives no indication, only continues to hover there, afraid to move, lest the fragile connection between us should burst like a bubble of soap.

"And you lived here? At the château? Were you mistress of this place?"

And as wary as I am, I'm surprised at how exhilarating it is, to have a kind of voice again. And someone to hear it.

Mistress of a chamber or two, where I swept and scrubbed.

"A maid!" he cries, as if it were the noblest occupation on earth, and I the queen of all maids.

Yes. One of many.

"That must have been a thankless enough task in this big place," says Beast. "Were you happy here?"

I would be frowning in confusion if I could. Jean-Loup cared no more for the feelings of a servant than he did for the beauty of a rose. And the chevalier would know better than anyone how little reason I had to be happy here.

But Beast continues to gaze at me, expecting an answer, in all apparent innocence. As I study his face, from where I've been stuck up here among the books, I also notice a spider busily spinning in a shadowy corner of this shelf just out of my light. Beast's gaze is too intent on me at the moment to see it. If he is playing some game, it is my turn to move.

I would be happier now down on the desk, where I could see you better.

Beast reaches for me, so eagerly he doesn't notice when his paw snags the new web—until the spider drops into his fur and starts scrambling up his arm.

I wait for his shriek of terror at the very least. But when Beast catches sight of the spider, he only pauses for a moment, arm still outstretched.

"Sorry, old goodwife," he murmurs, sliding his other

paw under the creature and lifting her gently back up to her shelf.

He takes me up and calmly sets me back down to the writing desk, not the least bit disturbed by the encounter.

But my thoughts are reeling.

The only time I ever saw the chevalier completely lose command of himself, shuddering in horror, was when an unfortunate spider touched him. He could not help his response at that time; it was an impulse he could not control. How could he now pretend not to be affected?

I can think of only one answer.

Somehow, as impossible as it seems, this is not Jean-Loup.

CHAPTER 16

The Storm

It's grown darker outside. A storm is gathering. The wind whistles like an eerie flute, and rain spits at the window like handfuls of gravel. The weather seems as disturbed as my thoughts.

How can I disbelieve the evidence of my own eyes? I saw the chevalier transformed into Beast! And yet, I have never sensed any of the chevalier's crafty slyness in Beast's words—or his actions—not since the night he shut me up in the attic cupboard. Jean-Loup has disappeared, with his cruelty and his handsome face and his fear of spiders. Beast is someone entirely different. How can such a thing be possible? But magic is alive in this château—no one knows it better than I—and magic obeys its own rules.

Beast, meanwhile, is pleased to have me at eye level again, sitting in the chair opposite me. He wants to ask me more questions, but I am intent on my own.

Beast, when did you come here?

He eyes me thoughtfully for a moment. "I don't know exactly. It was cold; that's the first thing I remember. I woke up out in the park, shivering under a bush. I wandered around the grounds for days before I dared set foot inside the château. I was certain that such a grand place must be full of people, but I never saw anyone go in or come out—not even to chase me off when I grew bold enough to enter the yard or cross the moat. At last I found my courage and came inside."

He sighs, thinking back. "But there was no one here. I poked my head into every room but could never find another living soul. One day, I worked up the nerve to climb up to the attic because I felt so strongly that there was somebody up there." He tilts his head slightly and raises one shaggy brow at me. "That is when I found you."

But how could you know I was alive?

"I don't know that, either, but I sensed it. It was not as if you were . . . *speaking* to me, as you are now." A brief smile plays across his face. "I never dared hope for that! But I felt the presence of an intelligence, a personality so nearby."

He shakes his head a little, unable to offer any more explanation.

"And what about you, Lucie?" he goes on more eagerly. "Tell me how you came to be here."

Fair enough, I suppose. I'm not the only one with questions.

There is little enough to tell. I come from a very small, very poor village. You won't have heard of it. My mother worked the landlord's fields.

"And your father?"

Cold in his grave these many years.

"Oh, I am sorry." Beast pauses out of respect, but he's anxious for our conversation to continue. "What was he like?"

He was poor. And good, and very, very kind.

Under Beast's sympathetic gaze, I permit myself to think back to my girlhood, before my stepfather ruled our lives and my mother's affections.

He worked in the stables of the alehouse in our village. Travelers on pilgrimage or off to the university stopped there to change their horses. I can barely remember. It all seems so long ago now. *All day he would listen to their talk. He lapped it up like — like their mounts drank from his trough.*

Beast lets out a soft whuffle of laughter.

That was why I wanted —

My thoughts come to an abrupt halt.

"What did you want?" Beast asks. "What did the stabler's daughter dream of?"

I haven't thought of this in years. *My father's stories were so exciting. I wanted to be a scholar, too. My father even found a learned woman in our village to teach me my letters. I wanted to learn things and be useful to people in some way.*

Beast considers this. "And yet, you came here."

It takes a moment to compose my thoughts. *My father died of a fever. My mother found another husband, with his own plot to work on the landlord's property and his own brood to raise.*

I don't like to think about my stepfather, his oily glances, the rights he thought he could claim over me. My mother kept me safe from him the only way she could.

So my mother sent me into service. She thought I would be better off here. She couldn't have known . . .

Beast's dark eyes are more alert than I would like, his muzzle slightly raised.

"Known what?" he asks very softly. "What happened to you here, Lucie? Why are you here all alone?"

I don't know if I dare reveal my secret to Beast. What would he think of me if he knew?

"It's painful for you," Beast says gently. "I'm sorry. I don't need to know."

But his dark eyes are so full of concern, his manner so gentle, I have a wild impulse to risk his opinion of me to be rid of the burden of my shame. "But—perhaps I can help in some way," Beast suggests. "Do something for you."

I muster my resolve. Doesn't Beast deserve the truth?

There's nothing you can do. It's already been done.

Beast's expression darkens. His face is very close, his eyes as sharp as stars. "Somebody hurt you," he whispers. His thick, tawny brows lower as if he's peering into my soul. "Jean-Loup."

And so, I begin to tell my tale, my thoughts halting at first. But the more I tell, the more I begin to feel a kind of relief to let it out at last. This is what my newfound voice is for. I've never had anyone to tell my story to; Mère Sophie already seemed to know about it in her witchy way. And the more I reveal, the more outrage I see kindling in Beast's eyes.

As my tale ends, he impulsively reaches out a paw but stops far short of touching me. His paw drops again into his lap, and he sits farther back in his chair, as if to make room for the horror that's burst into the room between us as ferociously as the storm outside.

"Monster," Beast rumbles at last, his voice low but fierce. "What a monster he was! I am so sorry, Lucie," he goes on, shaking his great head. "You deserve justice for what was done to you."

Justice has been done. Jean-Loup is gone.

"But you've lost your human form. How can that be just? You're not the one who should be punished."

But this was my choice, I insist.

He looks surprised.

To be free of my weak human body, so easily hurt. I became what I am out of vigilance, to witness Jean-Loup's downfall.

Beast peers at me, puzzled, trying to piece it all together. "But if Jean-Loup is gone, why are you still enchanted?"

To see that he will never return, I realize now—a far greater purpose than I had before, when watching him suffer was my only goal.

But before I can form these jumbled thoughts into an answer for Beast, a sudden volley of hailstones crashes against the high round window, like an alarm, a warning, making Beast jump. The howling of the wind seems to triple in strength and violence. Beast clambers out of his seat, scenting the air, his ears straining upward. Some mischief is afoot, but there are no other windows to see out of up here.

He pivots about to stare again at me. "Something is out there!"

I don't ask how he knows; I feel something, too, and his senses are far more acute than mine.

"We must see what it is," Beast exclaims, and springs for the desk. He grasps me again in his paw, and we head for the stairwell as the storm shrieks outside.

We racket down the little wooden staircase and into the attic corridor. We cross to one of the front-facing rooms, and Beast shoves aside the abandoned furnishings to get to the window that overlooks the courtyard. The rain is pelting down now, and deep explosions of thunder rattle the glass. Lightning illuminates the courtyard, and we see a shape, a figure out on the bridge that crosses the moat, beyond the gate. It cowers in the feeble shelter of the low stone wall of the bridge. A few paces away, a horse stands snorting and pawing, tossing its mane in alarm, but keeping close to its master. A human. A man.

Beast is all aquiver with eagerness, paw and snout pressed to the glass, watching. How long has it been since a human was in the château? Three months? More? It was autumn when I visited Mère Sophie, and we've already weathered the worst of the winter snows.

By flashes of lightning, we see the man creep almost all the way across the bridge, but the stone wall around the courtyard prevents him going any farther, its gilded iron gate firmly latched. He casts about in desperation for any other form of shelter as his horse jitters and whickers behind him.

"Please," breathes Beast. "Let him in."

The two halves of the iron gate unlatch and sweep open into the courtyard of their own accord. The man draws back in alarm, but his horse lifts its head and its tail and trots boldly into the courtyard. The man follows cautiously, and the two of them progress up the long driveway under the arch of roses. They emerge at the foot of the grand front steps, where the man pauses. But the horse canters off toward the east wing and the track that leads around to the back of the château as if he senses he'll find comfort there.

"Stables," whispers Beast. "Feed him and curry him." The magic seems willing enough to oblige.

The man can't hesitate for too long in the driving rain. Abandoned by his horse, he climbs the steps to the shelter of the colonnaded porch.

"Door," murmurs Beast, and I can hear the great double doors below us creaking open into the entry hall.

Beast's movements are stealthy as he creeps down the stairs to the second-floor landing. I, too, feel curious but wary, and I manage to dim my flames so we are concealed in darkness to get a better view of our unexpected guest. The stranger stands bewildered in the entry hall, below, gazing fearfully all around in the dark.

"Light," whispers Beast, and for the first time since the night of the transformation, flames blaze to life in the hall sconces. The stranger gasps and turns around again. He's an old man with a short grey beard, made straggly by the rain. His cloak is made of fine stuff but much worn with use. It leaves a puddle of water on the marble floor.

"Hello?" he calls out in a voice frail with apprehension. "Is anyone there?"

"Dry and warm him," Beast requests of the air, and a fire roars into being in the grate of the nearest sitting room, illuminating the doorway. The old man jumps at first, but then draws near, too wet and weary to wonder anymore where his salvation comes from.

Upstairs, Beast hurries to the dining salon and throws open the door. "Food!" he exclaims. "Wine!" The sideboard overflows with roast meats, tureens of soup, and platters of fish. Fruit of all sorts piles up in bowls, vegetables steam in silver pots, and a decanter of wine appears on the table beside a handsome setting of plate and silverware. At a nod from Beast, the sconces light, and a fire glows in the grate; then he crosses back to the railing overlooking the stairs, still gripping me in his paw.

The fire has gone out below, and the old man is drawn back into the lighted entry hall. "Here," murmurs Beast, and the stairwell sconces light up, illuminating the grand staircase. The old man hesitates for only a moment before obediently climbing the stairs. We fade back into the deepest shadows as the stranger arrives on the second floor. All is in darkness but for the blaze of warmth and light wafting out of the dining salon, along with the irresistible aromas of hot food. He goes straight there, never pausing to notice what might be lurking in the shadows.

Inside, he stumbles to the table, throws off his cloak, and slides into the chair where his place is set. Groaning platters arrange themselves on the table before him, and food dishes itself onto his plate. His hand trembles as he reaches for the decanter to pour himself a glass of wine; it sloshes over a little when he sets it down again, as full as it was when he first began to pour. But before he drinks, he pauses with his hands hovering before him in the air.

"Thank you," he quavers. "Whatever fairies or gods have done this, I thank you. I am in your debt."

When the old man has eaten and drunk his fill and begun to drowse by the fire, Beast causes his way to be lit to the nearest of the private bedchambers. Dust is banished, and a welcoming fire appears in the grate. The soft, down-filled quilt peels itself back, and our guest crawls happily into bed to sink upon the instant into untroubled sleep. He should scarcely look so peaceful if he knew what terrible visage was watching him from the shadows.

I wonder if Beast will keep this vigil all night, but at last, he wrenches himself away and carries me into the dining salon. The food has completely vanished, but Beast sniffs all around the table and chair as if to pick up the human scent, to accustom himself to the novelty of a person in the château again. Beast follows the trail downstairs to the entry hall, restless, probing everywhere, until he finally sets me down in my usual place on the windowsill.

"What are we to think of this, Lucie?" Beast murmurs.

No more do I know what to make of this unexpected

visitor, but I know how eager Beast is for human companionship.

Let him rest, I suggest to Beast. *We will sort it out in the morning.*

Beast nods at me and melts back into the shadows.

He's an old man who has lost his way in the storm. Really, what harm can he do?

CHAPTER 17

The Bargain

I find out the next morning.

The sun rises pale but resolute after last night's storm. Raindrops glisten in the red roses; it looks like a garden of rubies. The sound of tentative bustle upstairs tells me our guest has awoken and is making his way back to the dining salon. I have no doubt another lavish feast awaits him there to break his fast. I don't see Beast anywhere in his garden.

After a while, the horse appears out in the courtyard, his saddle oiled, his coat shiny, his head and tail held high. He waits patiently at the foot of the steps, and soon enough, the old man comes down the stairs into the entry hall. His cloak is clasped across his chest with the hood thrown back. His thinning grey hair is neatly combed back, and his sparse, pointed little beard is tidy and clean.

At the foot of the grand staircase, he stops once more to look around and marvel at the luxury of the place.

Then his eyes fall upon me, aglow in my window, my silver surface gleaming.

He glances at me as he moves toward the doors, then pauses and looks back, measuring me with his eyes. With one last swift glance all around the hall, he steps up and grasps me with one hand. I feel my flames rising up in outrage. How dare he touch me? The old man tilts my tapers toward him and tries to blow out my flames, but, of course, he can't do it. Undaunted, he swirls his cloak over me, lighted flames and all, and hastens through the double doors, out onto the porch, and down the steps.

At the bottom step, he signals his horse and, without ceremony, thrusts me into one of his saddlebags. But I don't fit all the way in; my tapers are too tall. He leaves the flap unbuckled and hurries to his horse's bridle to lead him down the drive. I am livid! I will scorch this saddlebag to smoking ruin before he gets as far as the gate!

But it's the glorious rose garden that halts him in his tracks. The gates stand open at the end of the drive, but he is too awed with looking to mount his horse. He crosses to the edge of the drive and gazes at the wall of roses soaring upward to arch over his head. His hand reaches out to touch one leaf; then his fingers caress a beautiful rose in bud, perfectly formed and dewy with rain. After another furtive glance all around the empty garden, his fingers close on the base of the stem, and he gently plucks the rose.

He has scarcely turned a single step back toward his horse when a thunderous roar splits the air, as if the storm were beginning again. Beast stands at the top of the steps, howling like a demon, his horns agleam, his dark eyes fierce, and his paws upraised, claws extended. He is swathed in a cloak of Jean-Loup's he has found somewhere, burgundy velvet, trimmed in gold. It falls to only a little way below his haunches, but the effect is both regal and terrible. He is a nightmare come to life, and the old man is so affrighted, he drops the perfect rose into the wet gravel.

"Human!" thunders Beast. "Why do you steal from me?"

The old man is so terrified, he can barely speak. "I—I . . ." stammers the old man. "Oh, forgive me, sire . . ."

"Silence!" roars Beast, striding down the steps. His hooves crunch menacingly in the gravel, and the old man, incapable of flight, falls to his trembling knees and cowers in terror as Beast approaches. "Have I not fed you, warmed you, provided you with the most civil hospitality?"

"M-more than civil; I . . . I should call it splendid," blathers the man.

"And this is how you repay me?" Beast demands.

The old man is bent so low, he can scarcely be heard. "It is . . . only a rose."

"But it is not yours," rumbles Beast. "And neither is this!"

The old man dares to raise his eyes to see this monster towering above him, a mountain of rage blocking out the sun, as Beast stamps to the horse's side and plucks me out of the saddlebag. I see the relief in Beast's eyes as he inspects me, cradling me in his paw, before he glares down furiously at the old man—whose face reflects stark terror at this proof of his thievery. He was in such a panic over Beast, it seems he forgot all about me.

"Oh, s-sir," he stammers. "Oh, please, my lord . . ."

"Never call me *lord*!" the monster roars. "I am Beast!"

"Please, Sir Beast, I beg your forgiveness." His nervous gaze jumps to me. "It was . . . foolish of me. I'm afraid I acted out of desperation. I—I meant no harm."

Beast glowers down at the old man, clutching me to his chest. I can feel his heart beating. "Did I not hear you swear yourself indebted to me?" Beast demands.

"And so I am, more so now than ever," agrees the old man hastily. "I—I confess myself financially embarrassed at the moment, but—"

"Your money means nothing to me," growls Beast. "But in return for all you have received in my home—and for all you presumed to take from me—I propose that you pay off your debt to me with your company."

"Stay with you? H-here?" The old man's voice quavers.

"Since you are so fond of my roses."

The old man lowers his face again to regard the one plucked rose, lying in the gravel where he dropped it. "It was wrong of me to take a . . . a souvenir without permission. But . . . the rose is not for me. It's for my daughter."

Beast frowns down at him. "You have children?"

"Three daughters, sir. And three stout sons, God be praised. Although my wife was taken from us many years ago." He straightens up on his knees and hurries on. "We have lately removed to the country in poverty after a cruel reversal of our fortunes. I was a merchant of some prosperity once, but—"

"Your family?" Beast prompts.

"My daughters are scarcely accustomed to country ways, poor things. They were so excited when word came that one of my ships had been recovered and that our fortune might yet be restored. I promised the two eldest to bring them back fine trinkets from my journey to the seaport where my last ship lay." The old man bows his head again. "But my venture did not pay off. I can't bring them what they ask." He risks a glance at Beast. "But the youngest asked me only for a single rose. She is as good as she is beautiful, poor child. This is the only promise I could keep."

Beast considers this. "And what of your debt to me?" he asks quietly.

"Good Sir Beast, I . . . I will pay my debt to you. I swear it!"

Beast gazes at him in silence, still clutching me close to his massive chest, as if to emphasize the enormity of that debt. With an ominous rumble of cogs and latches, the gilded gates at the end of the drive clang shut; the sound reverberates with awful finality under the arch of roses.

"Kind S-sir Beast," the merchant stammers. "I am an old man. My days upon this earth are numbered. I will share as many with you as you require. Only—" He dares to raise his face to implore Beast directly. "I beg you, allow me to return home to take leave of my children. I cannot simply disappear without a trace from their lives. Please, I throw myself on your mercy!"

Of course, he is a merchant, accustomed to bargaining; he calculates his chances in Beast's mute, dark eyes and presses on. "Accept my word, from one gentleman to, ah, another, that I will return to pay my debt."

Beast thinks it over. "One fortnight," he says at last. "Take your leave, settle your affairs, whatever is required. But at the end of a fortnight, you must return to me. That is our bargain."

"Thank you, oh thank you, Sir Beast!"

The merchant staggers to his feet and, somehow, commands his wayward limbs to hold him upright as he stumbles back to the support of his horse. As the old man clambers into the saddle, Beast goes low on his haunches and sweeps something up from the ground. The merchant reins up his horse and glances hopefully at the still-closed gates, but looking back, he is startled to find Beast standing beside him.

"Don't forget your rose," says Beast, holding it out to the merchant. The red rosebud looks impossibly fragile in his huge paw.

The old man takes it with nervous fingers and laces the stem carefully through the clasp of his cloak.

Beast reaches for the bridle, and while the man still cowers in his seat, Beast leads horse and rider down the gravel drive toward the gates, which swing open magically as they approach. At the foot of the drive, Beast turns to regard his guest one last time.

"Tell me," he rumbles, "your daughter, the beauty. Has she a name?"

"Rose," whispers the merchant. "She is called Rose."

BEAUTY

CHAPTER 18

Back inside, Beast returns me to my favorite perch in the window, but he is too agitated himself to take a seat.

"Are you all right?" he rumbles at me.

I am neither tarnished nor scratched. Yet it infuriates me that I was not able to do more on my own behalf.

"I hope you know that is not what I meant." Beast's paw trembles slightly on the sill beside me.

I know.

"I lost sight of him from the stairway," says Beast. "I didn't want him to see me, of course. So I didn't realize what had happened until it was almost too late."

So Beast was still hiding in the shadows, watching his guest.

You mean you didn't leave me there to tempt him into his bargain?

Beast is shocked. "I would never risk your safety like that!" He pauses, then glances at me sideways. "Although — perhaps if I had thought of it . . ."

I wish I could laugh; it would be a relief after the events of this morning.

Scaring him out of his wits was scarcely the best way to win a companion, I observe instead.

Beast shrugs. "Perhaps not. But he had to be made to know how serious his crime was. What if he had succeeded? What would have become of you?"

What indeed? Suppose I had been handed over by the old merchant to pay off some creditor, passed along from one bill collector to another until I ended up locked away in some cupboard of forgotten things. Or perhaps even melted down, my essence squandered for rings or coins. And no one would ever even know. No one but Beast.

Thank you.

Beast responds with a brief but decisive nod of his shaggy head.

But you can't really expect the old man to come back now?

"Perhaps not." Beast sighs in agreement. "But you are safe. That is what matters." He draws another breath and adds softly, "That is at least one thing I could do for you."

Yet Beast's movements about the château grow more aimless as the day passes. And the next. We go no more to the library, for fear he may not hear his visitor return. He occupies himself among his roses in view of the gilded gate. It surprises me that he would seek further acquaintance with this troublesome old man, no matter how lonely he is. But, surely, Beast can't possibly delude himself that the merchant will ever come back to this place. To him.

And when he does not arrive, what will Beast do? He's not a fairy or wizard, for all the otherworldly forces he can sometimes command. He can't fly through the air like a witch on his unresponsive wings to snatch up his prey, nor conjure him here through black arts.

For all his apparent menace, he is the lamb who's been tricked.

"Someone is coming."

Beast appears beside me at the window overlooking the rose garden. His shaggy ears prick up, and his nose quivers. I stare hard but can see nothing out in the garden; dusk is falling, and the shadows are long.

"There," says Beast, pointing out past the roses and the gilded iron gate beyond.

I lower my flame to make the glass less reflective, and we see a cloaked figure making its way up the hill from the vineyards below the château.

It must be the merchant, drawing his cloak closer against the chill of evening as he presses on. He comes on foot this time and will not condemn his horse to share his fate. His movements are clumsy, furtive, and yet determined.

Already Beast is vaulting up the stairs to ready a suite of rooms, order a meal, and prepare himself for his guest. I'm left alone in the window to watch the visitor approach the far end of the stone bridge over the moat. Across the bridge he creeps, stopping once to admire the swans and again to stare up in awe at the riot of roses bursting over the top of the château wall. But when the gates swing open before him, he draws back in alarm, as if he has never beheld such a thing before.

This is not the old man.

The intruder is in the garden now, crunching up the drive under the archway of roses. At the top of the drive, the figure pauses to gaze up at Château Beaumont in all its grandeur. Even in the half-light of dusk, it must be an impressive sight with its rows and rows of mullioned windows and carved balconies, its domed turrets and skyscraping tower. For a long moment, the stranger is too much in awe to continue, possibly losing his nerve and ready to flee. In that unguarded moment, the cloak falls partly open, and I spy skirts underneath. A woman! A woman in Beast's lair.

I see her straighten her shoulders, readjust her cloak, catch up her skirts, and begin her ascent. Only as she gains the porch do I realize that her eyes are on me, the only beam of warmth and light in this dark, forbidding place.

The grand double doors swing open, soundlessly this time, and the hall sconces light as she steps into the room. She turns around and around, taking it all in: the black-and-white marble tile floor, the brocaded walls, the golden sconces, the grand staircase with its ornate carvings. And as she turns, she pushes back her hood. She is young, with a heart-shaped face, large, liquid dark blue eyes, and long fair hair, artlessly drawn off her face with a single ribbon like a child's.

She is beautiful.

Why is she here?

On her final rotation, her gaze snags again on me. Then an ominous rumbling calls her attention to the stairway; Beast emerges out of the shadows at the bend of the stair-case as a chandelier suddenly flames to life. He gazes down at her, and she draws back where she stands. One delicate hand flies to her mouth, but she doesn't utter the cry that must be in her throat. For another long moment, they stare at each other. Beast is resplendent in a fine white linen shirt massive enough to confine and conceal his feathered back and furry chest, and breeches—breeches!—that must have adjusted magically to his girth. His burgundy cloak lined in golden satin is thrown back over his huge shoulders, clasped across his chest with a strand of pearls. But he is

Beast still, his great head maned and horned, his muzzle covered in downy fur, his paws savage, his hooves cloven beneath his breeches.

"Who seeks my hospitality?" he calls down.

Affrighted anew that the monster speaks, the girl loses her resolve and whirls about where she stands, only to see the double doors slam shut behind her. With a gasp, fingertips still at her mouth, she turns back to face her fate.

"Your name, girl," says Beast more gently.

"R-Rose," says she.

"So your father sent you in his place," says Beast. "I had not thought him so cowardly."

"My father is not a coward!" she cries. Then she thinks to lower her voice. "But he is old and worn down with his cares. It's my fault that he offended you; I'm the one who asked for a rose. I could not let him come back here to be . . . to . . ." She does not know what, or can't bring herself to say it. "So I slipped away before anyone could stop me," she says. "I only hope you will accept me in his stead."

Beast cocks his head to one side, regarding her. "You mean to say you are here of your own free will? No one has forced you to come here?"

"It is my choice." She lifts her pointed chin with a pretty show of spirit. "Our family keeps its bargains." And I see Beast's expression warm ever so slightly.

"Then you are welcome. *Rose.*"

Beast makes a little bow and comes down two steps. I see the girl tense, but she makes no other move. Beast pauses, eyes fixed upon her face.

"May I take your cloak?" he offers.

It's plain she fears him coming any closer, but she doesn't want to repay his polite offer with rudeness. So she unlaces her cloak, lets it fall from her shoulders, and stands uncertainly, holding it over her arm. Invisible forces lift it gently into the air, and this time, she can't suppress a little cry when Beast points one paw, and an ornate coatrack of polished wood suddenly appears at the foot of the stairs; the cloak flies through the air to hang itself on one of the hooks. Rose stands before Beast in a modest frock of blue homespun with a white apron pinned to her bodice and tied at the waist that sweeps nearly to the floor.

"Why, you are dressed like a servant," says Beast.

She glances down at her clothing. "These are all I have," she tells him. "We are poor now, and what few fine things we still possess belong to my sisters."

"You will find fresh garments in your room upstairs and a supper laid whenever you wish it. At eight o'clock— if you will permit it—I will visit you again."

She lifts her chin again and gazes frankly into Beast's face.

"You are . . . very kind. Sir Beast."

She favors him with a half smile, and he gazes back at her, his expression unreadable. Then he disappears into the shadows in a swirl of velvet and gold.

She looks after him in the gloom, then squares her shoulders and prepares to climb the stairs. But at the last minute, she comes back again to peer at me, although not with the same covetous look of her father. She does pluck me off my windowsill, however. Perhaps she doesn't trust the magical sconces to stay alight long enough to find her way upstairs. Or perhaps she feels safer with an object in hand she can wield as a weapon.

The small white hand that curls around me does not feel much accustomed to battle, but there is resolution in her grip as she mounts the steps.

I light her way upstairs. What choice do I have?

The sconces upstairs direct her to a cozy bedchamber dominated by a grand canopied bed. Spread across the counterpane, she finds a magnificent gown as blue as the one the stained-glass princess wears in the tower window and trimmed in creamy lace. She gasps when she sees it.

"But this is too fine for me," she breathes.

Who does she mean to impress with her modesty? There's no one here but me.

She sets me on the nightstand, and while there are no servants to dress her, her own clothes obligingly fall away, even as her hands rush to her bodice to try to hold them on. She looks all around in fear, expecting to be pounced on, I suppose. But instead a fine chemise floats down over her head, the embroidered material exquisite. Petticoats of equal quality follow, and then the gown itself, the bodice lacing itself up her back. With each new layer, her wide eyes grow more eager. She takes a pinch of shimmering satin between her thumb and fingers, expecting it to melt away like fairy dust. But it's as real as the roses in the garden that blossomed under Beast's care.

She fluffs out her skirt, adjusts her puffed sleeves, tosses back her hair, and turns to the dressing table across from the bed. Its mirror has been magically restored for her convenience. She peers into her reflection for a long moment. Then she smiles.

"Oh, sisters," she whispers. "If you could see me now!"

The hall sconces light her way, yet Rose will not venture out of her room without me.

Another fire roars in the dining salon. As we enter, music played by ghostly hands on unseen instruments sweetens the air, a wistful duet for lute and bass viol. Rose's eyes widen again at the extravagance of the feast laid out on the table before her. Then her face clouds over a bit.

"Surely he means to fatten me up and devour me," she whispers, and sets me nervously on the table but well within reach.

She's too frightened to indulge. She only picks at a fragrant, yeasty bread, nibbles at some sugared sweets, and scarcely sips the wine. The roast capon, jellied terrine, and poached fish swimming in lemon and tarragon all go untouched. From somewhere, chimes strike eight times — odd, for I've never heard a chiming clock here before — and Rose sets down her wineglass with a thump. When Beast's huge frame suddenly fills the opposite doorway, she tries not to gasp.

"May I join you, Rose?" he asks her formally. When she cannot quite find her tongue, he remains where he stands. "My supper does not please you?" he inquires.

"I . . . I'm afraid I have little appetite, Sir Beast."

"Because of me?" he murmurs, and withdraws back into the shadows.

She looks after him, alarmed. Should he be debating whether to devour her, she doesn't want to insult him into the bargain.

"No . . . Sir Beast! I didn't mean it that way. Please . . . come back."

He reappears slowly in the doorway, his hairy face etched in the firelight. "You have nothing to fear from me, Rose. I swear it." She glances up at him again, and places a paw upon his breast. "On my honor, I swear it."

Rose makes up her mind to relent and nods him to a seat at the table. Moving slowly so as not to frighten her any more, he seats himself at the far end of the table opposite her, arranging his fine cape and clothing with care. He glances at me, surprised, and perhaps pleased, to see that Rose has placed me nearby, next to her wine goblet.

"Will you not eat, Sir Beast?" she asks when he makes no motion toward the platters of food or the flagon of wine, which remain piled before Rose.

He gazes pensively at the food, human food fit for ladies and gentlemen; I know it cannot satisfy him.

"I have . . . dined . . . already. But do please help yourself."

She shakes her head. "I've had my fill, thank you."

Beast frowns. "But you've scarcely touched a morsel. Perhaps you'd prefer something else? Soup? Potted sweetbreads? A ragout?" As he reels off these names, the dishes themselves appear on the table, doffing their shiny covers to the startled Rose, enveloping her end of the table in savory steam until at last, she's fluttering her hands in the air like agitated moths.

"Oh, please, Sir Beast! It's all too much!"

And with a wave of Beast's paw, all the dishes vanish.

"I've upset you," he says anxiously.

"No, not at all," she replies hastily. "It's just that . . . all this . . ." And she makes a small gesture with her hand that seems to include the beautifully dressed table, the music, and the fragrant air itself, where the dishes were just a moment ago. She shakes her head in wonder, and unexpectedly, a soft syllable of surprised laughter escapes her. Beast peers at her.

"This will all take some getting used to," she explains. And then she smiles at him.

It's the first time he has seen her full smile, and I note the surprised pleasure in Beast's eyes. How eagerly he responds to even the barest hint of fellowship.

And I revise my opinion of this Rose, this innocent beauty.

She will break his heart.

CHAPTER 19

Constant Companions

Beast took his leave of Rose last night with the invitation to enjoy herself at his château.

"My garden, my grounds, all are at your disposal," he told her. "Whatever you desire while under my roof, you have only to wish for." He then asked her permission to visit her again tonight, at eight, and she cautiously agreed.

Rose keeps me nearby like a child clings to a favorite toy, for the reassurance of something familiar, and Beast does not interfere, anxious to put her at ease. So I spent last night on a night table next to Rose's canopied bed, illuminating nothing. And today, she and I are constant companions. Left on her own to explore the château, she needs my friendly light; spring rains have washed away the last of the snow, and the sun, when it shows its face, climbs higher every day, but there are gloomy corners in this place too ominous for her to venture into alone.

Upstairs, Rose investigates the cavernous ballroom with its plain, bare walls and doesn't know what to make of it, cannot imagine the rage and passion with which its fine mirrored panels were destroyed. She carries me down the grand central staircase, past the portraits of Beaumont ancestors, past the portraits of Rene and Christine LeNoir, Jean-Loup's parents, without even a flicker of interest. But she stops cold at the wall directly above the landing, where Jean-Loup's portrait hangs.

The tucked jacket and smooth breeches he wears beneath his tossed-back cloak emphasize his broad chest, slim waist, and long, shapely legs. His russet hair is loose and haloed in gold; his eyes are dark and cold, glittering with slyness. I note again how Beast's eyes are different, more thoughtful. More complex. But Rose sees only a splendid young knight of heart-stopping beauty. She stretches out her hand to touch the canvas, as if expecting to feel human warmth and life. She must wonder who this handsome knight is and what connection he has to this grand château. But of course, she could never imagine the answer.

It disturbs me to see how dreamily she gazes at this cold painted image, responding to its handsome surface alone, while Beast, a warmhearted creature of flesh and blood who so longs for her company, inspires only her fear and suspicion. I would not deny Beast the novelty of having another living soul about the place, but I find I dread how Beast might be hurt should she reject his offer of friendship.

It takes Rose a long time to tear herself away from the portrait and complete her descent into the great hall. There are receiving chambers and salons and sitting rooms and morning rooms of equal grandeur and anonymity in either direction; I have visited them all with Beast. I try to urge her instead toward the double doors. Perhaps if she sees again the outside world, she'll come to her senses and try to escape. Beast will not pursue her, nor will he keep her caged against her will. She has only to fly, and this charade will end.

I wish as hard as I might, and she does take a tentative step or two toward the doors, but she is less receptive to my thoughts than Beast. Abruptly, she stops and looks around in fear, perhaps afraid of Beast's magical powers. I peer out through the window, hoping to spy Beast asleep under the roses, sprawled in the dirt like the animal he is; if she sees him as he is in nature, without his elegant clothing, it might drive her away. But I don't see him anywhere; he's taken great pains to hide himself from her view.

At length, she sighs and turns around and carries me back into the hall.

Rose finds her way to the kitchen. Perhaps she means to find some honest work for her idle hands, to earn the splendor of Beast's hospitality. Or perhaps she only wishes to relieve the boredom. But the kitchen hums along in perfect order, pots and pans sparkling in their racks, cook fire crackling low in the grate, kettle warming on the hob. There's nary a crumb to be swept off the floor nor a stain of any kind to be scrubbed on the huge oak table. It's not at all like the chaotic days when messy human servants inhabited the place; magic manages everything so much more tidily.

After wandering from kitchen to scullery to formal salons, she takes a seat at last in one of my old chambers, weary from the explorations of the morning. It's midday, and a sturdy dinner of stew and bread and grapes and wine presents itself on the side table next to her. She eats more heartily this time and smiles to see the dinner things vanish when she is done.

At last, finding nothing anywhere that needs doing, nor any other amusement, she wanders out again into the entry hall. She's drawn to the sideboard against the wall, where Beast keeps his bowl of dried rose petals. The mound is higher than it was, with a few soft, still-red petals sprinkled over the dry brown ones. The fragrance is so delicious that Rose dares to dip into the bowl, crushing a few petals between her fingers and trailing her fingertips gently along the base of her throat.

A few more steps lead her into the vestibule behind the

staircase that overlooks the back of the estate. The doors are open, giving onto the smaller stone bridge that crosses the back of the moat and leads to the green park beyond. Beast has been at work here, for the bramble that threatened to swallow all not so long ago has now been banished deep into the woods. The pale sun has struggled free of the clouds for the moment and beams on the green, glistening trees and turquoise water.

Unable to resist, Rose is drawn out into the open air.

I've been clutched in her hand all the while, for the vestibule is full of shadows. But now, outside, she places me on the flat stone railing that caps the low bridge wall. I try to focus my thoughts, to urge her all the way across the bridge, into the park and the wood beyond.

But she dares only a hesitant step or two away, when she spies one of the swans fluffing up his feathers out in the moat. She trots another few steps down the bridge as the swan paddles away toward the far corner of the château.

"Wait!" she cries. "Oh, please, wait!"

Perhaps she hopes the swan, like Beast, can speak to her. But the swan isn't enchanted and won't obey, gliding on around the corner and disappearing from her view. With a great sigh, she flops down onto the stone railing beside me, shivering a bit as the sun, too, begins to disappear. Then she sits up straighter and lifts her chin.

"I am here for Papa's sake, and I will not be sorry about

it," she reminds herself. "But—if only there were someone to talk to. Someone else, I mean," she adds softly, with a wary glance back at the château. "It's so lonely here."

And with a charming melody of musical notes, a small red bird flies out of the park and over the moat toward us. He lands first on a window ledge on the third floor, then hops to a stone balcony above the bridge. He sings again and cocks his head; his bright black eye seems to look right at us. Then he flutters down to perch on one of my outstretched silver arms and gazes attentively at Rose. I would shoo him off if I could, but Rose claps her hands with delight.

"Oh, pretty bird! Do you understand me?"

He chirps again with a quick little nod.

"Can you speak?"

He sings another rhapsody of beautiful notes; every creature speaks, if we have the wit to hear them. But she's expecting human language, and her face falls a little. Still, the bird looks at her so keenly, she can't help but smile back.

"Do you live here, Redbird?" And her voice lowers and softens. "Am I right to be afraid?"

The bird answers with a cascade of pretty notes like reassuring laughter. And I realize where I've seen this creature before: in the rose garden, serenading Beast. I wonder if Beast has sent this bird to Rose, to help calm her fears.

"It is a beautiful place," Rose confesses, brightening a little, gazing up again at the towering château. "And . . . he did say I have nothing to fear from him."

The bird chirps merrily again, as if laughing off her qualms.

"I was being silly, I know," Rose agrees. She gets to her feet and smiles at the bird. "It won't be so much to bear."

She has a new gown to wear at supper, pale periwinkle blue, trimmed in tiny pearls. She marches into the dining salon with more assurance and samples more of the food; it delights her to send the platters and gravy boats flying with a wave of her hand. Indeed, she is bearing up wonderfully well.

At eight chimes, Beast appears again in the doorway, clothed and caped and groomed. Yet she can't quite stifle another little gasp at the sight of him. I should be glad to see her making such a fool of Jean-Loup, increasing his humiliation, but it irritates me that Beast must bear with her foolishness.

Rose recovers herself and graciously nods him to the table. Beast glances at me, surprised to find me still in Rose's company, standing by her plate. He then takes his place at the foot of the table, with several places between them at their opposite ends.

"Have you everything you require?" he asks Rose.

"You are very kind, Sir Beast."

"Have you visited my park?" he continues eagerly. "My rose garden?"

"I . . . I didn't know if it would be allowed." Her eyelids flutter down, and Beast draws back as if rebuked.

"But, Rose," he protests gently. "I have no wish to imprison you in this house. Please, go out of doors and enjoy the sunshine. I would be honored if you would visit my garden, as I understand you are fond of roses. And there are many handsome walks in my park. Please feel free to make use of them."

She raises her eyes again, as blue as an ocean. "I was afraid I would anger you," she confesses. "I didn't want to repay your hospitality with disobedience."

"But I do not ask you to obey me," says Beast. "I only wish for you to enjoy what I have to offer."

She nods and takes another small sip of wine.

"I would be very happy," he continues eagerly, "to escort you around my rose garden. Tomorrow, if you like."

Rose sets her glass down with a nervous thud and glances away to conceal the fear in her eyes from Beast— but not from me. It's clear she dreads the thought of Beast any nearer than a table-length away.

"But . . . Sir Beast, I'm afraid you would find me poor company."

A deft parry. She is more cunning than I gave her credit for, or else she is learning it out of necessity.

Beast scents the air between them and frowns very slightly. I know how sharp his senses are. He detects her true feelings, however hard she tries to conceal them.

"But I could wish for none better," says Beast. "It would make me the happiest of . . . of . . ."

He cannot say "of men," as the usual compliment goes, and her fragile composure wavers.

"Oh, forgive me, kind Sir Beast, but I . . . I . . ."

He rises so suddenly that she jumps in her seat, but he only means to back away from the table and make her a courtly bow.

"It is too soon. I know," he rumbles. "We scarcely know each other, and I have no desire to upset you, my dear Rose." His voice is pitched low and soft with concern. "I will leave you now. But, please, I beg of you, do not forbid me to come dine with you again tomorrow evening."

I dislike that Beast must beg for her approval. But Rose gathers her resolve and nods.

"You may come."

"Until tomorrow, then," he murmurs. "Eight o'clock." And with one last glance at me, he backs away into the shadows.

CHAPTER 20

Deliverance

Rose's mood is surprisingly sunny when she rises in the morning. She hums a little tune as she bathes at her wash-stand and allows more fine clothing to arrange itself on her person. She carries me into the dining salon, sets me beside the chocolate pot on her table, cracks open her egg in its china cup, and devours a sweet, rich pastry. She smiles up at the portrait of Jean-Loup as we descend the stairs.

Today, she dares to go through the grand front doors and down the drive under the arch of roses. She is now so accustomed to having me nearby that she takes me along. I'm useful to have in hand when she's thinking out loud: "Shall we go in here?" or "Let us see where this leads." Beast is nowhere to be seen; he forgoes the pleasure of his beloved garden during the daylight hours in deference to her. Neither is there any sign of Redbird.

At the end of the drive, Rose is drawn to the wide

stone arches of the carriage house, where she has not yet been. I have never been here, either; it lay outside the scope of my duties when I was a servant, and for all our rambling about the château, Beast never brought me here.

A breezeway under the arches connects a series of barnlike rooms. In the first one, I see the battered cart Beast filled with vessels of water for his roses. But a far more magnificent carriage draws Rose's attention, made of polished, exotic wood and trimmed in gold. The driver's bench is elevated to a disdainful height, the wrought iron back wheels are enormous, and a wine-colored curtain is drawn across the window of the covered cab. The Beaumont device is painted on the door, the Beast Rampant above a field of spearheads. The carriage has grown dusty since the servants ran away, but here and there the wood and gilt still catch the gleam of my light.

Rose decides to investigate the other rooms, mostly work and storage areas, that lead back to the château, thrusting me forward to light the way. In one, the shadows reveal an old ironmonger's forge covered over in cobwebs. Rose pokes me timidly into the gloom and utters a little cry when my skittering light picks out a shape in the far corner, not quite a figure but something more than a shadow sprawling amid a mound of straw bales.

It's an old suit of armor, dark and rusty, partially hidden among the bales. Some of the joints have separated so that it lies in pieces, broken rivets scattered here and there, a steel gauntlet like a severed hand lolling in the straw. A helmet with a pointed visor has rolled carelessly to the straw-covered floor, but the breastplate remains intact, propped up on one of the bales. It bears the Beaumont device, and although it's chipped and worn with age, I know where I've seen this armor before — in the portrait of Rene Auguste LeNoir, Jean-Loup's father.

But now it's tossed aside like an old rag in this forgotten corner. It's the only object of any value I've yet seen at Château Beaumont that is not pampered and revered. Given the reverence with which Jean-Loup always spoke of his father, I would expect to see it polished and glittering in the entry hall or the grand stairway, for all to see. And yet here it lies.

But Rose no longer shares my curiosity, hurrying through the last few rooms, where items not currently in use in the château are kept in chests. Rose steals a peek beneath a lid here and there; the daughter of a merchant, she must know the value of beautiful things. Outside, we cross the horse track that separates the carriage house from the main building and return to the château. When we are back in the entry hall, Rose makes her way to the foot of the stairs and gazes up again at the portrait of Jean-Loup.

"Chevalier," she whispers, "I hope I may dream of you again!"

I'm so shocked, I nearly jolt myself right out of her hand. How dare she come prancing in here, into Beast's domain, and start dreaming of Jean-Loup? He is gone, Jean-Loup, and I am sworn to see to it that no trace of him remains anywhere, not even in dreams.

A small musical peep interrupts us, and Rose looks up. Redbird is perched on the rail of the second-floor landing, peering down at us with his lively eyes. How did he get in the house? There must be a window open in the attic.

"Redbird!" she cries happily. "Have you come to visit me?" He gives a chirp of assent. But before she can say any more, Redbird suddenly flies up into the shadows of the stairwell, leaving only a cascade of tinkling notes behind.

"Wait, pretty bird!" she cries. "Don't go!"

His birdsong wafts down from above, and Rose climbs after him, following his song, until we come out into the gloomy attic. Rose hesitates, clutching me close, but Redbird chirrups again from the back corner. The little door in the turret stands open, and he's perched on its arched top. Then he flies into the dark passage within, and Rose makes up her mind to follow; she climbs the little carved staircase into the library.

It's eerie for me to be up here again. The last time was the night of the storm when I told Beast about Jean-Loup. The glass vase still stands on the writing table, but its water has dried up. A brittle stalk and a few crumpled petals littering the desktop are all that remain of the last rose. Beast can't have been back here. Perhaps he finds the memory of the last evening we spent here together too upsetting.

But Rose knows nothing of that. Sunlight pours in through the colored glass, and the image of the castle and its princess enchants her. While Redbird warbles his melody, she sets me on an open space on one shelf and inspects the books, peering at the spines, drawing out this one or that to riffle through the pages. When her father the merchant was prosperous, she must have had the advantage of a genteel education—music, embroidery, books. At last, she carries a few books over to the chair. She places me on the end table at her side and burrows into the cushions with her first volume.

"You have a lovely rose garden, Sir Beast," Rose volunteers that night at dinner after Beast has joined her at his place at the far end of the table.

"I am so pleased you think so," says Beast, trying to contain his eagerness that she has begun a conversation with him.

"My father spoke very highly of it," says Rose politely. "He also mentioned the splendid hospitality you had shown him."

Before Beast terrified the old man in the garden, I think to myself, but I doubt her father would have shared that part of the tale with his children. At least not the part that involved his attempted thievery.

"It was my pleasure," Beast replies. To make more conversation, he adds, "I hope he arrived home safely."

"Quite safely, thank you," says Rose.

Beast waits another moment and then gently prods, "Your family was glad to see him, I expect."

"Yes. Of course," murmurs Rose, but says no more. Even from this distance, I can see Beast's expression fall a little. Perhaps he thinks he ought not remind her of the loved ones she's had to leave behind because of him. Or perhaps he was hoping for a more spirited response.

Even Rose has now noticed how quiet Beast has become and casts about for a new topic to break the silence. "Sir Beast, I visited your library today," she begins.

Beast brightens on the instant. "Is it not lovely? I believe it belonged to the last Lady Beaumont. Please make use of it whenever you like."

"Thank you." Rose smiles, lifts her chin with some resolve, and gestures Beast one chair nearer in the line of chairs between them. "Please, Sir Beast, do sit a little closer. I can scarcely hear you!"

Beast, surprised, complies.

When the meal ends, Beast rises to take his leave but pauses when he sees Rose scoop me up again, as is now her habit.

"You needn't trouble yourself," he tells her, nodding at me. "The lights in this house will always shine for you, whenever you wish."

I begin to hope the girl will give me up at last. I would much rather spend my time in Beast's company.

But Rose, surprised, clutches me closer. "You are very kind, Sir Beast. But—I know it's silly, but there are shadows in my chamber." Indeed there are within the alcove where her bed and nightstand are placed. There are no sconces, and I provide the only light, although it embarrasses her to admit she is afraid of the dark. Then she looks at me, now gripped in both her hands, and warily back at Beast. "I . . . I hope you don't mind."

Perhaps she fears to be accused of stealing if she does not surrender me. This must occur to Beast, too, from his hasty reassurance.

"Of course not, dear Rose; you may do as you like. I only wish for you to feel at home here."

He backs toward the door, with a nod of farewell to Rose, who still clutches me in her hands. "And if you need anything, you have only to ask," he murmurs, looking directly at me. "You know that."

I read the question in his dark eyes as he lingers in the doorway.

"Thank you," whispers Rose.

I, too, flutter my flames a bit to show I appreciate him

thinking of me, but I am resigned to bear the girl's company a while longer. Only then does Beast bow his way out and leave the corridor unobstructed for Rose.

Rose spends all the next morning in the library, bathed in the shifting sunlit colors pouring through the window, absorbed in her private world of books. I stand beside her, providing light, while I stew in my own thoughts. She chooses fairy tales and romances, I notice, slim volumes with beautiful engravings, easily digested. Stories for children: princesses locked in towers waiting for deliverance.

By the time dusky twilight falls, Rose has returned to her room to refresh herself after the exertions of a day spent dreaming over her books. A new gown of silvery blue satin is draped over the painted screen beside her wardrobe, but for now she's dressed only in her delicate lawn chemise, dabbing rose water from her basin onto her temples and wrists. These tasks completed, she goes to stretch out on her bed to nap before supper.

But I am in turmoil over all the ways she seems to be settling in about the place; it's been gnawing at me all day. It's bad enough the way she disrupts everything, intrudes on our solitude. But ever since I learned that Rose has dreamed of Jean-Loup, I've been wrestling with something even more sinister: only a woman who agrees to marry Beast could ever restore Jean-Loup, according to

Mère Sophie's spell. It's impossible to imagine that Rose would ever marry Beast; she is far too terrified of him. Nor would he ever think to ask her. But over time she might learn to pity him. And any softening of her feelings toward Beast is cause for alarm. She has no idea of the horror she might possibly unleash, all unawares, simply by staying on here.

Yet how can I deny Beast the human companionship he so longs for? He asks for so little, and it means so much to him. But, I further argue with myself, doesn't Beast deserve more than her pity? And under no circumstances can we let Jean-Loup come back.

Because what then becomes of Beast?

Rose must leave here now, of her own free will, as she arrived. And it must be a quick, clean break. Beast must bear his awful loneliness, but it's for his own sake. Rose must not stay here. She must take her poisonous dreams and go.

I stand on the bedside table, gazing down at her in her white chemise, with her long, pale blond hair spread beneath her. There can be no better time to catch her so completely off her guard.

The sudden appearance of Beast, unbidden, in her private chamber, should be enough to convince Rose how foolish she was to come here. Of course, Beast would never harm her, but the fact that she might encounter him at any moment, not merely at their formal dinners together, might shock her to her senses.

Before I can talk myself out of it, I focus my thoughts on Beast. I don't know if I can reach him from such a distance, but I must try. For all our sakes. The sun sets outside, and violet darkness steals over the last of the day. It's the uncanny hour, when all of nature holds its breath, awaiting the night.

Beast, I think, *Beast, you must come. Come to Rose's chamber. Come at once. Rose needs you. Beast, come here now.*

The shadows deepen, and night falls, until I am the only light in the room. Rose sighs prettily and turns over in her sleep.

Beast, now! Come now.

Something crashes in the next room, and Rose starts in her sleep. The double doors to the bedchamber burst inward, and Beast looms there, panting.

"Rose!" he bellows.

She jolts awake and screams at the sight of him.

Heat and agitation and a gamy, sickening odor roll off him in waves, thickening the air in the room, and Rose cries out again, cowering into her pillows.

Beast staggers to the bedside into the pool of my light. He's a gruesome sight, clad only in a torn-open shirt splashed with red animal blood that hangs askew on his massive frame. His mane tufts up in all directions, clotted with burrs and leaves, and blood drips from his whiskers and beard. His bloody paws are raised, claws outstretched, his powerful furred haunches and ragged rows of feathers exposed beneath his shirttails.

Of course, he would be hunting at nightfall! How could I have forgotten? I was too intent on my own purpose. I only meant to give Rose a shock, not frighten her to death!

Worst of all are Beast's dark eyes, glinting gold in the light, grotesquely human and wild with fear.

"Rose, what's the matter?" he cries.

But she's gotten her legs under her and scrambles farther backward.

"You are a horrible beast, that's the matter!" she shrieks, dragging a pillow across her lap and clutching it like a shield. She's a tiny, fragile thing cowering beneath his hugeness. "And you're going to kill me!"

Beast teeters on his hooves, still panting, bewildered. "No," he gasps. "Rose, no, I would never . . ." He starts to raise one paw in supplication, and she jerks even farther away.

"Then why are you here?" she cries.

"I—I thought there was something wrong," he stammers. "That you . . . called for me—"

"I would never call for you!" she cries, and he backs up a step. "Go away!" And he backs up another.

"Rose, please, I . . ." The fear in his eyes is deepening

into profound humiliation as he sees himself reflected in her terror. He glances down at himself, makes a feeble attempt to wipe one bloody paw on his filthy shirt.

"Get out!" Rose shouts. "Out!" She's up on her knees now. She can feel the power she has over him. It's his turn to cower.

Beast clutches his torn shirt closed over his chest, eyes full of confusion and apology and shame. Then his gaze falls on me, for an instant of awful realization.

"Forgive me, Rose," he murmurs, backing away. "Please, please forgive—"

"Out!" she cries again.

With a groan, Beast heels around and gallops out of the room. The fireplace opposite blazes with comforting light and warmth the instant he is gone, but Rose won't be comforted. Tears she was too frightened to shed before now burst out; she throws herself across the bed, sobbing. She ought to be collecting her things, I think angrily, to shift my own thoughts away from this awful thing I've done. I promise I will make it up to Beast, somehow, if only she will leave.

CHAPTER 21

Open Your Heart

He will never imprison her; he told her so. But she won't resolve herself to a sensible course of action. Instead she cries and cries. Finally, she sits up and hurls her pillow across the room; when it knocks a jar of something off her dressing table, causing a cascade of powder, she leaps up to grasp me and stumbles to the table, wielding me by the base to sweep off the other bottles and potions. She plunks me down before the looking glass and sinks into the chair, then buries her face in her folded arms and sobs some more.

Can she not simply go? I am furious! Beast should have devoured her and gotten it over with! Besides, he'll hear her; her weeping must be echoing throughout the château, rebuking Beast over and over for the way he has frightened her, disgusted her. What purpose does it serve to keep hurting him with her tears? Hasn't he been hurt enough tonight? Did she not see his eyes?

But perhaps she did not. That wounded look wasn't meant for her, anyway. It was meant for me.

There was no thought of supper last night. Rose finally sank into her bed, leaving me here on the dressing table, and this morning, she is still too wary to leave her room. She tenses at every creak of wood in the château and every whisper of the breeze outside. But Beast does not come back.

This is not how I planned it at all! I thought she would be gone by now. What purpose does it serve for her to linger? The memory of last night will be a raw wound that Beast will never heal from as long as she is still here.

Rose circles back to the dressing table, plops down on the chair, and peers at her own image with still-reddened eyes. "I'm sorry, Papa," she whispers. "I'm trying so hard, I really am! But I'm so frightened!"

Perhaps she fears that Beast will take revenge on the old man or the rest of her family if she leaves him.

Overnight, the things she disrupted in her tearful blundering about have evaporated into thin air; there are new bottles and powders here on her dressing table and a new gown of pale violet silk draped over the screen. Bread and cheese and wine enough to sustain her appear on her bedside table, but she has no appetite. She washes and dresses herself in her new gown, but she does not seem to know what to do next.

The sun has been up for hours when she finally dares to open her door and peep out. All is silent within the château, but Rose lets out a small gasp at something I can't see. She opens the door wider, bends down, and carries something back into the room—a glass vase with a single red rose inside, which she places on the dressing table beside me. Her other hand grasps an elegant page of parchment, folded in half. She sits on the chair and unfolds the page. Her eyes scan whatever she sees there with a look of growing wonder, until at last she sets the parchment down beside me, her expression thoughtful.

I read the single sentence, written carefully in ink:

Your father's debt to me is paid.

The penmanship is far from elegant, but it can be read. How long it must have taken Beast to compose it.

My spirits lift. Surely now, at last, she will go!

Rose shifts her gaze back to the looking glass before her, slightly biting her lower lip in perplexity. "I don't know what to do," she whispers.

A milky image begins to swirl in the glass. Rose catches her breath and blinks at it in surprise. Perhaps the magical forces here will respond to her plea. Two faces swim into focus, two women I have never seen before. But Rose has; she sits up in attention.

"Blanche!" whispers Rose. "Violette!"

The women are both older than Rose, yet they resemble her slightly, handsome ladies with determined chins. But their eyes are harder, their mouths more prim.

"Our sister lacks the civility to send us word from the château," harrumphs the younger-looking of the ladies. She shakes something in her hand, a piece of linen she is attempting to mend with very bad stitchery. "Fine thing for her to run off and leave us with all the work!"

"Well, we couldn't very well let Father go after her," reasons the elder sister. "Then how should we live? Our brothers are content to play at farming, although their efforts yield up little enough. But as long as Father has livestock and furniture to sell, at least we shall always be clothed."

"In last year's fashion!" The younger sister pouts.

"Oh, hsst! Father still meddles in business affairs; one of his ventures may yet pay off." The elder sister adjusts her fine headdress, slightly worn about the edges. "Besides, what use was Rose to us?"

"No use at all, and now *she* lives in a château, while we live here like peasants!"

"A château ruled by a monster! Whereas we may marry princes one day, if we but bide our time."

This remark has a comforting effect on the younger sister, who smiles and smooths out her skirts as if in anticipation.

"Rose may be devoured by now, for all we know," her sister continues. Her careless shrug implies it's a matter of little importance to her. "And even if she is not, she must live in seclusion with a horrible monster. Either way, she is out of our hair for good, while we have Father here, alive and well. As long as he lives to mend his fortunes, we shall have prospects." The older sister arches a brow. "And we shan't have to share our dowries with Rose. We've made the better bargain by far."

Rose is now sitting up very straight as the scene begins to fade. She lifts her own chin.

"I have made a bargain as well. And I will keep it," she vows. "I shall not tarnish Papa's honor."

The image of Rose's sisters appears to have strengthened her spine. By suppertime, she opens her door and ventures out.

Eight chimes sound in the dining salon, but Beast does not come. Nor the next night. How humiliated he must still be, how shaken to the core. Has he run off to the wood, unable to face her, never to be seen again? Rose must certainly leave now out of sheer boredom.

Then an even more sinister thought occurs to me: Has

something happened to Beast? Has he thrown himself off the upper tower in shame? It makes a horrible kind of sense; he's taken his leave of Rose and absolved her father of his debt. I try to focus my thoughts, direct them to wherever he is, but there is no sign that he has heard them. I try to blame Rose, her frantic outburst, her endless tears. But I know it's not true. Rose has more spirit than I ever imagined. She has not run off.

No one here has hurt Beast but me.

Rose begins visiting Beast's beautiful garden again; she takes me with her as a perch for Redbird to keep her company. Everywhere we go, I search fearfully from my position in her raised hand for any sign of a large, shaggy body drowned in the moat or crumpled on the ground beneath the balconies, but there is never any sign of Beast, living or dead. Rose still visits the library now and then, but she wearies more easily of the silly romances that once diverted her.

This morning, Redbird's happy notes sang in the stairwell, luring Rose out of the library and down into the garden, while I am abandoned on a shelf, forgotten. I am idly watching the progress of the stained-glass figures across the carpet when I hear a solid tread on the stairs, and a familiar horned head rises up out of the stairwell.

Beast! The thought explodes within me, I'm so relieved.

He pauses at the top of the stairs, one paw on the railing, ears pricked. He turns his head to the corner where I stand, eyeing me cautiously.

"Lucie."

It's the first private word he has addressed to me since the day Rose came.

"I thought no one would be here," he says.

Rose has left me behind.

Beast nods. "As she soon will me." He says this without any particular malice, yet I experience a pang of shame. I would not blame him for stalking off, but he hesitates only another moment before stepping all the way up into the room. He perches his great bulk on the seat of the armchair with exaggerated care, patting his clean white shirt into place above his breeches. He looks calm enough, but it's plain he is still smarting from the fury of Rose's outburst. My shame intensifies for my part in it.

I'm sorry, Beast. I didn't think she would carry on so. And I certainly didn't expect her to hurt you so willfully.

Beast peers at me, his expression weary. "And what did you think she *would* do?"

I thought she would leave! Go home to her family, where she belongs! I try to put my thoughts in better order. *You know she must not stay here—*

"I know!" he barks. He turns away, shaking his head ruefully. "I know it," he says more quietly. "I was foolish to think she might ever be . . . content here." He sighs. "I suppose I could not expect her affection, but I thought she might learn to regard me with something other than fear, than *obedience*. I dared hope for an occasional honest smile, shared laughter, another voice to answer mine, if only . . ." His voice trails off. His warm, gold-dusted eyes lower in defeat.

"I can't bear to see the constant terror in her eyes," he mutters. "Of course, I should send her home."

That's not the only reason, as he ought to know.

But—what if he doesn't know? I am stunned by this new possibility: if he remembers nothing before waking up in the park in his beastly form, as he told me once, he may not even know about the spell that created him! He may not realize that this new life he has only just embraced might be taken from him just as quickly.

But how can I tell him in this moment? I have never seen Beast so despondent, so dispirited, so resigned to misery. What would it do to him to think that he had some connection to the hateful Jean-Loup? I remember how Jean-Loup raged inside of Beast, at first, when we smashed the mirrors and he shut me up in that cupboard. Beast has found the strength to overcome him since then. But Beast's grip on life may be fragile. What if the truth about his origin is too big a shock? What if Beast loses his hold, and Jean-Loup comes back?

I don't know the answer. But I do know the danger posed by Rose, even if she's proven she can never care for Beast as he is — with my help, I remind myself guiltily. If only I can persuade Beast to send her home now, perhaps he'll never have to know about Jean-Loup.

Rose is very attached to her father, I tell Beast. *It was very kind of you to forgive his debt, but perhaps she fears it will shame him if she leaves without your permission.*

Beast considers this. "Would you have endured so much for your father's sake, Lucie?"

As much and more. If only he were still here.

And out of nowhere, I hear my father's voice again, warm and humorous.

"You are the light of the world, my Lucie," he would tell me. *"Open your heart to life."*

I stop abruptly. What would my papa say to see me now?

"You must have loved him very much," murmurs Beast.

Yes. I pause to get hold of my thoughts, sensing my opportunity. *Beast, you must send Rose away. Send her home to her father.*

"Agreed." Beast sighs again. "I will never be more than a monster in her eyes."

She simply doesn't know how to see who you are, I protest. *You have far more humanity than the chevalier ever had.*

This from some hidden generosity of spirit, so long

untapped inside me. It must be the memory of my papa. *Open your heart.*

But Beast frowns at the mention of Jean-Loup and turns his great head away. Then he musters the nerve to face me again. "It has haunted me every day, Lucie, what ... was done to you here. I would give anything, *do* anything, to erase that moment of horror from your life. But I haven't found any magic spell for that."

He shakes his head, his expression intent. "I should send you away from here too, Lucie, but I can't manage it. I have tried every way I can think of to beg or bargain or bully the magic of this place to release you from your enchantment, to send you back to a life you deserve, but it all comes to nothing."

Release me? Have I ever sought release? Such an idea has never even occurred to me. Where would I go? I try to imagine myself in human form again, that dull, plain girl, friendless, ill-used, and abandoned. Had I fled with the other servants, I might have been welcomed down in Clairvallon for a day or two, perhaps a week. My tale of the chevalier's hideous transformation should have ensured me companions for a time who might have purchased my story for a meal or a bed. But sooner or later, I would be alone again, with no living nor any prospects, to sell what little I possessed—my wretched body—or starve in the road. Perhaps both. No, I am far better off the way I am.

The sudden trilling of Redbird downstairs startles us both and signals Rose's return in the entry hall. Beast rises quickly.

"I mustn't let her see me," he rumbles. And, with a last, poignant look at me, he turns and disappears down the stairs.

CHAPTER 22

Predators

Two more nights pass with Rose taking her meals in restless solitude. On the third night, Rose and I are once again in the dining salon before the warming fire, serenaded by unseen musicians. When eight chimes fail to produce Beast, Rose sets down her goblet next to me on the table and sighs.

"Please, Sir Beast, do come back to me," she addresses the air. "I shall die of loneliness."

The doors open slowly, and Beast stands in the entryway; I wonder, does he wait there each evening, hoping to be summoned? His fine gold-worked cloak sparkles in the firelight. His mane is groomed, and his paws are almost hidden by long, embroidered shirt cuffs. His bulk is arranged in a posture of humility, and his eyes are downcast. He does not enter the room.

"Sir Beast." Rose gasps, and he draws a step back. "No, wait! Please . . . come in."

He comes as near as the doorway again. "Please accept my apologies for . . . my appearance the other night," he rumbles. "I mistakenly thought you were in danger, that something had happened to you, or I should never have burst in like that. I would never frighten you for all the world, Rose."

Beast does not glance at me, but I feel another pang of shame.

Rose draws a breath. "I behaved very badly myself," she says. "It was all a terrible mistake, as you say. I am willing to forget it, if you are."

Beast does not know what to say at first. He does not actually sniff the air, but I see how alert he is.

"Whatever you wish, of course," he says at last, watching her. "But . . . you are not obliged to remain here."

"I know I am not," says Rose. "It is very kind of you to forgive my father's debt, but I will not betray his honor by running away like a child. I will stay until his honor is satisfied. And my own," she adds, lifting her chin. "With your permission, Sir Beast."

I have underestimated her, this frail-seeming girl. She is learning that courtesy and kindness mean more to her fearsome host than an ocean of tears.

Beast continues to peer at her. *Now, I think, now is the moment to tell her she has acquitted herself with honor and send her home.* But after only a moment of hesitation, Beast nods, disarmed.

"You are welcome here for as long as you like, Rose."

"Thank you." Then she favors him with one of her radiant smiles. "Oh, please, Sir Beast, do come in."

He steps tentatively into the room and reaches for his chair at the opposite end of the table. Rose makes a grand gesture and motions him two chairs nearer. Beast looks surprised but takes his place as directed.

"I pray you are . . . content, here, Rose," says Beast. "That it's not too unpleasant."

"But it's very pleasant to have everything one could ever want!" She smiles at him again. "All I lack of late is your company. I've . . . missed you."

This time, Beast does raise his perceptive nose to the air but apparently scents no deceit. *The girl's resolve must be strong indeed.* "Have you?" Beast considers this. "In spite of . . . everything?"

"You have ever been a most gracious and civil host," she replies, choosing her words with great care, her dark blue eyes keen. "So long as you maintain that humor, you shall always be welcome at my table."

Her table? Who is she to order him around, demand

civility? He is master here; he could split her eardrums with a single roar of his sovereignty! But he only gazes at her in quiet contemplation.

"Then I shall endeavor to be civil, Rose . . . for your sake."

They chatter on in their civil manner, the two of them, saying nothing about nothing in words with no more weight than the down of a swan, floating in the air. Another hour passes before Beast senses Rose's weariness and excuses himself.

Beast and I have no opportunity for a private word, now that Rose is speaking to him again. Night after night, at the sound of eight chimes, she allows him to sit at the table while she joins him in conversation. I watch in mute anxiety as Rose allows herself to be charmed. Not by Beast himself—she is still too frightened of him physically— but by her own ability to charm him. And every now and then, she allows him to sit one chair closer.

Beast never speaks to Rose about his passion for the natural world at these dinners, nor reveals to her the tenderness with which he has learned to care for his roses, nor confesses to her the fullness of heart that once drove him to attempt poetry. Perhaps he believes she would not care about these things, and I suppose she would not. Or perhaps they no longer mean as much to him. It angers me that Beast seems to have mislaid the parts of himself that felt those things—at least, he has when Rose is around. But it's far more alarming that Beast does not try to send Rose home as he agreed he should. Instead, she seems to be warming to her place in this household.

By day, Rose tours the rooms of the château again, with even more attention than before. If the afternoon is fine, she crosses the moat in back to wander in the park. The trees are in fresh green leaf, and every now and then, she spies a hind or a hare amid the trunks. But the black wood that stretches far beyond the park frightens her still, with its dense, gnarled trees that shut out the sun, its sinister animal noises, and its dark, surging river. She never goes there.

The rose garden is in more glorious bloom than ever. Each climbing branch supports dozens of blooms, heads lifted to the sky, their red velvety petals unfurling with lazy abandon, reveling in the spring sunshine. This morning, Rose has brought me into the garden as a place for Redbird to perch and sing to her.

"It's like heaven here!" she exults as she carries us down the drive under the archway, a fragrant tunnel of lush red blooms. At the bottom of the drive, Redbird hops up to a crossbar on the gilded gate and warbles his merry song.

"You were right to encourage me to stay," she agrees.

I suppose she views Redbird and myself the same way, a chorus of support for any random idea that enters into her head. She steps to the gate and gazes out past the moat and down the steep slope of green hill to the valley. Far, far beyond the orchards and vineyards, the tiny stone buildings of Clairvallon huddle together under their red-tile roofs. A brave church spire rises from its hill at the far end of the town.

I wonder how the townsfolk are faring since the night of the witchcraft. There is every appearance of industry and husbandry continuing on as usual—fields are being cleared of their winter debris, planting has begun, church bells toll. Without the lord of Beaumont to collect their quarter rents and call in their debts, they must relish the freedom to work their plots of land and pursue their commercial ventures in some prosperity. The gentlemen of his suite and his companions-at-arms must have dispersed back to their own estates. All of their lives go on.

The town nestles in a fertile basin dwarfed by vast green and gold wheat fields trimmed in evergreen. Deeper green patches farther in the distance conceal even tinier villages dotting the broad, gilded fields that stretch away to the blue horizon. It all seems so far away from up here.

Rose turns her back to the gates and looks up at the riot of roses growing so much higher than the wall. "It's even more beautiful up close," she exclaims.

Her words strike me like a slap. Of course! Beast's roses are visible for miles and miles up on this hillside; tales must be rife in the villages about their strange magnificence. Rose must have known her father would have to come here when she asked for her gift; where else could he find a rose in the depth of winter?

The splendor of Château Beaumont and the wealth of its masters, the LeNoirs, has been legendary for generations. Whatever tales the fleeing servants spread about the town after that night may be forgotten or disbelieved by now. But the chevalier is gone; that much is clear. Soon enough, someone might wonder what's become of all that splendor and wealth. Someone used to fine things who suddenly finds his — or her — fortunes reversed.

I reconsider Rose, with her backswept golden hair and guileless blue eyes. And I wonder: *Who is the puppet master here? Who is the predator?*

She climbs thoughtfully back up the drive, Redbird perched on my silver arm, singing his cheerful tune.

"It's not so gloomy here, is it?" Rose wonders aloud. "He would never hurt me. He's far too . . . gentlemanlike." Redbird pipes a few more agreeable notes. "I'd have only to bear his company from a safe distance," Rose goes on softly to herself, "and Papa need never want for anything again."

CHAPTER 23

Two Grotesques

Rose carries me up the front steps and into the château, eager to see what new gown awaits her upstairs and prepare herself for the evening meal. But my thoughts churn with dread. Since Beast is so gentlemanlike, as she says, she must believe some portion of his splendid wealth might be spared to care for the father she adores. She knows by now that Beast will deny her nothing.

But she can never care for him in any way that matters. She will never appreciate Beast for himself: warm, reflective, caring. Noble in fact, not only in station. So worthy of the companionship he so desperately craves. She can't know the beast that once lived here, with his angel's face and form and his evil nature or the agony he inflicted so carelessly on others.

She sees only the poor, tragic Beast: So hideous. So melancholy. So romantic. Foolish girl—foolish *maiden*—who knows nothing of life but what she finds in books.

She sees Beast as a task in a fairy story and believes the reward will be worth her sacrifice to this courtly monster. But she can't know the horror she might set in motion, should her ambition bear fruit—if she positions herself to become mistress of this place.

Would she ever spare a thought for my Beast if he were poor?

Rose's happy mood from the garden continues into supper. The tune of the invisible musicians is livelier than usual, bending to her pleasure, and she brings a flourish to all her movements, whether buttering her bread or raising her goblet. Beast joins her at eight chimes. Her gaiety amuses him as much as it terrifies me, for, of course, I am there at her place on the table.

"Rose," he asks after she has supped her fill, "do you dance?"

"I was counted a fine dancer once," she says, "before Father lost his fortune. We've had little in the way of balls or amusements since then."

"But I've an entire ballroom at your disposal!" Beast declares. "You shall have whatever music you like!"

The ghostly music all around us subtly rises in tempo, and Rose can't help tapping her foot.

"It would please me very much to escort you there," says Beast.

She smiles, decision made, gets to her feet, and takes me up out of habit, although the sconces are already lighting the way to the ballroom. Beast rises, too, and hopefully offers her an elbow, but she balks. With an inward sigh, he bows and sweeps an arm out the door into the passage. Rose gathers up her skirts and glides past Beast to follow the lights.

The golden chandeliers are all ablaze, and the unseen orchestra plays an irresistible tune, the music filling the cavernous white hall as if it were wafting down from the angels. Rose is swaying to the music even as we arrive, setting me on a little side table by the door. She takes up her skirts in one hand and begins to whirl herself around the room. She's a comical little figure in frosty blue, swirling around and around in the vast, empty room. Beast follows us in, his eyes on Rose, and gives a single wordless nod.

Panel after panel of gold-veined mirrors suddenly appear on the white wall behind him, racing to cover its entire length. When they reach the corner, more panels appear to cover the side wall, and still more proceed along the distant wall at the opposite end of the hall and back up the other side. Rose is too absorbed in her dancing to see it happen. She only knows that as she whirls around, she's suddenly facing her own image in the gilt glass, her hair and gown shimmering in the light, her cheeks aglow. It surprises a laugh of pleasure out of her to see her reflection, all of her reflections, as she dances around the room to beautiful, unearthly music.

As she comes rotating back toward Beast, he takes a step forward into her orbit, one paw aloft, the other fisted at his waist. He makes an extravagant bow, and while her first instinct is to swirl a bit farther away, she turns back and smiles and nods. He enters into the rhythm of her dance, stepping his hooves with care. For a moment, her free hand lights upon his outstretched paw, and they swirl around together—until she catches sight of the two of them reflected in the glass, his hulking frame towering above her, his horns glinting in the light, her delicate fingers touching his huge, furry paw.

She jumps away from him with a gasp, shaking her hand as if her fingers have been burned. Beast staggers back as if from a blow, stunned, humiliated yet again. The music coughs and sputters to an uneasy halt, and Rose continues to back away from Beast, wringing her hands. She's sensible of the wound she's given him, perhaps shamed by it, but she can't take back what she's done.

"Sir Beast . . . I . . ." she begins. "I—I'm sorry, I didn't mean—" But there's nothing more to say. Unable to repair the damage, she turns and flees out of the room. The sconces outside obligingly light her to her chamber.

Beast is left standing in his blazing hall of mirrors, his own image reflected back at him in every panel, slumped and dejected, horrible in his finery. There's something far beyond rage or sadness in his eyes now: a desolation so profound, it would crack my heart if I still had one. What would she do if she saw it? Would she even notice?

He turns back toward me on the table near the door where she has forgotten me for once. "I've seen enough," he murmurs. The chandeliers dim behind him, throwing the mirrored ballroom into shadows, and he takes me out into the passage again and back to the dining salon. The wine decanter, ever full, still sits on the table, and he grasps it in his other paw and carries us both upstairs. I cannot bear to nag him in this moment about sending the girl home. Even he must realize it by now.

It's gloomy in the library at this hour. Beast sets me and the wine bottle on the writing table next to the empty vase with its dry rose stalk, then seats himself on the chair. He gazes at the vase for a moment, leans forward, and with one deep, melancholy breath, he blows the dry, dead petals to the floor. I see resignation in his eyes, eerie in my flickering light, as he reaches for the wine.

"Men often find comfort here," he rumbles, regarding the glass decanter, its facets glinting red in my light. "Or oblivion. Let's see if the charm works for me."

Beast withdraws the frosted glass stopper, but when he tries to lift the fluted bottleneck to his mouth, his muzzle intervenes. Unable to reach his own lips, he throws back his head, but his attempts to pour the wine down his throat only result in a red sodden shirtfront. He sets the decanter down again, claws open his shirt, and shrugs out of his cloak, peering around the room. Several spent candles are placed about the bookshelves. Beast shambles over to one, tosses aside the candle, and blows the dust out of the dish that contained it, wider and deeper than a saucer, which he brings back to the table. He pours a measure of wine into the dish, lowers his head, and begins lapping it up, turning his muzzle first to one side, then the other, his tongue filling the dish with every lap. The dish is empty in seconds, and Beast lifts his head and smacks his tongue in his mouth, tasting the last of it.

"I didn't know it would be so bitter," he says. Then he pours himself another dishful and laps that up as well.

There's no moon tonight to shine through the colored glass. My light alone illuminates Beast's face as he broods over his wine. He laps up another dishful—I've lost count how many he's had—sighs again, and props his tufted chin on his paws. I wish I could think how to comfort him, to let him know it's all for the best.

She is only a child, Beast. She doesn't know enough to appreciate you, I tell him. *It doesn't matter what she thinks.*

He shakes his shaggy head. "I will always be a beast in her world. The human world."

He pours himself another dish, but he makes only a

few idle laps at it before lifting his muzzle and cocking his head again at me. "But I am not even a natural beast," he says with a snort of derision. "A true wolf can enjoy his wolfishness; a lion may revel in his feline majesty. A true stag may look to the leadership of his herd. But I am a thing of mismatched parts, a patchwork, a nightmare. I can't even seek comfort from others of my kind; there are no others of my kind. There is nothing else in nature like myself." He lifts the decanter in a shaky salute. "I am unique." He lowers his head and laps at the dish with grim resolve.

You have a human heart, Beast. That is what sets you apart.

"That is my curse," he agrees.

True enough. A beast in nature does not consider such things. The lowliest dung beetle does not know he is ugly or ill-formed or outcast. He goes about his business as nature directs and is perfectly content. He has no capacity to be haunted by what he is.

"And yours as well, Lucie," he adds quietly. "Why should you be cursed to share this fate?"

Cursed? It's dangerous to consider myself in such terms—not as a strong, impervious vessel of enchantment, but as a mere thing. I was once vibrant and alive; I had blood in my veins, a beating heart. Now I am reduced to this: a cold, dead instrument of revenge.

The specter of Jean-Loup hangs over us both. We are two grotesques, Beast and I, because of him.

But I forfeited my own humanity readily enough, and never have I better understood the reason until this moment. I must retain my vigilance and see Rose gone from here, once and for all. We have thought her on the brink of departure before, and yet she always finds the nerve to stay. And Beast allows it, out of kindness, out of his hopeless craving to make a friend of her. But I'll no longer stand by and let Beast be hurt and humiliated again and again by that girl. This can't go on. He must know the truth.

It's not a curse, I tell Beast. *It is my mission. Remember when I told you it was my choice to witness Jean-Loup's downfall?*

Beast nods.

I am also here to see that he never returns.

"But—Jean-Loup is gone," he whispers.

I pray that is so. Unless . . .

"Unless what?"

Unless . . . a woman should marry you.

"*Me?*" Beast sits as still as death. "Why? How?"

A spell was cast on the chevalier, and you appeared. I wish I had a voice to soften, eyes to convey sympathy, but there is nothing to do but plunge ahead. *If a woman agrees to marry you as you are, the spell would be broken. Jean-Loup could come back.*

"What?" Beast's eyes fill with horror. "Back from where?"

From . . . wherever he went. When you . . . appeared in his place.

Beast's voice is low and stark. "You mean there is still some part of Jean-Loup alive?" His expression darkens. "In me? I knew that he was gone, and I was here. But I never thought . . ." He shakes his head slowly, as if to shake off a dream; then his gaze rises again to me, bright and intense. "How could you not tell me, Lucie?"

I'm sorry, Beast. I knew it would upset you. I . . . hoped I would not have to.

Beast sighs heavily and nods. "Well, you were right to tell me now," he agrees, frowning over what this might mean. "But . . . how do I know he doesn't have some kind of . . . control over me?"

I thought he did at first, I admit. When Beast looks even more horrified, I hasten to reassure him. *But you are nothing like Jean-Loup! From the moment you took me out of that attic cupboard, you have proved to me in a thousand ways how different you are. I searched for evidence of Jean-Loup in your every word and deed, to be sure he was suffering as he deserved.*

But I could never find any trace of him anywhere in you, Beast. You would never behave with such cruelty. You have far too much honor and compassion and sense. You have defeated him!

"Unless he comes back," glowers Beast.

I am glad his response is so spirited; he is far from giving way to despair.

Jean-Loup is never coming back! I have dedicated my life to it.

Beast sits up straighter, muzzle raised, eyes fierce. "And I will dedicate mine as well! From this moment on."

You see now why you must send Rose away.

"Of course we must! It is far too dangerous to have her here!" His glance falls to his paw sitting on the desktop, the one she could not bear to touch. "Although there's little chance of her becoming my *bride*," he adds wryly.

No chance at all if she is gone.

"Yes," he agrees. "If she, for any reason . . . if Jean-Loup . . ." But before he can complete this dreadful thought, he draws away with an abrupt hiccup and then another. His paws fly to his mouth, and his shoulders begin to heave. He scrambles off the chair and leaps across the room for the stairs; a moment later, I hear him retching in the dark passage below.

CHAPTER 24

Plots and Visions

Beast does not return for me, but I am busily plotting. Rose must leave here; that is the only way to preserve Beast and see that Jean-Loup stays buried. I can think of one way for it to be done, but first she must find me.

Rose has toted me all about the château since her first day here as a kind of lucky charm. She must have missed my light in the shadows of her bed last night. I wait until the soft glow of dawn shimmers in the colored glass window, for Rose would never prowl the château alone in the dark.

Rose. Come to me. It is my only thought, and I repeat it over and over like a spell, with all the force of my being. *Rose. Come.* She does not understand that I'm alive, as Beast does, yet some spark of common humanity might connect us. *There is nothing to fear. Rose.*

I hope that Beast took himself off to some hiding hole after last night and is not collapsed in a drunken stupor in the stairwell. He has endured enough humiliation.

Please, Rose.

I banish every other thought until I hear, at last, a soft, timid tread upon the stairs. Rose's head rises cautiously from the stairwell, and she glances around. Satisfied that no one else is here, she climbs up into the room and hurries toward me and my comforting light. She must have cried herself to sleep again last night, ashamed, perhaps of the way she treated Beast; delicate tear tracks have dried on her cheeks, and she's still dressed in her pale blue gown. She doesn't know why she is here, but she reaches for me like an old friend.

"I wondered where you'd gone," she murmurs.

With another guilty look around the room, she hurries back to the stairs and carries me down. To my relief, there is no evidence of Beast slumped and miserable in the shadows as we enter into the passage through the gloomy attic corridor and down to her own room on the second floor, where she feels safe. She sets me on her vanity table, where the looking glass reflects the warmth of my flames into the room, and sits on the chair before me.

"I must be strong for Papa's sake," she tells her reflection in the glass, then shakes her head sadly. "I never meant . . . It just happened." She sighs. "If only Sir Beast can forgive me."

Her remorse feels genuine enough; I believe she would not hurt Beast's feelings on purpose. But it's disturbing that she still hopes to stay. So I concentrate on my goal and abandon myself to the unseen otherworldly forces that thrive here. They have shown Rose her family before, the life she left behind. The natural powers — witchcraft, miracles, whatever they may be — will do their work well when there is enough at stake.

Rose's deep blue eyes suddenly widen with alarm. "Oh!" she cries out. "Papa!"

She sits up straighter, eyes fixed on the vision that swims into being in the glass, an old man, weary and white-haired. It takes a moment to recognize him as Rose's father, the merchant, his face is so creased and drawn and tired, his cheeks so hollow. He reclines on threadbare pillows, a bedraggled nightcap slipping off his white head. I hoped to conjure her father, but I had no idea we would find him in this condition. I only thought to make her so homesick, she'd wish to go home.

Turning this way and that, he moans, "Rose! Rose! Oh, my poor child!"

"Papa!" Rose cries again. "I'm here! I am well!"

"Oh, Rose," groans the old man, and sinks back into his pillows, spent.

She can't scramble to her feet fast enough. She roots out her walking boots and pulls them on, grabs her old grey cloak off its hook by the door, and catches me up to ward off the early morning shadows before racing out into the hallway.

"Sir Beast!" she cries, poking her head in at the ballroom door, then hurrying to the dining salon. "Sir Beast! Come quickly!"

She's hovering around the staircase, uncertain whether to go up or down, when Beast's head appears, peering down from the third-floor landing. Even from here, I see the disarray he is in after last night's attempted debauch, his clothing wrinkled and undone, his mane spiking out in odd twists and clumps. But Rose doesn't notice.

"Sir Beast!" she cries when she sees him. "Oh, please, forgive me waking you. Forgive me . . . everything." And she bows her head in shame and curtsies so low in her gown, the great mounds of blue silk all but engulf her. Beast claws back his unruly mane as he stares down at her.

"Rose," he says, "please rise."

But she only raises her head enough to fix him with her eyes. "But I must beg your pardon for last night, Sir Beast. I behaved horribly. I am a very foolish girl."

"Of course you are pardoned," rumbles Beast.

"And . . . I must beg yet another favor, if you would be so good as to hear it."

"Please get up, dear Rose," Beast insists. "I will come down."

By the time he trots down the stairs, he has found his wine-colored cloak, which he is hastily swirling over the bulk of his shoulders; I notice bedraggled black-tipped feathers trembling below the hem of the long, rumpled shirt, its bib still stained red from last night. Rose rises only to her knees as he joins us.

"Please, good Sir Beast, my father is very ill," she pleads. "He may be dying." She points me vaguely in the direction of her room, where she saw her vision.

Beast slides a sidelong glance at me.

"Please, please, let me go to him!"

"Of course you must go," Beast says. "I would never try to keep you here against your will. You must go at once."

Rose blinks up at him, surprised. Clearly she expected an argument. "But—of course, I will be back. And soon!"

"But your father's welfare comes first," Beast agrees. "I understand, Rose."

He extends a paw, and with only an instant of hesitation, she places her trembling fingers upon it and rises to her feet. She withdraws her hand immediately once she has regained her balance, but Beast seems to appreciate her effort.

Then he pulls out the thin red ribbon from around his neck, on which hangs the golden ring with the tiny red jewel heart—the one he found in the library. He lifts the ribbon over his head and holds it out to her.

"This is an enchanted ring," he says. "You have only to place it on your finger, and it will carry you wherever you wish to go."

This is the first I've heard that the ring is enchanted. Is there some connection between Beast and Jean-Loup's poor, sorrowing mother that gives her ring a special power?

Rose's eyes widen. "Will it take me home?" she asks eagerly. "Now?"

"You have but to ask."

"Oh, thank you, Sir Beast!" Rose cries, drawing the ribbon over her head; the long ribbon seems to shrink a little, to accommodate her, as it once expanded for Beast.

"And please accept this present for your family," Beast continues, and with a wave of his paw, a small ivory box appears on the floor beside me where Rose has set me down. At a nod from Beast, the lid lifts partway up on its hinges; coins of gold and silver and some jeweled trinkets sparkle in my light before the lid closes itself again, and the box sails up into Rose's hands.

"Buy your father whatever he requires," murmurs Beast. "With my compliments."

Rose can scarcely utter her thanks. At Beast's direction, she tucks the box under her arm and swirls her cloak around herself.

Beast gazes at her a moment longer, mixed emotion in his dark eyes. "Rose," he says gently, "thank you for your company. Your father has every reason to be proud of you. I wish you and your family well."

"But, Sir Beast, I will come back to you!" Rose insists. "You kindly gave my father two weeks to settle his affairs; I will ask for no more. I shall return in a fortnight, I promise!"

With the long ribbon still around her neck, she slips the ring over her finger. And Rose and her cloak and the chest vanish into the very air.

The silence in the hallway is profound as soon as Rose is gone. Beast sweeps me up from the carpet where Rose left me, carries me to the staircase, and places me on the wide, flat railing around the second-floor landing. I see sadness in his eyes, but his expression is resolute as he rests his paws on the railing beside me.

I'm sorry, Beast. I know how difficult that was for you.

"It had to be done. We both know it." Beast sighs. "I'm glad you were wise enough to find a way to do it." He shakes out his tawny mane. "The consequences of letting her stay would be unthinkable."

Especially for Rose, I agree.

He gazes at me. "For all of us." He frowns slightly. "You don't think she will actually come back, do you?"

Rose is . . . unpredictable. Only moments ago, in her room, she seemed to be making plans. *Did you know that ring was magical?*

"It has great power; I've felt it ever since the day we found it in that book. It gave me such a sense of comfort, of courage."

He has worn it every day since. *Did you know it would take Rose home, or did you only . . . wish for it?*

He shakes his head, considering. "Neither. I just suddenly felt so strongly that it was the right thing to do."

And it was very smart of you to send her off with that box of riches for her family, I tell him. *Very generous, too.*

Beast shrugs this off. "Those things mean nothing to me. It was far more important to remove the danger of having her here. Did you know her father was ill?"

No. I only hoped she might begin to miss her family. I never thought we would find her father in such a state.

"How did you do it?"

She has seen visions in the glass before with no help from me. We know how lively the forces of magic can be here, and she had a decision to make. I only tried to . . . help.

Beast smiles. "Because your feelings are so strong! Because . . . you opened your heart to that girl," he adds softly.

I am touched that Beast remembers the words of my father. *I was not thinking only of Rose,* I confess.

Something warms in Beast's gaze. He straightens a little before me.

"The forces of magic here pay attention to you," he

whispers. "In a way they don't always to me. Not when it really matters."

But what about your beautiful roses?

"Trifles! Ornaments," says Beast with a wave of one paw. "You seek justice, Lucie, and look what's happened. Jean-Loup is defeated. We've seen that girl safely home." He presses himself away from the railing. "But—there is still justice to be done, I think," he murmurs. "If only a way can be found."

And with a last, wistful glance at me, he turns and disappears down the stairs.

From my perch, I can only look down the narrow stairs, but there's nothing to see. Beast does not come back to me. Night follows day follows night, and I stand here alone, illuminating nothing.

It's the loneliest I have ever been here. I was shut up in the attic cupboard longer than this, but then I had my revenge for company. Beast may go up and down the turret stairs to prowl the lower floors. Or it may be that he's forsaken the house altogether for the park and grounds. Perhaps he is tending his roses, remembering again the joy they brought him before that other Rose came. I try to call him, but he no longer responds. Why doesn't he come?

I begin to be alarmed that I can't reach Beast. Surely

Rose has not come back? And no sooner does this thought occur to me than an image begins to form in the looking glass on the wall opposite the stairway. Two women. Rose's sisters, Blanche and Violette; I recognize the dissatisfied whine in their voices even before their images take shape.

"Our little sister parades about like a queen in her silken finery," says the younger, Violette, with a pout. She sits primping at a dressing table, an array of jewels sparkling before her. Jewels that must have come from Beast's box. "I shall be glad when she goes home to her monster."

"Only an addlepated goose would say such a thing," observes Blanche. She stands behind her sister, adjusting a headdress top-heavy with ruffs and pointed peaks in the glass.

Violette turns to stare up at her, her fisted little face full of reproach. "Surely you don't want her to stay?"

"Only think," says her elder sister. "If she keeps her bargain and goes back to her château, these are the last of the monster's riches we shall ever see." She sweeps a hand toward the baubles spread across the dressing table, and Violette casts them a wistful, covetous glance.

"But . . . what can we do about it?" Violette whimpers.

Blanche throws her veil behind her back, places her hands on Violette's shoulders, and bends forward to address her in the glass. "Rose told us she promised to return to her monster in a fortnight. She insists he will die without her. If we keep her here past that time, perhaps he *will* die. And his lovely château will stand empty."

Violette nods slowly, although her face remains scrunched up in bafflement.

"We have seen only one box of his riches," Blanche goes on. "Think what wealth and jewels and finery he will leave behind unprotected in his château? No one ever goes there. We'll be the only ones who know. All his treasure could be ours!"

"But what if he isn't dead?" worries Violette. "What shall we do? How will we know?"

"We shall take our brothers with us," says Blanche. She has obviously thought the whole thing out. "And they shall bring their swords! If we find the monster still alive, they shall cut off its head and bring it home for a trophy! No one could begrudge them slaying the monster who imprisoned their sister. And only think"—and here, her expression goes sly, still regarding her sister in the glass—"think of Rose's face when we bring home the head of her monster, and the château is no longer hers to command. That will put an end to her fancy airs!"

A vague eagerness dawns in Violette's empty blue eyes, but it turns just as quickly to alarm.

"But . . . Rose says the place is bewitched," she whispers.

"Oh, pooh! Rose's head is full of fairy stories!" scoffs

Blanche. "The chevalier is too ugly to be seen; he lives in seclusion with all his finery, and Rose conjures up a monster in a magical château out of dreams and fancy! I promise you, whatever fairies haunt the place, his treasure is real enough. The fairies don't need it. It shall be ours, if we but play our hand wisely."

"What must we do?" says Violette.

"We must beg Rose to stay with us."

"Oh, but I can't!" cries Violette.

"We must show her we are too heartbroken to let her go again," Blanche insists.

"She will never believe it," says Violette.

"We shall be *very* convincing." From the folds of her full skirt, Blanche produces something small and round and yellow, and places it on the dressing table.

Violette frowns. "What is that?"

"It's an onion, you goose!"

"What am I to do with it?" whines Violette.

Blanche produces a small paring knife and slices the onion open, right on the dressing table. Milky juice forms on each cut surface, and Violette shrinks back, wrinkling her nose.

"It smells vile!"

"Breathe in," Blanche instructs her. She grasps her sister by the scruff of the neck and holds a juicy onion half up to her nose. Violette's mouth puckers. She scrunches up her eyes, but they are already turning red with tears. Blanche releases her sister, holds the onion under her own nose, and inhales deeply. The noses of both women are running, and their eyes are gushing tears in no time.

"It's horrible! I can't see!" sobs Violette.

"Just follow me," Blanche says, sniffling and pulling her sister to her feet. "We'll find her straightaway. Just look at the state we're in! Rose will never have the heart to leave us!"

Their images dissolve, and I am alone again, perched on the railing. I'm glad to think that Rose is less likely than ever to come back, but I ought to warn Beast about her scheming sisters.

Where is he?

· CHAPTER 25 ·

Restoration

At last, a tread upon the stair. Beast's shaggy head moves cautiously into view at the bend of the stairwell on the first-floor landing below me. He peers up hopefully but comes no farther when he sees me here. His expression seems to fall a little.

Beast! Where have you been?

"I've been trying to free you." He sighs heavily. "Spells. Prayers. Incantations. Obviously, I'm not very good at it." He shakes his head sadly. "I swear to you, Lucie, had I the power to restore even a fraction of all that's been taken from you, I'd do it in a heartbeat. But my efforts come to nothing; here you are still."

Where else should I be?

"In your human skin!" Beast exclaims. "At home with your mother. With your friends."

I haven't any friends! I haven't anywhere else to go.

Beast looks stricken, his eyes teeming with feeling. "But you will, Lucie, I know you will, and a life of your own, as soon as you are free of this place."

The finality of his words, his demeanor, chills me. *What do you mean? What are you trying to do?*

Beast lifts his muzzle, an aching determination in his eyes. "I could not simply disappear without a word of farewell. That would be cruelty worthy of Jean-Loup, and cowardly besides. And you deserve so much more! I want you to know how much you've meant to me. Sharing your thoughts and dreams with me. Showing me your . . . friendship . . . all this time." And he shakes his shaggy head, with a small smile. "I hope you will think well of me." He starts to turn away.

Beast! You must stop this talk! Please, don't leave me!

That stops him. He turns back, stung. "I would never do anything to hurt you, Lucie! But it's clear to me that you can never be free as long as Jean-Loup . . . exists. Somewhere."

Jean-Loup? What has he to do with anything?

"You were enchanted in the moment he was enchanted. Your sole purpose now is to prevent his release. So long as Jean-Loup exists, so you must exist, too, in your current form. But there will be no further need of your enchantment when Jean-Loup is gone. Your purpose will be fulfilled." Beast shakes his head. "It's the only thing I have not yet tried."

Suddenly, with an awful shock, I realize what he means to do. The guilt in his eyes, just before he glances away, confirms it. He'll destroy Jean-Loup by destroying himself!

Beast, no!

"It's the only way! Jean-Loup festers inside me like a wasting disease. Who knows by what future spell or witchery he might be transformed out of this body, as I was transformed out of his? I could never bear to be the agent of his return. I'm the only one who can stop him. It's the only way to free you."

No! Not like this! We will find some other way—

"There is no other way!" Beast is shaking his head, holding up a paw as if to stop my protest; I see how it trembles. "Please, let me do this one last thing for you, to give you back one thing that Jean-Loup stole from you. Your freedom is all that matters."

But what will I do without you?

"You are strong, Lucie. You survived Jean-Loup. And you will survive this."

Beast! Wait!

But he turns and clops again down the stairs, despite my pleading.

I am frantic! All this time, I've been so intent on

thwarting Jean-Loup, but it's Beast who has suffered so much humiliation, Beast who pays the penalty, Beast who will die! Suppose Rose's sisters and brothers find their way back here, like a plague of invading rats, and find Beast dead. I imagine Beast's mighty head, dripping blood, on the point of a sword, carried away in triumph to decorate the battlements of some gaudy palace that Rose's family buys with Beast's treasure.

How can I lose Beast after all we have been through together? He is the only one who knows me for who I am, my only friend. How can I let such a noble soul die for my sake?

His hoofbeats have stopped echoing down the stairwell and across the marble floor below. The silence is overwhelming. I can't tell where he went, nor how he means to do it. Cursing my useless immobility, I try to call out to him, over and over again, but he no longer responds. I am fearfully alone. Desperate to control the chaos inside me, I shut out every other thought but one: *Where is Beast?*

It seems to take an eternity, but at last, another hazy image begins to assemble itself in the mirror opposite the stairwell. First I see Beast's shaggy mane and horned head and a swirl of burgundy and gold as he draws his cloak around himself in a bed of mossy green. He must be out in his rose garden; fading red petals dapple the moss. He settles farther back, closes his eyes, and sighs deeply under his beloved roses.

More of the image resolves. He is stretched out at full length, breathing in the fragrance of his roses that he has always found so soothing. The perfume of roses gives him courage, he told me once. Slowly, he slips one paw out from within his cloak, and something catches the sunlight: a small bottle full of dark purple liquid.

Madame Montant's drops! We found this bottle the day we toured the old servants' quarters so long ago! The housekeeper took drops to help her sleep, but what if someone drank the whole bottle at once? Would their sleep be permanent?

Beast! No!

He does not respond, but he has not yet unstoppered the bottle, either. He still grasps it in his paw as he draws another deep breath.

"Farewell, Lucie," he whispers.

Beast! Don't do this!

But my pleading is useless; my thoughts have no effect, and there's so little time! It may be too late already; he may raise the bottle to his lips in the next heartbeat! I cannot lose Beast! I can't let him die for my sake!

I have no power to stop him. But someone else might.

Rose, I command from within the depths of my own

desperation. *Beast is dying, and only you can save him. Come back, Rose. You are my only hope!*

Can she still hear me?

Hurry, Rose! Beast needs you! Don't let him do this! Please, Rose! Save him!

I swear I can feel my heart pounding in my throat, blood thundering in my ears — savage, stubborn life such as I've not felt in months. I'm in darkness, and I feel myself falling. My eyes fly open — my eyes! — and I see the lower stairs racing up to meet me as I teeter on the railing. My hands — human hands — lunge for the railing, and I push myself back from the open stairwell and collapse on the carpeted floor behind the balustrades.

My legs are all askew beneath my plain grey frock. I try to pull them up under me, but they're too awkward to manage after so long. Finally I grip the balustrades with both hands and haul myself up. I'm not yet standing; I'm leaning all my weight on the railing, but random points of feeling are beginning to return to my legs. Pain first, the ache of disuse, and then the sharp pinpricks of returning life.

Is it Beast's death that's released me as he hoped? No, it can't be true, not yet! I never made such a bargain. There must be more time!

I creep unsteadily to the corner newel-post, struggle down the stairs to the first landing on jellylike legs, and half tumble down the rest, sprawling at last out into the entry hall. I crawl across the cold marble tiles to the glass panels overlooking the rose garden, but the rosebushes have grown so thickly together and are so dense with blooms, I can't see anything beyond the first rows nearest the house. I pull myself up by the window frame, trying to rub more life back into my legs. Where can he be?

My legs bearing me up at last, I stagger out the grand double doors and out onto the colonnaded porch. I steady myself by one column, then let myself down by holding on to the ceremonial urns that decorate each step. I manage to cross the gravel courtyard at the foot of the steps under my own power, but still too slowly! I hobble to the end of the first row of bushes and crunch around to the open space between this row and the next. But there is no Beast. At the end of that row, I come around to the next, struggling to see or hear anything as I hurry from bush to bush.

When at last I spy a solid shape and a glimpse of burgundy two rows ahead, I rush to the end of the row and double back. And there he lies, on an expanse of mossy green halfway down the next row, near enough to the drive that the high central vault of roses bloom almost directly over his head. The sun sparkles turquoise on the water of the moat, out beyond the gilded gate, and the swans can be heard softly nattering in the distance. It's a lovely spot, a tranquil, peaceful place to die.

"Beast!"

It is my voice, my own human voice. But even as I push myself forward, a shadow falls across Beast, a shadow thrown by nothing that I can see. Then Rose is suddenly standing at his side, blocking my path to the place where he lies. She's dressed in one of the fine gowns he gave her; it dazzles in the sunlight. She wasn't there a second before. She's appeared out of the very air and rushes to Beast, flinging aside something that sparkles momentarily in the sunlight. I recognize the magic ring by the red ribbon trailing behind it as it disappears in the gravel.

But I am still several bushes away from them. *Rose! Stop him!* I plead with all my heart, my newly beating heart; it's still more natural to call out to her this way than to trust my rusty voice. *Throw that bottle away!*

Rose falls to her knees beside Beast, snatches the bottle out of Beast's paw, and hurls it away. From here, I can't tell how much liquid flies out, if any does. "Sir Beast!" she cries, shaking him vigorously by the shoulder. "It's me, Rose!"

Beast lets out a bark of surprise. "Rose?" He sounds confused.

"Sir Beast! I've come back to you!" She grasps his paw in both her hands. "I never thought you would truly die without me!"

"Rose . . . what?"

"Oh, Sir Beast, do not die! I'm sorry I was delayed, but I promise I will never leave you again!" Her voice is earnest, full of feeling. "I will do anything you wish, but you must get well! Oh, stay with me, Sir Beast, and I . . . I will be your wife!"

I'm so stunned, I trip over my feet at the nearest bush; Beast's startled cry, "No!" fades to a groan as I half fall to my knees, staring out between the branches. Rose is so caught up in the moment, she's begun to sob, bowing her head over Beast's paw. So she doesn't notice how Beast's mane is shortening; his horns disappear, his muzzle flattens, and the whiskers and tawny fur vanish from his face.

Beast is gone. Jean-Loup reclines in his place!

No! I want to scream, but I've lost my voice as this nightmare vision unfolds before me. Not Jean-Loup! The chevalier, in all his cold glamour, peers intently up at the girl who is still bent over his hand, softly sobbing, "I'm Rose! I'm here!"

But only when she realizes the hairy paw she's been clutching has become smooth human flesh between her hands does Rose open her own eyes and see the transformation.

"Oh!" Rose drops his hand and sits back on her knees, flustered.

Jean-Loup scrambles to sit up. "Please, please . . . do not fear me."

"But . . . but . . ." She stares into his face. "But . . . where is Sir Beast?"

"Beast," echoes Jean-Loup; he sounds puzzled but recovers himself swiftly.

"Beast is gone," he says more decisively. "But I am here." He rises to his knees before her.

Rose remains where she is, staring at his face, bewildered and awestruck, then dares to let her gaze slide over the rest of him. His shirt and his breeches have adjusted to his human body again and fit him beautifully; their dishevelment gives him the air of a rakish young knight at the end of a quest. "I know you," she whispers at last. "You're the man in the portrait. I dreamed of you," she breathes, eyes wide with awe.

"Jean-Loup Christian Henri LeNoir, Chevalier de Beaumont." He smiles at her again, pretending to doff a hat in the air. "At your service, mademoiselle. And . . . and you must have known me as Beast!"

He does not seem to remember the time when Beast was here, but he's trying to piece it together.

Rose's hands flutter in astonishment. "But . . . how is it possible?"

Jean-Loup shakes back his russet hair the way he used to do. "An evil witch cast a spell on me," he tells her solemnly. He remembers that much, although I'm angered at his slander of Mère Sophie. "I was to pine away all the rest of my days as a hideous beast unless a virtuous maiden might consent to marry me." He smiles at her, ardent, triumphant. "And you have—Rose." He pronounces her name with some hesitation; he may have only just heard it on her lips, but he understands what has happened. "You have set me free!"

Now it is he who grasps one of her white hands in both of his. He lowers his lips to her delicate skin, then slowly lifts his handsome face to gaze at her again, still cradling her hand in both of his.

"Are you very disappointed, my dear?" he murmurs.

Yes! Rose, tell him, my thoughts erupt from where I stand; speech still feels strange to me. *Send him away! He's not half the man Beast was!*

But Rose no longer responds to my thoughts, dazzled as she is by the chevalier's handsome face and the touch of his perfect mouth. She stretches out her other hand to him and dares to caress a lock of his hair. Her trembling fingertips trail gently down his cheek. "I . . . shall bear it." She smiles.

Jean-Loup bows his head again and presses her hand fiercely to his mouth. "Then everything in Château Beaumont, including myself, belongs to you," he declares, his gaze rising to hers again. "If you still consent to be my wife."

"Yes!" she cries as my heart sinks. "Oh, yes, Sir . . . Sir . . ."

"I am only a knight at court, my dear," he tells her with a gentle smile. "In private life to my intimates, I am simply Jean-Loup."

"Jean-Loup," she murmurs, savoring the taste of it.

The chevalier gets to his feet with enough vigor that I realize Beast must not yet have drunk much from the bottle. Jean-Loup shakes the petals out of his cloak and throws it back over his shoulders. He stretches out both hands to Rose. She places hers eagerly in his, and he draws her to her feet. He kisses each of her hands in turn, pauses, then draws her one step closer. She does not protest. He leans forward, seeks her mouth with his, and kisses her slowly. He lets go of her hands, and his own hands reach for her waist.

"Jean-Loup," she murmurs, but then she presses him an inch away.

"Rose," he whispers urgently into her hair. "Marry me now, today!"

"But there's so much to do!" she exclaims. "People to invite, arrangements to be made. We must tell my family and post the banns. I must have a dress!"

He gazes down at her and says nothing for a moment. "Of course, my dear," he murmurs, "whatever you wish. Only let it be soon."

He takes her arm and turns to propel her back to the château. Only then do I realize I'm no longer free to watch in anonymity. Stripped of my own enchantment, I'm but a plain, dull girl again, a voyeur to their perfect romance. I am the intruder now.

I stumble back for the protection of the rosebushes, keeping out of their sight. Not that Rose would likely take any notice of me; she has eyes only for her handsome chevalier. I might as well still be a candlestick, for all the difference it makes to her. Jean-Loup sweeps her to the far end of the row, out onto the gravel, and up the drive under the archway of roses. And I am left to huddle here alone, choking on my misery. I've regained my human heart only to feel it shatter.

They climb the front steps and disappear together into the château. I wander down to the place where Beast so recently lay, the moss crushed flat under the canopy of blooms, almost as if he lay there still, but invisible. After turning away, I see a glittering in the gravel track nearby— the ring with the tiny red heart, forlornly cast off, its long red ribbon stretching away across the tiny stones. For Beast's sake, I crouch down and pick up the ring that seemed to mean so much to him. It brought him comfort, he told me. I close my fist around it, squeeze it tightly, and feel warmth and courage stealing into me. There is power in this ring. I can feel it.

But for all its power, the ring cannot bring Beast back.

I spread open the red ribbon, slide it on around my

neck, and tuck the ring into my bodice. Rising on my unsteady limbs, I gaze up one last time at the magnificence of Château Beaumont. Then I hurry to the far end of this row and up the side path until I gain the horse track that leads across the side moat and around to the back of the château. Past the well, I begin to run through the green trees of the park and deeper into the black wood beyond, away from the château, away from the happy couple. But I can't run away from myself, my thoughts.

Beast is gone! That noble soul, that gallant heart, gone forever. All of his wisdom, kindness, humanity, now lost.

That foolish girl, that beauty, has won her storybook prince. But I have lost Beast.

BEAST

· CHAPTER 26 ·

The Changeling

It's dark night when I arrive at the side of the river; it bubbles and boils in agitation to match my own turbulent mood. But I'm no longer the ignorant, timorous chit I was the first time I came here. I know the forces that work in this wood much better now, appreciate their power and their mystery.

"Mère Sophie," I murmur, "show yourself."

And the dark little hut of thatch and bramble sprouts like a mushroom on the riverbank only a few paces away. I walk to the low, arched front door with its mysterious carvings, turn the handle, and gently nudge it open; that the cottage appeared at all is invitation enough to enter. All is as I remember inside: the same warming fire, the same tidy kitchen corner, the same calico cat purring happily among the bed pillows. Mère Sophie wears the same grey gown, tending a pot of something on a hook over the fire. Simmering meats and slow-cooking beans, a snap of thyme, a pungent hint of mustard, all release their fragrance, and my newborn human stomach responds with a twinge of longing. Mère Sophie does not look up as I enter.

"Finished, is it?" she mutters over her pot. "Happily ever after, I suppose?"

And all my resolve, my outrage, drains out of me in a great torrent of misery, and I burst into tears like a child.

"Oh, hush, hush, my girl," she clucks at me, and comes to put her arm around me and guide me to one of the stuffed chairs before the fire. "Sit," she murmurs, and when I do, she procures from the folds of her apron an enormous handkerchief, into which I sob and sob.

"I've been expecting you," she says after a while, stroking my hair as she perches on the arm of my chair.

"Then you should have given me legs," I sputter between raspy gulps of air, "to do your bidding faster."

"My bidding?" says she. "What has my bidding to do with it?"

"You . . . enchanted us. You should have given me the power to change back sooner!" If only I could have gotten to Beast in time.

But Mère Sophie stands abruptly with an exasperated sigh. "Your power is yours to command, my girl, not mine!" And she stalks back to her pot.

I fling away the last of my tears with the back of my hand. "Then why couldn't I help him?"

"But you did help him. Did you not call for Rose?"

I frown at her. "How do you know that?"

She glances at me. "My dear, who is the wisewoman here?"

"But I didn't want her to bring back Jean-Loup!"

Mère Sophie stirs ferociously in her pot and shakes her head. "It's always the same," she mutters. "Folk pine for a thing and wish for a thing, and then they find it's not at all what they want."

"But can't you change him again?"

She lifts her wooden spoon, dripping with thick broth. "With my magic wand?"

"A charm!" I cry. "Another spell!"

She lifts the pot off its hook and sets it down on the hearth to simmer. "You credit me with too much power, my dear." She bustles over to her little kitchen corner, and I follow.

"I saw you change Jean-Loup into Beast once," I say as Mère Sophie takes two pottery bowls out of her cupboard. She hands them to me to set on the table. "I saw it with my own eyes. Can't you cast another spell to make him Beast again?"

"Oh, my poor, foolish girl, have you not guessed by now?" The wisewoman sighs. "Jean-Loup *is* the spell, the

changeling, the figment of magic. Beast is the true chevalier."

The bowls slip from my hands and clatter against the
table. I can't imagine what I must look like.

Mère Sophie sighs again. "Let me tell you a story," she
murmurs, "about a woman who gave birth to a monster."
She nods me to a chair at the table and lowers herself into
another.

"Beast's mother, Christine DuVal, the last Lady
Beaumont, was a dear, sweet girl. Her mother had been
a great friend of mine. I was Christine's godmother. She
was born in the country and loved countryfolk and country
ways."

"I saw her portrait." I don't mention my vision, the way
she sobbed for my help, although it would not surprise me
if the wisewoman knows that, too.

"Her marriage to the seigneur de Beaumont was
arranged. Her father was a wealthy merchant elevated to
the office of receiver of the royal tax. He grew wealthier
still in fees and bribes but was not considered noble. He set
aside a vast dowry in lands and income for Christine and
sold her to the seigneur."

"Rene Auguste," I say, recalling the grim-faced portrait
and the cast-off suit of armor.

Mère Sophie nods. "He had fortune enough of his own,
amassed over time by the cruelty of his ancestors—tactics

he learned all too well. In the late wars when the noble families of France battled one another in the streets, the seigneur sold his men-at-arms to whichever side paid most handsomely. In one conflict, he gathered together a company of disgruntled men spoiling for more rights and privileges and rode off in service to the Reformers. But Rene Auguste professed to have a change of heart on the eve of the battle and took his men home. The late king, a staunch defender of the Old Religion, granted him command of the gendarmerie of Clairvallon for his loyalty." Mère Sophie pronounces this last word with grim precision.

"The seigneur was a hard, cruel man born into privilege and luxury," Mère Sophie continues. "He was eager enough to get control of the DuVal holdings Christine brought to the marriage. But he grew fond of his new bride and indulged her. He furnished the château with grand, beautiful things, copying the luxury of the Italian style so popular at court, hoping to please her." She shakes her head a little. "The wedding present I gave her must have seemed odd amid so much splendor, a rocking chair fashioned out of bentwood from the forest."

"But I saw it!" I exclaim. "She had it painted into her portrait." Mère Sophie smiles. "I believe it was her favorite thing besides her books."

The wisewoman nods. "Her books," she murmurs. "It was considered a great scandal among the nobility when

Christine had the tower chapel at Château Beaumont converted into a library."

I remember the library with a little pang of longing. What a sanctuary it was from the cold, formal beauty of the rest of the château. Beast found comfort there, too, under the image of the stained-glass princess and her dragon.

"It was her private room," Mère Sophie explains. "But it was prudence on the seigneur's part as well. In those days, when men were murdering one another over which face of God they chose to worship, the seigneur was glad to remove any element that might link him to one faction or the other—the wrong edition of a prayer book or an altar too ornate or too plain. What had once been a chapel became instead a temple to folklore and fantasy and poetry and magic, for those were the things the new Lady Beaumont loved."

"But what has this to do with Beast?"

"I am coming to that," says Mère Sophie. "Christine and the seigneur tried and tried to have a child, but their efforts never came to fruition. Some folk said it was because of the chapel, a punishment from God. Others said the line was cursed by witchcraft, black arts conjured by some enemy. But I know better." She fixes me with her black gaze. "The LeNoir bloodline has become too corrupted over the generations and will no longer prosper." She gives a single, significant nod. "Nature wills it."

"But," I whisper, "I carried the LeNoir seed. You helped me to . . . to . . ."

She shakes her head. "I did nothing but calm your fears," she tells me gently. "I knew the babe would never quicken. They never have; I told you you were not the first woman to flee into my wood in that condition. But their fears come to nothing. Jean-Loup is the last of the line, no matter how heroically he scatters his seed."

"But . . . if that is so . . . how was Beast born?"

Mère Sophie heaves a deep sigh. "My dear Christine wanted a child with all her heart. And her heart was so large, not even Nature could resist her." The wisewoman shakes her head slowly, ruefully, looking backward in time. "Christine wanted so much for her unborn son, as all parents do—she wanted him swift and agile, strong and generous, stouthearted, kind. But he was born Beast, monstrous and ugly, and all her other considerations vanished into the air."

An image swims into my memory: a christening gown like a tent, a cap large enough to conceal the misshapen head that wore it. Sewn for an infant Beast.

"The seigneur blamed her, of course," Mère Sophie continues bitterly. "He swore he would take holy orders in penitence. All the servants who had been present at the birthing were sent far away, but there were soon rumors of a Beaumont Curse. He hid his son within the château walls, consulted doctors, mountebanks, conjurers. An alchemist was brought into the household to effect a transformation." The wisewoman shakes her head again. "But it was far too late for all that. Generations of LeNoir villainy had poisoned the bloodline, and poor, monstrous little Beast was the result. It was time for the LeNoir tyranny over the Beaumont seigneurie to come to its natural end."

"But then—where did Jean-Loup come from?"

"Christine loved her monster son as fervently as a mother can," Mère Sophie goes on. "She came to me, begged me to give her son a pleasing human shape. Nothing else mattered to her. She couldn't bear to see him hurt, shunned, reviled all his life—even by his own father." The wisewoman frowns. "There is no end to the folly of parents who wish a life without adversity upon their children. It's adversity that shapes character and makes folk strong. I pleaded with Christine not to interfere, to give little Beast a chance to meet life on his own terms. But she was heartsick that Rene Auguste could not bear the sight of his own son. When the child did not outgrow his monstrosity by the time he could walk and talk, she begged me to make him beautiful—as beautiful on the outside as the lovely spirit that was growing inside him. Her pleas were heartrending. She was like a daughter to me. I—I could not refuse."

The kettle is singing on the hob, may have been doing so for this last quarter of an hour for all the notice I took of it. But Mère Sophie welcomes the distraction and goes to retrieve it, while I rise to get cups and saucers out of the cupboard.

"But I thought you said it was the will of Nature," I remind the wisewoman as I slide back into my chair.

She brings a dish of ground chocolate to the table and a pinch of spice, and we pour ourselves steaming cups. Her cassoulet on the hearth is temporarily forgotten.

"There are some forces stronger than Nature," says Mère Sophie, "and she loved him that much. But it cost him dearly." She nods at her worktable with its orderly rows of plants in pots, strings of herbs, and bark covered in river mold. "The forgery that was Jean-Loup became like a beautiful fungus that attaches itself to a host plant. He used up all the air and light. All the generosity of character that Beast had developed as a child, blossoming in his mother's love, was smothered deep within." Mère Sophie shakes her head. "Although she acted out of love, she made over her sweet beastly boy into the image of his father, of all the handsome, cruel lords of Beaumont before him. And yet, her desperate gamble did not reconcile her husband to him after all. His father did not love him any more as Jean-Loup than he ever had, and it drained away

Christine's strength and her spirit. Rene fostered the youth out to all his relations and dependents, to be rid of him, knowing what he'd been."

So that's why his father's armor lay discarded among the hay bales in the carriage house; Jean-Loup would not have had it anywhere in the house.

"It broke her heart." Mère Sophie sighs.

"I have seen his mother sobbing," I confess at last.

Mère Sophie nods sadly. "My poor Christine. She died of it, what she'd done to him."

I recall the plain little room in the château, where the vision of Beast's mother first appeared to me, rocking sorrowfully in her bentwood chair. All of her sadness comes back to me, like another rebuke. She wasn't sobbing for Jean-Loup. It was *Beast* she wanted me to help, *Beast* she wanted me to save. And I failed her.

"And what became of Beast's father?" I ask her.

"Rene made good on his threat and returned to the faith of Rome, became a zealot, and joined the Holy League in the siege of Paris. Jean-Loup gained his majority, gathered his companions, and rode in the cavalry of the prince of Navarre against the Spanish invaders. After the prince became the new king, Jean-Loup retired to Château Beaumont. His father had died during the siege — starved, diseased, or driven mad, no one knew. All of the seigneurie of Beaumont belonged to Jean-Loup, and he devoted

himself to enjoying his birthright at last and to promot-
ing the glory of Beaumont by whatever means necessary."
Mère Sophie sighs. "But that much you know."

I nod, wearied and saddened by the tale. "His mother,
Lady Christine," I say at last. "Could she never . . . wish
him back?"

Mère Sophie shakes her head. "Jean-Loup became
very strong. That much willfulness, unchallenged—it's
very hard to overpower it."

"But . . . you did it once," I remind her softly. "You
brought Beast back."

She lifts her cup to her lips and takes a long, thoughtful sip. "I did not say it was impossible."

How had she succeeded in turning Jean-Loup back
into Beast? I remember the scene as I watched it from my
hiding place behind the doorway: Jean-Loup's romantic
guile as he closed on his prey, the beautiful stranger who
was Mère Sophie transformed seeming to slip helplessly
under his spell. I remember my heart filling up with rage.
And I draw a deep, shivery breath.

"You had me," I whisper. "I hated him so much."

Mère Sophie lifts an eyebrow and offers me a wan
smile. "Yes," she agrees, "your hate, your thirst for revenge,
were very useful to me in the moment. But it would have
crippled you, Lucie, all that hatred, had you not made
room in your heart for something more."

"But why did you give Jean-Loup the chance to return? Why not put an end to him once and for all when you had the chance?"

Mère Sophie frowns into her cup. "I found that he had become too strong for me to banish him completely; I could only narrow down the means by which Jean-Loup might yet escape to a single task I thought would be impossible." Mère Sophie shakes her head. "I did not think he would ever see another woman, let alone one who would consent to be Beast's wife."

But the wisewoman reckoned without Rose, her taste for romance, her innocence. Her devotion to her father.

Her ambition.

"A maid of good virtue, heaven-sent to break the spell," I mutter. "But Beast was going to die! Who else could I have called to save him?"

"We can never know all the consequences of our actions," says Mere Sophie with a rueful sigh. "But by summoning Rose, by that single selfless act, you regained your own human heart. And that is no small thing."

And my human limbs as well, but by then, it was far too late. I remember how often I resented Rose, that she could walk and laugh and smile, all those things I could no longer do. And I recall how desperately Beast tried to find a way to free me by magic. "Beast thought his death might set me free."

"Only you could do that," says Mère Sophie gently.

Open your heart.

"If only I'd known," I fret. "If only I'd regained my human body sooner, I could have saved Beast! But now Beast is gone. Because of me. Because I couldn't reach him in time."

But the wisewoman shakes her head. "Beast would have ended his life right there in his garden had you not sent Rose to stop him. She may have unleashed Jean-Loup, but she did save Beast's life."

My breath catches in my throat. "Beast is still alive?"

She nods again at me. "The fungus needs its host to survive. Some spark, some essence of Beast lives on. Because you sent Rose to save him."

My thoughts are reeling: joy that some part of Beast may yet survive warring with grief that he is trapped inside the illusion of Jean-Loup once more.

"What is it like for him . . . where he is?" I ask Mère Sophie. "Does Beast know what's happened to him?" I can't bear to think that he might suffer.

It's a long moment before she speaks again. "He feels—and knows—nothing," she murmurs at last. "He sees nothing, nor senses anything. He is scarcely more than a dream of the creature he once was, buried inside the shell that is now Jean-Loup. There is not room in the vessel of the body they share for more than one at a time."

I frown at this. "But when Beast was restored, Jean-Loup raged inside him for days." I remember the savagery with which we smashed all the mirrors.

"He'd had possession for twenty years, and Beast had been dormant just as long," says Mère Sophie. "Jean-Loup clung to life within Beast out of sheer willfulness for a short while. But without the constant reassurance of his own good looks, his physical superiority over other men, he lost his will. His beauty—the illusion of beauty—was everything to Jean-Loup. His new monstrous shape destroyed his sense of himself, and Beast was able to emerge."

I remember Beast's wonder, exploring the château as if discovering it all anew, inspecting everything, every room—the family portraits, his mother's library. Did some deeply buried part of himself remember living there once as a child? Is that why he restored the ruined garden with such loving care? The roses he used to bring to the library—did he do so in memory of his mother without even knowing why? It's no wonder he was so drawn to his mother's ring. And I recall Beast's horror the more evidence he found of the shameful way Jean-Loup had lived his life.

"But why was Jean-Loup able to come back so fast when Rose found him?" I ask.

"Because in that instant, Beast was letting go of his life," Mère Sophie tells me gently. "He was ready to die."

"For my sake," I add miserably. "But if some spark of him still exists, somewhere, could it not be possible for Beast to come back again?"

Mère Sophie smiles sadly at me. "Jean-Loup must be driven completely out—as we once almost did, Lucie—if Beast can ever reclaim the vessel of his body, again, and himself," she says. "If we had done it with love instead of hate, maybe we could have banished Jean-Loup forever."

I grasp at this idea, that love might set Beast free. "What if Rose has a change of heart?" I ask her eagerly. "Say her feelings for him, for the memory of Beast, deepened over time. Might she not . . . bring him back?"

"It is possible, I suppose," says Mère Sophie. "If her love was strong enough."

Her tone suggests how little hope she holds out for such a prospect.

"And not likely, now that Rose is so smitten with her chevalier," I agree sadly. How long before Rose forgets that Beast ever existed? "She ought to have had the sense to fall in love with Beast," I mutter. "She does not deserve a life of misery wedded to Jean-Loup." Another thought occurs to me. "Should I not try to warn her somehow?"

Mère Sophie draws a slow, thoughtful breath. "We cannot know what their married life will be like," she says. "Rose is likely to suffer his infidelities. But sadly, that is not uncommon among wives of the nobility."

And Rose has her family nearby—three stout brothers, as I recall—as I did not. Nor will her reputation be ruined, as I feared for Lady Honoree, when Rose is his lawful wife. And why would she take the advice of a disgraced servant, in any case?

Mère Sophie gazes at me for another moment. "You have earned a great deal of wisdom," she goes on gently. "So many learn nothing for all their troubles. It would make me very happy if you would stay here with me as my apprentice."

I glance up into her face, astonished. I haven't had a moment to think what my life will be like now that I am human again or where I will go. How enticing it would be to enter into sisterhood with Mère Sophie, to dine here at her table, to make a place for myself before her comforting fire. To share her work and her wisdom and her knowledge. To feel myself at peace at last with nature. A part of me already loves this wood better than the world, for all its dangers and enchantments.

Something burns near my heart. I realize it is Lady Beaumont's ring still tucked into my bodice. I finger the red ribbon to shift it, but Mère Sophie stretches out one gnarled finger and gently tugs at the ribbon. The golden ring with its tiny red jewel emerges from my bodice, and her gaze softens as she lets it dangle into her palm.

"His mother's ring—" I begin.

"I know. I gave it to her," murmurs the wisewoman. "I found an artisan to craft it for her when we learned she was with child. One perfectly heart-shaped stone, an object of wonder, as wonderful as the babe she carried. She wore it on the day she gave birth to him and all through his childhood."

Mère Sophie puts the ring back in my own hand. "You keep it, Lucie," she murmurs. "I'm sure Christine would be pleased."

I remember when Beast found the ring in a book in the library after so many years, how awed he was. How it comforted him. And my heart aches again.

"I'm too foolish to ever make you a suitable apprentice," I tell her. All this thinking makes my poor head too heavy, and I lower it into my hands. "I've lost Beast. I've lost my virtue. I'm not—"

"Nonsense," the wisewoman interrupts me crisply. "Maiden you may no longer be, but you are as virtuous now as the day you were born." My head bobs up, and she smiles again. "Virtue is yours to make of what you will, by your actions, by your character. No one else can ever take it from you."

She has quietly taken my hand in hers and gives it a gentle squeeze, and I feel her strength and warmth pumping into me. Perhaps I am not ruined. Perhaps my life has value still.

"But—I don't know what to do."

"Eat a bowl of my stew," suggests Mère Sophie. "Stay here and rest for a while. Things may look different in the morning."

· CHAPTER 27 ·

Christ and His Monsters

There's never any smoke from Mère Sophie's fire, although it burns cheerily in the grate all night. She conjures a second bed for me, piled high with quilts and pillows and a cat of its own, an elegant brindle that curls up in the small of my back and keeps me warm throughout the night.

It's the first night in nearly four months that I've had eyes to close and felt the urge and the ability to surrender to sleep, and I long for that sweet release above all things. Yet I can't quite let go. I've been alert, wakeful, watching for such a long time; if I give myself over to human sleep, human dreams, what chaos might engulf me? Still, I murmur a prayer for Mère Sophie's protection and surrender at last. And I sleep soundly that first night, untroubled by dreaming of any kind. My newly restored human body needs its rest.

In another day, word seeps into the wood that the Chevalier de Beaumont, so recently returned to the château and reassembling his household, has already departed with his bride-to-be. They escort her father to the healing springs at the Cluny Abbey, for his health, where they will receive the blessing of the abbé on their upcoming nuptials. Wedding preparations, we are told, proceed at a furious pace at the château.

I cannot bear to think of Jean-Loup so completely in command again of the life he stole from Beast, and so I throw myself into my studies with Mère Sophie. Many folk, but especially women, both highborn and lowborn, make their way into the wood seeking her healing remedies. It's not witchcraft, as I once feared, as put about by slanderous rumors, but a skillful knowledge of natural things that might bring ease and comfort to those in distress. She teaches me the lore of her plants and how the cycles of the moon affect them—new moon for sowing, full moon for growing, waning moon for the harvest. I help her gather wild herbs and dry them by her fire, and I learn to assist in mixing her potions and infusions. Each day, I discover the depth of her knowledge and the patience with which she passes along each tiny morsel of it to me, as awkward as I often am.

"All you need is time, Lucie," she assures me. "You have the heart for it and the wit. I can teach you the skill."

I have never had such useful work to do, nor felt more at home in any place, not since my father died. I imagine him smiling down at me now. I hope he is pleased that my life has some value at last, that his confidence in the child I was then was not misplaced. And gradually, I allow the calming rhythms of Mère Sophie's life to bring me a kind of peace.

I have begun to dream again. And most nights, I dream of Beast, his warm, gold-dusted eyes, his husky laugh, his animal smile. I wake from these dreams giddy with so much happiness, such relief—until the cruel truth dawns on me again. I worry that mine might be the last memories of the dream that was Beast. Rose may have already forgotten him, in her rush to marry the chevalier.

And every night, even my dreams of Beast grow more faint.

We are on the cusp of the new moon, the time of beginnings, on the morning Mère Sophie asks if I will run an errand for her into the town. "My dear friend, Madame LeBoeuf, keeps an inn at Clairvallon. I brew a special tisane for her rheumatics, and I would appreciate it if you would deliver a new packet of my brew to her."

"Of course," I agree, always glad to return a favor for my tutor and benefactor.

"She will offer you lodging as well, for my sake," says

the wisewoman, "if you need it; it's a long walk to town and back." And she bustles off to her worktable to measure out her herbs.

When the manicured trees of the outer park behind Château Beaumont come into view, I make a long, wide detour around the grounds, along the uneven track worn into the earth by peasants and wayfarers who dare not trespass on Beaumont land. By midday, I am far below the château, halfway down the hillside that overlooks the town. From here, the red-tile roofs of Clairvallon cluster together like kneeling penitents in the shadow of the church tower that rises up at the opposite end of the town. I travel down the hill and into the town and stop at the inn where I first came as a green serving girl.

I introduce myself to Madame LeBoeuf, a plump, merry woman, who is delighted to get the packet from Mère Sophie. The innkeeper doesn't know she has ever served me before. She doesn't remember me as the timid little chit who spent a night in the common room on her way to a life of service at the château. She knows me only as Mère Sophie's assistant and insists that I stay for a midday meal. She is eager to share all the gossip about the chevalier's wedding; folk talk of nothing else. She tells me the chevalier is now back in residence at the château, along with his bride-to-be and her family.

"And we're to have a great deal more excitement, too, mademoiselle," she exclaims.

I glance around the room, at the local folk meeting their friends for a cup of wine, at the travelers taking their meals and gossiping with the serving girls. The place is a hive of expectation.

"More excitement than this?" say I.

"Oh, much more! The abbé himself has decided to come from Cluny to perform the wedding ceremony tomorrow!"

So soon? I've lost track of the days.

"It will be a great day for us to see the abbé right here in our town."

"Such an illustrious person, here?" I ask her. "Will the local curé not perform the ceremony?"

"But my dear mademoiselle! The LeNoirs held the very first Beaumont lands in fief from Cluny Abbey back in the old times. They have always been powerful allies. It's a mark of great favor that the abbé himself will join the bride and groom in matrimony, and the chevalier would accept none less. The chevalier knows no other mortal man as close to God."

She bustles off to carry the happy news to some other guest, hoping to persuade them to stay an extra day or two to celebrate the great event. But I can scarcely find joy in her news. They will be joined in the sight of God, Rose and her sham husband, who should be Beast. Once the church has blessed their union, Jean-Loup's triumph will be complete.

The wedding preparations at Château Beaumont have the entire town abuzz. From the inn, I can see the barrels of wine carted up the hill to the château and the herds of hogs and sheep driven up for the feast. Armies of cooks, waiters, housemaids, seamstresses, gardeners, and stable-boys stop at the inn on their way to their new employment. There's no longer any talk of the château being cursed. The Beaumont fortune cascades down the hill and into the town like a spring rain, and all talk of monsters and fairy curses is washed away.

After my meal, I leave the bustling town behind and follow the steep, winding path upward to the ancient stone church of Clairvallon, being readied for the nuptials. I have never been here before, but I want to know more about this God who would sanctify so unnatural a union. The Basilica of Mary Magdalene, they call it, dedicated to the Magdalene, patron saint of sinners who have mislaid their virtue on their journey through life. Pilgrims from provinces far and near have climbed this steep hill on bleeding knees to pray to the Magdalene, so they say. I have forgotten my prayers, if ever I knew any, but folk come here seeking comfort, and I would be comforted.

But I find this place, too, all abustle over the coming

ceremony. Young monks are on their knees, not in prayer, but scrubbing the broad stone steps beneath the huge arched portal. Others are trimming the lush greenery in the yard. Berobed men scurry in and out of the doorway beneath the portal under the supervision of a senior monk with a sour face. I dare not disturb the scrubbers, nor risk the wrath of their superior.

Yet, as I stand here below the steps like generations of pilgrims before me, I find my gaze drawn up and up to the massive portal carved in stone above the doorway and the tall, narrow Gothic windows above. All are alive with carvings to show folk the ways of the righteous. Giant figures of saints and kings gaze down from the niches of the upper windows, but my eyes are drawn back to the lower portal, an enormous half-moon lying on its side above the doorway.

The scene carved in the portal is Judgment Day, with Christ seated at its center, surrounded by His holy people. They are the apostles, I suppose, with the Virgin Mary and the Magdalene among them. Surely whatever local noblemen paid for the building of the church centuries ago, and the abbé who dedicated it, had their portraits etched in stone in Christ's company. But what captures my attention is the long lintel that serves as a base for the half-moon, supporting the scene. Two lines of smaller figures march to meet in the center, eager to be resurrected under Christ's benevolent gaze. But these figures are not priests and merchants and princes. They are the lame, the poor in rags, the disfigured. Some have hollow, staring eyes, lost to madness. Some are hunchbacked, some clubfooted. Some have the heads of monsters.

I swallow hard. Monsters at the feast of Judgment Day. The hand of the Christ rises above them one and all, offering His blessing.

Perhaps Beast will be welcome in the next world as he is, if not in this one.

But how unfair that he must wait until then.

The senior monk peers over at me with suspicion, and I hastily bow my head. When I notice that the gold ring on its red ribbon has jostled loose from my bodice in my journey up the hill, I grasp it in my hand. Twisting it in agitation, I gaze up again at the frieze of monsters. What became of Rose's sisters, I wonder, and their plot to slay the monster of Beaumont?

And before I can draw another breath, I find myself standing before the massive gilded gates of Château Beaumont. I can't be dreaming now; it's the middle of the day! Yet here I am, standing on the stone bridge across the moat, which is jammed with carts and drays of all sorts making deliveries to the château.

"Watch yourself there, ma'amselle!" cries a carter as he drives his mule past me, and I grab at the low stone wall to get out of the way. I feel it cold and rough against my hand. A wave of heat from the lathered animal washes over me along with the stinging odor of its sweat. How can this be real? Then I look down and see, to my amazement, that I have somehow fidgeted the enchanted ring over my finger. Its magic has brought me here!

After pressing myself to the wall, I remove the ring hastily from my finger and slide it back inside my bodice while I peer around. Some of the vehicles crowding the bridge before the gate carry supplies, but many are delivering wedding gifts. The gatehouse is occupied by a new, less ferocious gatekeeper in Beaumont livery who must weigh the merits of each request for entry before signalling the two robust footmen inside to throw open the gilded iron gates.

Through the gates, I see that the red roses still grow in the terraced beds that fill the courtyard garden, high enough to be seen above the wall. But the bushes have been trimmed and bullied into severe formal patterns, and the blooms do not burst with the same energy they once had under Beast's loving care. I suspect Jean-Loup has given the task back to his gardeners.

On the far side of the rose terraces stand the familiar stone archways that front the east wing and the carriage house. The rooms in this wing, so long unused, are filling up now with wedding gifts and supplies and servants to see to them. Footmen in livery bustle about in the breeze-way under the arches, attending to each new arrival. I glimpse the Beaumont carriage gleaming in renewed glory. Another figure bustles about in an official manner. I realize it is Rose's father, the old merchant. He is back in looks again, ruddy-cheeked, clear-eyed, his pointed little beard now white but neatly trimmed.

A wagon halts before him, and servants are ordered to unload the chests it carries. Rose's father marches out to examine their contents.

"Lace!" he barks to a nearby footman. "Not the best quality, although finer than that stuff the Comtesse de La Roche sent. Tell Jacques to make a note."

I return my attention to the archway of roses vault-ing over the broad gravel drive and notice that two female figures now stand at either side of the driveway nearest the gate. They are both clothed in grey gowns the color of stone. It's not servants' clothing; the silken fabric looks too fine. Still, their dress is almost a kind of livery, with their matching silver lace collars, untrimmed robes, and tall felt hats with modest brims to keep off the sun. They might be taken for statues, but for the way they fret and fidget at their appointed posts. I can't imagine what purpose they serve until a cart is let through the gate and directed to the lady at the left of the drive. From a purse at her waist, she extracts a coin and hands it to the carter, then gestures him down the side track for the kitchen wing. They are here to dispense the Beaumont munificence, I see, to impress the tradespeople with the chevalier's generosity.

Although I have never seen these grey women before, not even when I was in service here myself to Jean-Loup, something about them tugs at my memory. Then I realize where I've seen them before: they are Blanche and Violette.

Another wagon is let in and directed to the right to Rose's eldest sister, Blanche. We are near enough now that I see her fumble in her little purse, eyes downcast, her expression stony; she produces a coin and hands it to the driver.

"For your trouble," she mutters. Then lifting her chin a little, she adds in frosty tones, "The Chevalier de Beaumont and his lady welcome you."

So this is how Rose repays her scheming sisters! They are forced to stand and watch the endless parade of servants and sycophants and revellers come to pay homage to their more fortunate sister and her handsome chevalier, doling out coins like common almsgivers in penance for their pride.

But I was just thinking of them, not a moment ago, at the Basilica of the Magdalene—far, far away from here, at the opposite end of the town. Is that what brought me here to them? In response, the ring warms a little against my skin. I had scooped it up that day for Beast's sake because it was important to him, but I'd forgotten until this minute that it was enchanted. Now I realize how powerful it is— infused with his mother's love.

Weary, now, of the revelry and anticipation all around me, I make my way into the shadows behind the gatehouse and withdraw the ring on its ribbon. I slip it on my finger and wish to go home to Mère Sophie.

· CHAPTER 28 ·

Lady Beaumont

I have little appetite for Mère Sophie's simmered onion broth at supper. The wedding will take place tomorrow morning, and all the town is invited up to the château for the celebration to follow. We've known this day was coming, but I suppose I had not let myself believe it until I miraculously saw the bustle up at the château today with my own eyes. Jean-Loup thrives, and Rose will marry him. That is the simple truth. All else is foolishness.

It's impossible to believe that I will ever sleep. Yet I am so weary and heartsore, I crawl into my bed as soon as darkness falls. It must be defeat that weighs me down so, a longing for oblivion that stops my thinking. In truth, I cannot bear another thought.

It's full dark when I waken again, and profoundly quiet, but for the low, rumbling purr of my brindle cat. I realize it's a slight warming of the ring on its ribbon around my neck, inside my chemise, that has wakened me. I roll over to face the shadowy wall away from the fireplace, and I startle to the soles of my feet at what I see.

A figure sits in the darkness, a woman. It's not Mère Sophie; I can hear her murmuring softly in her sleep from the other side of the fireplace. The face of the woman before me is bathed in a peculiar light from above, a light that has no source — pale shades of pink, blue, and green. I recognize the careless spill of her curls, escaping their jewelled net, her lovely face, her dark, expressive eyes. They no longer well with tears as she gazes at me, but I know Christine DuVal LeNoir. Beast's mother. She is moving ever so slightly in the darkness, back and forth, as she was when I first saw her in a mirrored room at Château Beaumont, in a chair made of bentwood, although I can't quite see it in the darkness. The pale colors on her face are the same ones I saw reflected in my own polished silver surface in her library not so long ago.

"Lady Beaumont," I whisper, sitting up in my bed.

She nods at me. "Lucie."

I remember my terror when she first called me by name, but I no longer fear her. I feel a kinship with her now because we both care so much for Beast. And I share her sorrow over what we have allowed to become of him.

"We tried to bring him back," I tell her, lowering my voice even further. "Mère Sophie and I."

"But you did." She offers me a soft, sad smile. "He became himself again in your company. My little one, grown so big and strong! It gave me such joy to see it. After what I'd done to him."

My heart aches for her, for this lovely, heartsick woman who can never forgive herself, who cannot rest in the next world because of her tragic mistake in this one.

"He doesn't blame you," I tell her. "He may not even realize what happened. But I know that he has very tender feelings for you." I remember the roses he brought so faithfully to her library.

She gazes at me, her expression wistful, perhaps wondering if she should let herself believe me. Is this what her eternity will be like, hovering between two worlds, paying in sorrow for accounts she can no longer settle in life?

"You are very kind to say so," she murmurs at last.

"I should have been kinder, sooner," I say ruefully. "I'm sorry I failed you, my lady. I failed Beast."

"*I* failed him," she corrects me gently. Her warm brown eyes are so like Beast's, so full of feeling. She nods at me, and I feel the warmth of the ring under my chemise. I draw it out, and she smiles.

"I always meant for him to have it," she tells me, "if . . .

by some miracle he might ever be restored. So I kept it on a ribbon for him. A poor enough token of my love, I suppose. But this was all I had to give him. Especially now that I can no longer embrace my child in this world."

Her expression sinks into melancholy for another moment before she turns her eyes back to me. "I came here to thank you, Lucie. You were a friend to him for a time — something I think he had never had before. I will treasure the memory of his happiness."

I would tell her I don't deserve her thanks, that I let Beast slip away again, but Lady Beaumont's image is already fading again into the shadows. But I am far too agitated now for sleep.

Lady Beaumont's misery is like a knife blade in my heart. It cannot be possible that there is nothing I can do to help send her to her rest at last, nothing I can do for Beast, now that I have arms and legs and a heart of my own.

Mère Sophie said a permanent transformation could be done only with something stronger than hate. Lady Beaumont still loves her true child so much, her ring burns with it, although she is gone these many years. I have felt the power of this ring. I felt it this very afternoon — a tiny vessel that contains the vast ocean of Lady Beaumont's love.

Jean-Loup may be stronger than all of us. But is he more powerful than love?

~⸾~

I must have slept, for I'm wakened by the clamor of distant church bells. It's full day outside, and I know the bells are from the basilica, tolling for the wedding of the chevalier and his bride. I annoy the brindle cat by shifting myself away from the light while I wrestle with what I must do.

My plan is desperate indeed, especially now that the chevalier has claimed his bride and the seigneurie has a new Lady Beaumont. The entire town of Clairvallon must be wending its way up the hill to the château at this very moment for the wedding feast. If I meant to find a private moment to see Jean-Loup, it will not be today. Yet every moment I delay, there may be less and less of Beast to save.

Plagued by these thoughts, I drag myself out of bed. The brindle cat rolls over into the warm spot hollowed out by my body and sinks back into contented slumber. But Mère Sophie and I are scarcely full awake when there's a hammering at the door. A woodcutter begs the wisewoman to come to his cottage to treat his feverish child. She takes me with her to help with her balms and infusions, and I spend the rest of the morning at her side, until the fever is broken and the boy made stable.

It's midday by the time we return to our cottage, and my thoughts return to Beast. We have been victorious today for this child, a stranger, and I am more resolved than ever to win a victory for Beast. I may be completely addled to think I can do anything at all for him now, and yet I must try. I can't let Beast spend the rest of his life suffocated within the illusion that is Jean-Loup, not if there is any possibility, however remote, that I might have the means to free him. Beast was ready to end his own life in hopes of releasing me. I must find the same sort of courage for him.

I'm lacing my boots again when I find Mère Sophie standing by my side.

"You are leaving me," she says.

"Beast needs my help," I tell her. "I'm the only hope he has left."

Mère Sophie nods thoughtfully. "Be very sure of what you want, my dear," she says at last.

I finish lacing my second boot and run my fingers through my hair. I stand and smooth out my skirts, dull and grey and plain.

Mère Sophie eyes me up and down. "I believe there is a celebration in progress where you are going," she says, and nods toward the bed where I've been sitting. Across it now is spread a modest gown of soft mossy green, the color of the river, with a bodice worked in coppery-colored embroidery. The cat slumbers on undisturbed beside it. I notice a traveling cloak the rusty color of autumn leaves hanging on the hook by the door.

"Thank you, Mère Sophie," I whisper. I unlace my old grey frock, pull it off, and put on the green. I feel as if I am wearing the wisewoman's colors into battle, the colors of the wood. They are nothing fancy, nothing fine, but decent, durable clothing for the task I undertake.

"Know that there will always be a place for you here by my fire," Mère Sophie tells me at the door, as if she has been listening to my thoughts. "But you must follow your heart. There lies a power greater than any enchantment."

CHAPTER 29

Reunion

I draw out the ring on its ribbon, but I'm not sure where to go. I need to find where Jean-Loup is, if I mean to unlock Beast, but I cannot very well appear out of the air beside him, as Rose did in Beast's garden—especially if he is doing some public thing, like standing to receive a toast to his health. So when I slip the ring on my finger, I desire only to join the wedding feast.

Instantly, I am standing in the courtyard before the grand front steps of the château. The courtyard is so thronging with people, nobody even notices when I am suddenly among them. At least half the folk of the town are still here, roaming about, feasting to their fill from long, narrow tables laden with roasted meats and bread and cheeses and fruit that are set up between the newly formalized rose beds. Brewers' and vintners' wagons are parked under the arched porticoes alongside the east wing, and legions of servants, some in Beaumont livery and others attached to the wagons, wander among the crowd, pouring wine, ale, and mead out of large, full-bellied country pitchers.

More formal tables for invited guests are set up to one side of the steps. Rose's father sits at the head table, chatting happily among some of the chevalier's titled guests, but Rose's sisters and three young men I take for her brothers — the would-be monster hunters — are seated at a middle table, not as close as the nobler guests, but not so distant as to show disrespect. Musicians playing horns and bladder pipes and crook-necked lutes stroll between the tables, sweetening the air with their lilting harmonies beneath the general din of talk and laughter and toasting.

At the center of it all stands an elevated platform, like a mummers' stage, on the other side of the château steps. There the wedding party is enthroned, under a canopy of burgundy and gold. It's an imposing structure, trimmed in flounces and rosettes and bearing the Beaumont device.

In the middle of the long table sits Rose, radiant in a gown of palest blue silk the color of moonbeams. She is flanked by a few of the chevalier's closest companions-in-arms and their ladies, although some of the chairs are empty now. And as I circle nearer in the crowd, I see their table is littered with the remains of much feasting: fruit pits, cheese rinds, various small animal bones, and many,

many kinds of drinking vessels, from delicate crystal and pewter goblets to more formidable steins.

Most noticeable about this grand table is that the chevalier is not sitting at it.

I peer all around, but I don't see Jean-Loup anywhere. A half-dozen ladies and gentlemen knights still occupy places at the table, chattering idly at one another, but the thronelike chair beside Rose is empty. Rose herself is occupied with being charming to a line of supplicants and well-wishers from the town who come bowing and scraping to the chevalier's table. She has a smile and a friendly word for every ironmonger or lace maker or washerwoman or shepherd who dares to approach her.

But I see the way her eyes dart fleetingly from side to side between these brief interviews. I notice one of the noble ladies at the table speaking behind her hand to the gentleman knight beside her, who responds with a sly look. No doubt they are wondering why the Lord Beaumont is not here beside his new bride.

This may be the perfect opportunity for me, perhaps the only one I will ever get. I duck behind a rosebush thick with blooms and muster out the ring on its ribbon. A dream of Beast still exists somewhere, but to find it, I must go to wherever Jean-Loup is. And so I seek the chevalier and slip the ring on again.

I open my eyes inside the sitting room, in the middle of Jean-Loup's private apartments upstairs. I shudder to find myself here again, in my human form, but I know I must confront Jean-Loup in person if I'm to have any prayer of reaching Beast. Still, I keep the ring clutched close in my palm, ready to slip it on again in an instant if I need to escape.

His sitting room is empty but shows all the signs of habitation. The wardrobe door is partly open with a jacket thrown over it and muddy hunting boots discarded beside it. An empty wine decanter sits beside a goblet on the table next to the armchair. The carved stags still vault over the marble fireplace, and the mirror beneath them has been restored. An unlit pipe trailing ashes lies abandoned on the mantelpiece, and a plumed hat has been rakishly hung on the stone head of the god in its center. But even without these objects, these clues, I would know he is nearby. I can feel him.

No servant will dare to enter without the master's permission. Jean-Loup and I will not be interrupted.

The doorway to the bedchamber stands partly open, but no sound breaks the quiet. Is he sleeping? Is he ill? I creep to the doorway and see articles of fresh clothing—breeches, doublet, linen, smallclothes—neatly laid out across the foot of the bed in preparation for the wedding night. The chamber does not appear to be occupied, yet the very air crackles with his presence; I can feel him nearby, and yet I can't see him. Where is he?

But as I pause, heart hammering in my throat, I hear the soft, placid lapping of water. The gentle rippling sound fades away, and I hear a deep human sigh of contentment.

Jean-Loup is in his bath.

The mirror above the fireplace opposite the bed reflects the far side of the room that I can't see around the door, including the half-drawn velvet curtain. Behind it must be the bay window where the tiled bathtub is located; I remember gazing down into it from my cupboard in the attic. I grip the ring more tightly in one hand and step around the door into the room.

"This way, mademoiselle," comes Jean-Loup's most honeyed voice as he pokes his head out from his bathtub beyond the partly drawn curtain.

But his voice falls away as his eyes rise to me. His jaw gapes open for an instant as he straightens up in the water. The carpeted steps leading up to the level of the inset tub suggest a throne, and Jean-Loup looks regal enough as he peers out at me, even though he is naked and up to his rib cage in bathwater.

"Lucie," he whispers. He remembers me, but I don't seem to be the one he's expecting.

His hair is loose and mostly dry, except for the ends

that cling to his neck and scatter across his shoulders in wet curls. His damp skin has a golden sheen in the afternoon sunlight as his arms rise to rest along the rim of the tub. How peculiar his chest looks, slick and naked, without its covering of fur or a long mane curling over it. He seems unformed, somehow, an embryo, not yet born.

"Chevalier," I respond with a nod.

He glances at the door for an instant, then back at me. "And what are you doing here?"

"I've brought you . . . a wedding gift," I tell him.

"Why, you astonish me, Little Candle." I bristle inwardly at the smugness in his voice, but I don't let him see it. "I thought you cared little enough for my charms."

He pushes aside the curtain and stands up. He looks like a fairy king rising there, naked, dripping water, haloed in sunlight, like one of the perfect godlike statues carved in marble on his fireplace.

I forbid myself to shrink back or recoil in disgust as he comes down the three short steps, although I grasp the ring more firmly. At the bottom step, he plucks up a wine-colored dressing gown thrown over the back of a chair and wraps it around himself.

"You mistake my meaning, chevalier," I say, pleased at how calm I sound. "The gift is not from me; I bring it on behalf of . . . a friend."

I step back into the sitting room, eager to be out of

his bedchamber, and he cautiously follows, suspicious, yet intrigued. I'm not completely sure what to do next, but I pray that the ring itself, burning with Beast's mother's love, will guide me.

But I have scarcely opened my hand to reveal it when a soft knocking comes at the door behind me from the outer salon of the chevalier's suite of rooms. The door opens, and there stands a pretty girl from one of the vintners' wagons below, carrying a jug of wine on her hip. Her eyes widen at the sight of the two of us standing here.

"Monsieur le chevalier!" She gasps and comes no farther in. Her gaze darts to me and back to Jean-Loup. "But . . . I thought . . . oh, apologies, monsieur!"

She turns and flees back out into the salon. And then we hear her gasp again.

"M-my lady," we hear her stammer. "I was told . . . the chevalier said . . . I never meant . . ."

And as the girl's voice fades away out into the hallway, Rose marches into the sitting room, crying, "Jean-Loup, who was that girl? Where have—"

But she freezes on the spot to see me together with her husband. "Who is this?" she demands of him.

"She is nothing, no one." Jean-Loup waves me off, turning to his bride.

"Really, Jean-Loup, how many more are there? They multiply like the roses in your garden. And on our wedding day! In our home! Have you set out deliberately to humiliate me?"

Surprised by her anger, Jean-Loup slips into the placating tone with which he is so accustomed to getting his way. "Now, my love, you know you mean everything to me—"

"Who are you?" Rose rounds on me again.

I squeeze the ring in my palm. "My name is Lucie, my lady. And I have a message from Christine DuVal LeNoir to her son."

Jean-Loup looks shocked. Rose whirls on her husband. "You told me your mother was dead! Is every word you speak a lie?"

"She is long gone, my lady," I say to Rose. "But her spirit haunts me. I was employed here as a chambermaid not so long ago. I was here on the night Beast appeared."

I hadn't thought Rose's blue eyes could widen any further, as she gasps, "You know about Beast?"

"Beast is gone!" Jean-Loup glares at us both.

I ignore him, speaking to Rose. "I remained in this place until—until the day he left us."

"But there was no one else here!" Rose cries.

"I, too, was transformed by magic," I tell her. "I was a silver candlestick."

Anyone else would think me raving to make such an outlandish claim, but Rose knows far better than anyone else what enchantments took place here. Her hands fly to her mouth as her gaze darts from me to her husband, then back again to me. "You saw everything," she whispers.

I squeeze the ring again and focus my thoughts. *I could scarcely help it. You took me with you everywhere.*

Rose stares at me, shocked to hear my voice in her head. "You are the one who called me back here!"

I nod. "Beast would have died," I tell her. "It was the only way I could think of to save him. And we *did* save him, you and I. Some part of Beast still exists inside your husband."

"Nonsense!" Jean-Loup scoffs. He turns to his bride. "My dearest love, don't listen to her foolishness. She is only jealous of our happiness!"

"Happiness?" Rose spits out the word. "Receiving women in your dressing gown? Insulting me in front of our wedding guests? Leaving me on my own for an hour or more? You think we are happy?"

Jean-Loup rounds again on me, but his voice is less sure than it was. "How dare you come into my home with your lies and your hate—"

"You are not worth hating, Jean-Loup. You're not even real." I wave my hand at him the way you might brush off a gnat. "I'm here for Beast's sake. And his mother's." I unclench my fingers so the ring is visible in my hand.

"She saved this all these years for Beast. It's a token of how much she loved him."

I don't know what I expect to happen next—a thunderclap and lightning, perhaps; a chorus of angels. But all that happens is Jean-Loup cries, "Stop this nonsense! There is no Beast!" But despite his commanding voice, there's an edge of uncertainty in his manner as he reaches for his bride. "It's all lies! Rose—"

But Rose backs away from him, pulling her arm away. "Don't touch me! Don't ever touch me!"

"I am your husband!" he shouts again. "And now that we are married—"

"I find I have married a horrid beast!" cries Rose. "After all I have done for you, after what you were before—" She stops and shakes her head. "No, no, that was not you. Sir Beast would never treat me so!"

"Of course he would not!" I chime in, eager to make an ally of Rose. The more she turns against Jean-Loup, the more fondly she may feel toward Beast. "Remember how kind and gracious Beast was?" I remind her. "He was so concerned with your comfort and your well-being. Your happiness was all that mattered to him."

It seems I cannot stop myself praising Beast's virtues once I've begun. "He is good-humored and thoughtful, with a sense of justice so profound, he cannot bear any kind of cruelty. He would never raise a paw in anger. His passion for life is strong, and his feelings run so deeply, yet he is always quick to laugh."

It warms me even now to think of his husky laughter and his animal smile, to recall the zeal with which he brought his garden to life, and his respect for all living things. I am shaking my head as my heart swells with feeling. "I love his mismatched animal parts and his poet's soul. I love his warm eyes sprinkled with gold."

Rose and Jean-Loup are both staring at me as I clutch the ring on its ribbon to my heart.

"I . . . I love Beast!"

There is the plain truth of it. I feel it welling up inside me even now, flooding through my blood. How could I not know it before now? I have overestimated the power of this ring, and yet by its magic I find the strength to speak the truth that's in my heart.

"He was a monster!" Jean-Loup yelps.

"You are the monster," I tell him angrily. "Beast is the true chevalier. And you are nothing!"

"No!" howls Jean-Loup, his eyes full of panic, his face full of horror. He howls again, but his voice has deepened as he hunches forward, covering his face in his hands. His hair grows long and tangled, and two small, curved horns sprout from the top of his mane between two pointed, furry ears. He grows more massive beneath his robe, which falls away as his soft, whiskered muzzle rises up from behind his paws. He plants his hooves, stretches out his paws, shakes out his tawny mane, and lets out a blistering roar of triumph.

CHAPTER 30

The True Chevalier

"Beast!" I cry, even as I hear Rose faintly gasp, "Sir Beast!"

I want to fly to him, but I dare not, checked by the enormity of what I've done. What must Rose think? What does Beast think? He has never even seen me in my human form—does he even know who I am?

"Lucie," he whispers in the tenderest voice I've ever heard in all my life. Awe and delight dance in his gold-dusted eyes. "You are human again! You've been restored!"

I can't resist grasping his paw in both my hands. "Oh, Beast, when I think of how close I came to losing you! But there was no way you could have undone that spell, however bravely you tried. Only I had the power to free myself."

"And you came back," he rumbles. "For me." He glances at my hands gripping his paw and back at me. "But you risked so much to come here. You had to face *him*."

"I would have risked anything for you, Beast! I . . . I was so afraid I would never see you again. I was so afraid that Jean-Loup had won."

Beast's gaze intensifies. "But—he's gone! I can feel his absence in a way I never could before. It's like a weight lifted off my heart." He covers my hands gently with his other paw. "We've defeated him at last, Lucie! Jean-Loup is gone!"

"Sir Beast." Rose's voice trembles, recalling us to the moment. "I don't understand. They . . . they all told me this place was cursed, that you were cursed. But they said I broke the curse!"

Beast turns to her. "But . . . I *am* the Beaumont Curse," he says, his dark eyes bright with sudden understanding. He glances at me again. "I was so little when it happened the first time, when I was first transformed. I didn't remember. But the memory lives inside this body. And now that he is gone, I know it in every one of my senses." He raises his paw again to stare at it. "This is what I am, how I was born. I *am* the true chevalier."

"And far more worthy of the title than Jean-Loup ever was," I say to Rose.

She nods slowly, frowning slightly. What must she think?

"I know this must be a terrible shock to you, Rose," says Beast softly. "But I shall not force you to honor vows you made to another man."

Rose peers at him with more resolution in her expression. "No, Sir Beast, I made my first promise to *you*," she corrects him. "And our family keeps its bargains."

We fall suddenly silent. Rose is Beast's lawful wife, after all.

"But Jean-Loup is never coming back?" Rose asks. She does not sound displeased.

"Never," says Beast.

Rose's gaze falls to my hands still entwined with Beast's paw. "And you are in love with him," she says to me.

It's too late now to pretend otherwise. "Yes, I am," I confess.

"And you are in love with her," she says to Beast. It is not a question.

"I am," says Beast, closing his other paw gently over my hand again.

"So perhaps we can come to some . . . arrangement?" Rose says delicately.

Her plans may lie in ruins, but the merchant's daughter is ready to bargain. I rather admire that she can remain so clearheaded in spite of everything. For my part, I can't imagine what will happen now. One last chance to release Beast had been my only goal; I've given no thought at all to what might come next.

"My dear Rose," says Beast gallantly, "in return for all

you have endured, of course I am prepared to see you and your family provided for. What would you ask of me?"

Beast behaves as honorably as ever, and Rose considers his offer. I wonder what she will choose? A trunk of riches? Some sort of annual stipend to be shared from the profits of the seigneurie once Beast has lowered the taxes and rents and restored prosperity?

But no sooner do I have this thought than something far more disturbing occurs to me: How can we expect the people of the seigneurie to accept Beast as their new chevalier? All they will see is what Rose and her father saw at first, what all humans see: a hideous monster. How will they ever give him a chance to govern?

"Beast," I tell him with sudden inspiration, "give this château to Rose!"

"What?" says Beast.

"What?" says Rose.

"Who better?" I go on. "Rose, you are now Lady Beaumont, the rightful mistress of the château. No one will dispute you."

Rose looks surprised, but I can see she is thinking it over. It's Beast who looks doubtful.

"But . . . this house, these things . . . Lucie, I have nothing else to give you . . ."

"I don't want things! All I want is you. Safe and alive!"

I tighten my grip on his paw. "Jean-Loup was nothing without his fine possessions. They are all that gave him worth. But you are different."

Beast begins to nod slowly. "The seigneurie deserves a new sovereign," he rumbles at last. "Promise me, Rose, that you will treat them well, after all they have endured — when Château Beaumont is yours."

"I promise, Sir Beast!"

A commotion of servants startles us from out in the hall. Housemaids' voices rise in alarm over the roaring they heard and wondering what's become of Lord and Lady Beaumont; they are missed downstairs. Rose hurries to the door.

"Wait here," she whispers to us. "I'll send them away."

As the voices move off, Beast raises his paw to stroke my hair with awkward tenderness. He leans closer, his breath warm on my cheek as he nuzzles my face, learning my new human scent. "But how can you want me like this, Lucie?" he murmurs. "How is it possible?"

"I might ask you the same thing," I say, sliding my fingertips gently through his mane. How soft it feels. "There was no room in my heart for anything but revenge until you came along. I lost track of who I was inside. But I found myself again because you cared for me. You gave me a reason to open my heart."

"And you gave me someone to come back to, Lucie,"

he rumbles. "My faithful companion, my light in the darkness. My illuminator, who knows me better than I ever dared to know myself."

I lean my cheek into the soft fur of his chest.

"I will make mistakes—I am only human, after all." He chuckles softly. "But they will be *my* mistakes. Not Jean-Loup's."

I glance up again. "But do you not think after all we've endured together that we might encourage what is best in each other's nature?"

Beast's dark eyes shine with humor. "I think we might at that," he agrees.

I close my eyes, but a shrill yelp startles them open.

"Beast!" a voice bleats nearby. "Monster! Murder!"

CHAPTER 31

Flight

We look up to see Madame Montant quivering in the doorway in her sober black gown, fluttering a white handkerchief about her mouth. Although she was in the house the night Jean-Loup was transformed into Beast, she never actually laid eyes on him; witchcraft drove all the servants off in terror. Now her sense of duty wars with horror in her wavering expression, finding herself face-to-face with Beast.

"W-where is my lady Rose?" she cries. "I heard her voice! If you've harmed her in any way . . ."

"My dear Madame Montant, calm yourself," Beast tries to reassure her in his most conciliatory tones. "No harm has been—"

"The Devil knows my name!" shrieks the housekeeper. "I am a marked woman! Oh, help! Murder!"

Beast is too dumbfounded to respond as both her hands fly up to her whitening face to ward off the evil eye. When he takes one anxious step toward her, she reels backward, half turns, and collapses to the floor of the salon in a pool of black skirts. Beast glances nervously back at me.

"By Christ and all His saints, am I so hideous a sight that people die of it?"

"There is nothing hideous about you," I tell him firmly, squeezing his paw. "It's her own fear that overwhelms her."

Rose appears breathlessly in the outer doorway to the hall, pulling it shut behind her. "What has happened? I heard a shout—" But she freezes when she sees the figure sprawled on the floor. "Madame!" she gasps, raising wide eyes to us.

"Fainted dead away," I tell her, trying not to smile at the notion of ferocious Madame Montant swooning like a girl. But more agitated voices from below sober me at once.

"They heard her shouting, too," Rose says urgently.

Already we hear housemaids' voices, crying, "Madame!" and "Lady Rose!" A clamoring erupts downstairs of servants and guards drawn by these alarms. No one is running away this time, not if they perceive their new Lady Rose to be in any mortal danger.

"Don't let them find you!" Rose urges us anxiously. It may be that she's merely protecting her interests as new mistress of the château, but I believe she really does care something for Beast. She would like him to be happy.

"She's right, Beast. We must flee!" I exclaim. "I know where we can go, but we must go now!"

Heavy footfalls of a distinctly martial character on the marble floor of the entry hall below echo up the stairwell. Beast's body tenses.

"Lucie," he rumbles, "put on the ring! Go far beyond these walls, and I will meet you there as soon as I can."

But I grasp the ring on its ribbon and tuck it firmly back into my bodice. "I am not leaving you, Beast. I am never leaving you again! We will do this together."

Something indescribably sweet warms in his dark eyes as he gazes at me for another instant; then he reaches out his paw and takes my hand. We dash out to the second-floor landing of the grand staircase. Voices are shouting and yodeling below, but we dare not try the back stairs, where we might find ourselves trapped in a closed turret. Beast lowers himself to all fours.

"Beastliness has its uses," he growls, nodding to me.

I climb astride his back, squirm in between the feathers, dig in my knees, and press myself flat against him, knotting my fingers in his mane.

We move down to the bend in the stairway, keeping to the cover of the portrait wall, past the glazed eyes of Beaumont ancestors, staring out in haughty impassivity.

But as we creep by, one by one, the paint in each portrait begins to melt. The colors all run together, and their faces dissolve into masks of gaudy paint. All but Lady Christine, Beast's mother; in her portrait, she smiles radiantly. I can feel her warmth as if she were standing here beside us on the stairs, sorrowing no more, peaceful at last. I know we have pleased her. Beast feels it, too. We pause for a heart-beat to look at her portrait and say farewell.

But as we descend to the landing, Beast pauses again. He is looking at the last portrait in the row, the portrait of the present chevalier, but the old Jean-Loup, cruel and beautiful, is nowhere to be seen. In his place, elegantly outfitted in his suit of burgundy and gold, stands the true chevalier: my Beast, mane, horns, hooves, all captured in oil, his expression fearless. Warmth and humor shine out of his gold-flecked eyes, so like his mother's. He is ready to claim his place in the family at last, now that he is leaving it forever.

I feel tension in Beast's sinewy muscles beneath me, and he springs from the landing and gallops down the last of the stairs, bounding over four or five at a time. Guardsmen with swords race toward us across the black-and-white tiled floor, and servants and stableboys shake clubs and fists, faces contorted with yelling, eyes huge. But they balk and stumble backward to see this terrible beast in all its monstrosity hurtling toward them. And their weapons, if they have the wit to use them, miss their marks; swords sweep harmlessly; clubs drop in confusion.

I hide my face in Beast's thick mane as he leaps off the stairs and gallops for the open double doors. It feels like flying, sailing out over the porch and down the wide front steps. I hear his hooves crunching gravel behind us as we race across the flat upper courtyard, amid the shrieks and shouting of wedding guests. I see Rose's sisters on their feet at their table, throwing themselves together in terror, clutching each other like children. They have heard their father's stories and Rose's, but perhaps they have not truly believed them. Until now.

"Our sister's monster!" Blanche gasps, calculating, perhaps, how the sudden appearance of this apparition might have changed their sister's fortunes — and their own.

"He will eat us!" cries Violette, whose concerns are much more practical.

"Perhaps he has eaten our sister," Blanche chimes in hopefully.

"Help! Save us! The monster has eaten our sister!" they shriek together, adding their voices to the din that rages behind us.

I would laugh if I had time; Blanche and Violette are far more likely to make a meal of their sister than Beast ever was.

We make for the driveway into the protection of the

arch of roses. I can smell their heavy fragrance as we pass beneath them, and I wonder if Beast suffers much to be leaving them behind. As we speed down the drive, I dare a glance backward and see a marvelous sight. All the glorious red blooms on every stem in every terraced hedge and the arch overhead all turn toward us as we gallop by. And every one we pass releases its scarlet petals into the air, like a flurry of snow, like a shower of rice thrown over a bridal couple, so the air is thick with fluttering red rose petals. It's a farewell to Beast from his beloved roses, a cloud of red petals to camouflage our escape. And the wonder of it momentarily freezes our pursuers. The mob of servants and guardsmen and a few brave guests clatters to an uneasy halt on the steps behind us, struggling against their own amazement before they dare to spill down the rest of the way after us, rattling their weapons.

But ahead, the gilded iron gates have clanged shut; we are trapped like one of Jean-Loup's deer. And the gatekeeper leans out the upper window of the gatehouse, a long-handled crossbow at the ready in his shaking hands, pointing at us.

"Halt!" he shouts.

Beast stops, animal muscles stretched out at the gallop freezing on the instant, with scarcely a stumble. He rises up slowly on his hind feet, shaking me gently to the ground behind him; he spreads his arms and raises his paws, feathers rising slightly along his back. He is Beast Rampant, in all his terrible glory.

"If you mean to kill me, Man, you are welcome to try," Beast rumbles at the gatekeeper, who is too stupefied to respond. "But harm this lady in any way, and you will answer to me—phantom or flesh, dead or alive!"

The weapon wavers in the gatekeeper's grasp; his hands can scarcely steady it, and his nervous finger barely stretches to the trigger. He can't think what to make of this nightmare that speaks with a human voice. Beast remains on his hind feet, and I realize it is to shield me, his feathers fanning out nearly to the ground.

"If you let her go through," he growls to the gatekeeper, nodding at the gate, "I will consent to be your prisoner."

"You will not!" I cry, and I dart in front of him.

"But let us pass, and you will sleep well all the rest of your days," Beast goes on, catching me gently by the waist from behind, "knowing you have done a great kindness for your fellow beings."

The gatekeeper stares at us, astonished to hear a cornered animal plead so eloquently for its life. He can't know this frightful beast is the chevalier who employs him. But the gatekeeper appears to have no desire to kill a creature for sport, especially one who can reason and speak so persuasively, and the tip of the bolt in his bow dips slightly. That the creature speaks at all must be evidence of a miracle, or perhaps witchcraft, and it's plain the gatekeeper doesn't know which possibility to fear more.

The mob is cascading down the gravel driveway behind us, but even as the gatekeeper lowers his weapon in confusion, I realize there will never be time for him to throw open the gates again. But in the next moment, I feel myself swept up in Beast's great, padded paws. Gripped in his strong arms, nestled against the warm fur of his chest, I feel we are rising in the air, higher than Beast could possibly leap. The ground is falling away, and, angling my head to look at his face, I see his two enormous feathered wings rising up behind him. The deep *whoomp-whoomp* of their stately beating echoes in the air as we are carried higher still, until we are sailing over the gilded gates. He glances down at me, joy and awe sparkling in his dark eyes; then he leans again into the task, cradling me snugly against himself. I can feel the taut power in his animal body as we gain the sky under his angel wings.

He is beautiful!

Over the gate we go, and then we are above the bridge across the moat. With another few heavy, measured wing beats, we are gliding out over the moat. Then we descend again to earth at the far end of the stone bridge. The swans natter at us as we land, and they puff up their own feathery wings in salute. I slide out of Beast's arms, he folds his magnificent wings, and I climb aboard his back once again.

We gallop into the cover of the trees, down the trail along the ridge that overlooks the town. Behind us, the gates remain closed, shutting in the mob, even as they clamor to pursue us. Perhaps it is the last of Mère Sophie's enchantment.

Farther below, well out of sight of the château, we take refuge in a budding apple orchard that borders a steep, sloping vineyard. Beast slows to a trot and then stops to rest. I slide off his back and stand beside him, stroking his unruly mane as he pants from his exertions. Despite his powerful haunches, his spine is not made for galloping on all fours over too great a distance. He rises up and straightens his back as we gaze out at the placid landscape.

Deep in the valley at the foot of the hill far below us huddles Clairvallon. Soon enough, hysterical tales of the monster that terrorized the chevalier's wedding will be all over the town. Whatever townsfolk did not witness our flight to freedom will be infected with all the same fears and prejudices as those we've just left shut up at the château. They must all be pressed against the gilded gate, shouting and cursing now that the danger is well past; their harsh human noise still echoes down the green hillside to us.

But we turn our backs on the din and set off down the dusty track that skirts the outer edges of the Beaumont grounds. The spring rains have given way to green summer. Insects hum lazily in the tall grasses, and untended wildflowers sway in the light breeze as we double back along the outskirts of the park well behind the château. We stop often to listen to the exuberant song of a mocking-bird or watch the drunken path of an orange-and-yellow butterfly skittering playfully along in the air. Once Beast freezes in place so as not to fright a small brown hare nib-bling at a shoot of greenery. The little creature freezes, too, angling its head to take us in with its large, liquid brown eye, wriggling its tiny pink nose. Then slowly, so slowly, it finishes its task, puts down its delicate front paws, and scampers silently away.

We wander deeper below the park, where the trees grow wilder and closer together, until the tittering of birds, the rustling of busy squirrels, the murmur of leafy branches on the breeze, and the distant burbling of the river are all that can be heard.

Beast stretches out a paw to take my hand, and I smile up at him.

And we start down the hill into the wood. Together.

AFTER

The Heart of the Wood

That's not the way folk tell the story now.

Fearful minds invent tales to conceal what their eyes have seen, to explain away what's too frightening to understand. Stories are whispered in the shadows, across the hearth, at the well — but never in the hearing of the magistrate or the priest, I'll wager. They seep into the wood like the distant cooing of a dove in the velvety fog — in the idle chatter of peasant girls picking blackberries or boys fishing in the river or the ribald old goodwives from other villages who visit Mère Sophie for her potions and possets.

Some say the handsome young chevalier was bitten by an enraged beast while on a hunt, that he sickened and died of his wound. They say his body was burned in secret to prevent a vile contagion from running riot throughout the seigneurie, and that is why he was seen no more. Others whisper that his poor bereft bride was cursed for her beauty by a jealous witch who wanted the chevalier for herself and whisked him away to the fairy world. They say this prodigious witch and her animal familiar were seen flying away from the château on the wedding day.

I might count myself defamed, or more likely flattered, by that part of the tale, if I cared anymore what others think of me. But only one other's opinion matters to me, and he is far too sensible to worry over such idle talk.

Beast thrives in the wood, as I thrive in my studies with Mère Sophie, learning her skills and her secrets. She would gladly have made room for us both in her enchanted home, but Beast prefers to build us a cottage of stones dug out of the riverbank, mortared with good, loamy earth. The paws that found it so awkward to manage a pen are perfectly suited to mashing up the glue of mud and twigs and waste and setting the stones in place. We thatch it over with sturdy evergreen limbs that offer concealment as well as shelter.

Beast finds a wild climbing rose of the softest scarlet tangled up in the bramble behind our cottage. We cut back the bramble and train the rose to arch over the little plot of earth where I plant my vegetable garden. Small red buds explode along the mother plant, relishing their freedom. We hang the ring that belonged to Beast's mother by its red ribbon on the highest branch, in her memory.

Christine's restless spirit, finally at peace, troubles me no more.

Mère Sophie introduces me into the vast sisterhood of wisewomen who live on the outskirts of all the villages, caring for the folk. And when I am off about the fetching and gathering that she finds so tiring on her own, or the chopping, measuring, and mixing I am learning at her worktable, Beast busies himself building a hearth for the fire in our home out of leftover river rock piled up outside. It gives him such pleasure to build useful things after so many idle years imprisoned within the illusion that was Jean-Loup. He makes a bed beside the fire, lined with straw and swansdown. I creep in beside him at night, into the sheltering warmth of his body, where his soft fur and the deep, rumbling hum of his breathing give me more contentment than I have ever known.

The woodland creatures fear him at first, sensing how he is not one of them. But Beast behaves with such deference in their presence, be they badger, buck, or butterfly, that they grow more tolerant. He hunts for our food when he must, learning again to eat meat that I have cooked, but he's come to consider himself the caretaker of the animals. He will not countenance sportsmen in the wood hunting for amusement and drives them off. But he won't interfere with a poor man hunting for food; that is nature's will. And he watches over travelers in the wood who have lost their way—discreetly, from the shadows—to protect them from whatever predator, two-or four-legged, might trouble them in the night.

Beast finds it prudent to retreat into the shadows whenever folk are about in the wood. But as time passes, those who have caught a glimpse of him spin their own tales, and these, too, find their way to us. They call him Green Man; or Pan; or Silvanus, the Horned One, lord of the animals, heart of the forest. Once in a great while, a traveler finds a striped feather that Beast has dropped in the wood. These are considered objects of rare good fortune, Mère Sophie tells us, prized by the folk. Sometimes a feather is seen woven into a necklace or a belt or hung up in a place of honor inside a cottage for protection. Now and then, we find offerings left on the little pile of river rock outside our cottage, as if it were an altar: cups of mead or cow's milk or milled wheat, a garland of garden flowers, a joint of fresh meat in the slaughtering season. Sometimes, we find bits of brightly colored cloth, berry-dyed, that I stitch together into quilts and curtains.

We make a place for ourselves in the wood, Beast and I, as cold and damp, dark and treacherous, and full of forbidding shadows as it often is. Here he belongs in his natural skin, free to enjoy and explore his animal power, and yet he has companionship to satisfy his humanity. He also has a purpose as useful as mine, as I partner Mère Sophie in her vital work. We have found our place in the world at last. Together, in the wood. We ask for nothing more.

Rose stays on at Château Beaumont. The rumors and whispers filter down to us over time. Kind, beautiful, and exquisitely tragic, she is beloved by all. There are few enough who knew the chevalier before who would dare to associate him with the beast seen fleeing the château on the day of the wedding feast. Whether he was gored by a wild animal or murdered by a jealous husband, or if he simply abandoned his dewy bride, Jean-Loup is spoken of no more. The LeNoir bloodline goes no further.

Rose is good to her servants, so they say, and they protect her with fierce loyalty. She is wise enough to leak a generous portion of the Beaumont fortune into the coffers of the cheese seller, the draper, the wine merchant, and the dressmaker, and the seigneurie falls under her administration. The folk marvel at their good fortune in the new Lady Beaumont, after the generations of LeNoir knights who ruled the region for centuries. The wheat crops, the vineyards, the orchards, and the livestock all flourish under her benevolence, and the whole of the region prospers. Only Jean-Loup's lawyers go unpaid, his suit against the Villeneuve estate withdrawn at last. There is no longer any talk of a curse, but for those hushed fireside stories of Lady Rose's bewitched wedding feast.

In time, the legend of the beautiful young widow spreads far and wide throughout the country. Much is made of how sad it is that she lives all alone in such forlorn splendor. A handsome young princeling from a neighboring duchy journeys all the way to Château Beaumont to seek her out. He pays her court, and in due time, she consents to accept his suit. They marry in a wedding by all accounts as lavish as the first one, although without quite so dramatic a finale, and he sweeps her off to a palace even grander than the château. But Rose and her new prince keep Château Beaumont as their secondary estate, so all the servants remain employed and the town continues to benefit from its operation.

As more time passes, gossip insists that the handsome prince she married with such happy results was once the same monster rumored to have haunted Château Beaumont in the dark times. They say it was the purity of Rose's love that redeemed him.

That's the sort of story folk love—a clear moral, a happy ending. It comforts them to think the barriers between virtue and evil, love and hate, beauty and beast, are so clearly defined. The tempest of emotions that roils in our hearts every day, the struggle that never ends to master the monsters within, to love, to live, to survive—those stories are not so comforting, nor so easily told. Happily ever after takes hard work, but folk don't like to hear about that.

The heart is a dark wood—dangerous, compelling, and profound. Its pathways can be frightening, but only by plunging into its depths are we fully alive.

The heart revels in its mysteries. Defy them at your peril. Embrace them if you dare. That is where magic begins.

THE END

Who doesn't love *Beauty and the Beast*? It's irresistible, the tale of the tragic Beast and the brave girl who sees through the outer monster to the noble soul within.

But the moment that all thinking women dread is the climax when the marvelous Beast transforms back into the bland, handsome prince. Indeed, when the actress Greta Garbo saw Jean Cocteau's excellent 1946 film, *La Belle et la Bête*, it's reported that her response at the end was: "Give me back my Beast!"

Readers who love the classic fairy tale expect the restored prince to be the hero and Beast to be the spell that needs undoing. But, like Ms. Garbo, I never found that story satisfying. It's Beast, after all, who earns Beauty's love, not the prince.

So why is it the prince who gets the "reward" of Beauty's love? And why is Beauty so ready to forget the Beast she says she loves and marry the prince? Doesn't Beast himself deserve to be the hero?

As someone who's always loved Beast more than the prince, I thought: wouldn't it be more interesting if there was another woman involved, one who wants to preserve Beast and make sure the prince never returns? So, in my version, there is a good reason the young chevalier is transformed into Beast: his handsome face conceals an evil and corrupted nature. And no one knows it better than my heroine, Lucie.

My story includes all the elements of the traditional fairy tale, but it begins earlier and ends sometime after "happily ever after." But it's Lucie's story I wanted to tell. My heroine is willing to sacrifice her own humanity to pursue her revenge against the prince — until she discovers that Beast is someone entirely separate, with a heart far more human than the prince's ever was.

How would she feel when Beauty arrives on the scene, with the power to restore the prince and banish Beast forever?

As much as Beast deserves to be the hero in my book, I wanted to create, in Lucie, a heroine openhearted enough to care for Beast just the way he is — and strong enough to fight to preserve him. In *Beast: A Tale of Love and Revenge,* they both deserve a happy ending.

· ACKNOWLEDGMENTS ·

Thanks to my wonderful editor, Kaylan Adair, for all the tough love, helping me make this the best Beast he can be.

Thanks to my agent, Irene Goodman, the first one to fall in love with Beast.

And, as always, thanks to James for being my touchstone through all the strange enchantments of a writer's life.